The Inn
at
Walnut Valley

A Gift from
JoAnn

Best Wishes

JoaN Lewis
October 3, 2009

The Inn
at
Walnut Valley

Joan Lewis

To order additional copies of this book, contact:
Xlibris Corporation
1-888-795-4274
www.Xlibris.com
Orders@Xlibris.com
52776

PART ONE

CHAPTER 1

ZORITA'S BIRTH

Zorita was the infant of Pearl and Miss Ada's. No one ever knew who the baby's real daddy was because she was conceived by the doings of the older woman, Miss Ada, and the willingness of young, lazy Pearl.

Miss Ada, and everyone called her that, was a regular at Lou's Tavern in Macon, Georgia. It was at Lou's Tavern where she first spotted the petite, eighteen-year old Pearl Frazier. She knew she had to make the pretty, honey-brown skinned girl hers. All of Pearl's young friends teased her about the older lady's unwanted affection. Even so, Pearl figured she would take the thirty-year old woman for whatever she could. Pearl discovered Miss Ada could give her much more than the jive, young men she'd been dating. She knew, even if she wasn't a gay lady, she could adjust to being Miss Ada's plaything.

Pearl was trifling and loved being cared for. When she convinced Miss Ada she was interested, the woman immediately rented a side by side house and put Pearl next door. The large woman assured Pearl she had provided the home for her with no strings attached. However, most every night while the neighborhood slept, Miss Ada would slip out of her door and into Pearl's open arms. Something which started out being a convenient way to live for Pearl soon became a deeply involved relationship.

It was Miss Ada who insisted Pearl get herself pregnant by a white man so they could have a baby. The older woman found such a man in the bar of a neighboring town. Miss Ada did not know the man was really a half-breed with hard hair. He paid his sister to give his hair permanents in order to pass himself off as white. On February 22, 1945, when Baby Zorita was born, Pearl and Miss Ada were happy to have their little girl. The old woman never even knew the man's name or where he lived, and that was the way Miss Ada wanted it. She was happy to know they had a tiny, pretty, fair-complexioned baby girl. As the little, yellow baby got older, her hair became very hard and course. It didn't matter, she still had the brightest color Miss Ada had ever seen and she was proud of the child.

For Zorita, life as she could remember started at the age of four. At that age she recalled chasing butterflies in the park which was located a little ways from their one story house. At the age of six her memory of life fully developed and her little mind held on to most all it could. When she turned seven years old, Zorita knew even though she did not have a daddy, there was another grownup around to fill the void; that was her mother's best friend, Miss Ada.

She spent almost every waking moment listening to her mother and Miss Ada as they sit on the porch drinking their beer and smoking their cigarettes. There was never a subject the two women felt was too taboo for their daughter's ears. One day Miss Ada said to the child, "Zorita, we know we're talkin' some nasty stuff for those delicate ears of yours, but believe me girl, what we're talkin' about on this porch is your life lessons. Everything we tell you, do not repeat to anyone because it's only meant for you to hear."

"That's right Miss Ada, you tell her. This gal's gotta learn sooner or later what life is all about. Do you think I'm gonna be talkin' baby crap around her? Hell no." Zorita looked up at her mama. "Yeah baby, you heard what I said. Trust me, this world ain't gonna give you nothin', 'specially if you're a colored person. That's why I made sure I picked you a white daddy to have your little ass. Maybe you might have a better chance in this Godforsaken place bein' half-white." It was a lesson she'd learned early in her life as she sat beneath her mother's legs getting her thick, hard hair plaited.

As Zorita got older Pearl would tell her daughter of all the fine boyfriends she had in high school. She'd tell the child how the boys would give her gifts because they liked her and nothing more. Her mother explained if she liked them enough, she would let them kiss and feel on her to show appreciation. One day, when the big woman was away, Pearl told Zorita, "Child, it's hard to find a man that's got a good job to give you beautiful things. You gotta get nice stuff anyway you can. Zorita, I learned this old sayin' a long time ago, *There is nothing to fear, but fear of no money.* It's the truth too. You got to get what you want any way you can. But remember, it's a man who knows how to make a woman feel good. They just do. It's a natural thing. Ain't nothin' like a man takin' care of a woman if he's got a good-payin' job." The mother gave Zorita another one of her clever gems of wisdom, "Listen little girl, *all's fair in love and money*; and don't you forget it." Whenever Miss Ada was in Pearl's company, her mother never mentioned the boyfriends or the gifts. It was a secret the mother and daughter shared. Even though Zorita was only seven years old, she knew not to repeat any portion of her mother's life lessons to Miss Ada.

As Pearl cleverly informed her daughter the wonders of having a man around, Miss Ada tried to engrain in the child's head the adversaries of the opposite sex. "Men, they're all such dogs. You can't trust them, the dirty bastards. That's why I don't have any of them sniffin' around me. Ummp-ummp! They'll never be jiggin' in me, and beggin' me for money too. Best to leave them alone. That's right, Zorita. A man can't do nothin' for you that you can't do for yourself."

Zorita was a quick learner. She took bits and pieces of her lessons from each of the women. If she could use some of what her mama taught her, she did. If she could use pieces of what Miss Ada taught her, she would. At age nine she had already learned the art of extracting presents from the little neighborhood boys. By the time she was ten, she'd been well schooled by her mama and Miss Ada the advantages of being fair-complexioned. Miss Ada would tell Zorita, "Girl, I sure wish I was bright and fair. I'd have everything I ever wanted. I tell you Zorita, you sure are a lucky little girl. You better thank the high heavens you got such a pretty skin tone."

When the dark-skinned children came around to play with Zorita, her mother would holler at them. "Get outta this yard, Zorita ain't got no time to be playin' with you." She'd shoo them away every time. This went on until the age of eleven. Zorita questioned why she couldn't play with the other kids. Her mother would explain, "Why Zorita, you're too good to be wastin' time with those no-account kids." It was Miss Ada who devised a plan to keep Zorita's mind off of the darker-colored, neighborhood children. She informed Pearl to feed their daughter all of the cakes and pies she could whip up, and fill her up with ice cream as well. Miss Ada was a big woman and she loved the sweets as well. When Pearl would fix the goodies, Miss Ada sat on the porch with Zorita and they both ate as much as their bellies could hold. The older woman wanted Zorita to be a happy child, and it would not work as long as the girl constantly reminded Pearl she had no one to play with. That's why Miss Ada insisted Pearl keep baking the delicacies. Food became her daughter's friend instead of the neighborhood children. By the age of eleven and a half Zorita was a good one-hundred and forty pounds. Her once small frame had become nice and round. Zorita had come to love the taste, the smell, and the texture of food in her mouth. However, she still longed to have friends. When she adamantly voiced her opinion on how unfair her mother was being, Pearl told Miss Ada of Zorita's concerns. The older woman gave her approval to let Zorita invite her favorite cousin, Sally Mae, over to the house. Sally Mae was two years older than Zorita, and though her skin was brown, Pearl and Miss Ada felt she would be good company for Zorita. Even with Sally Mae playing in the yard with Zorita, Pearl kept the food piled high and the child's life lessons coming. By age twelve, Zorita learned every trick a girl needed to know about the beauty of having a good, dependable man from Pearl; and how low-down and underhanded all men were from Miss

Ada. The porch's life lessons from her mama and Miss Ada kept coming; and she learned how to survive from both. The lessons had been detailed and entrenched in every segment of Zorita's brain. She picked up many lessons from the two masters of the porch, enough to take her through the rest of her life.

Zorita always knew the big woman next door as her mother's best friend. However, shortly after she turned twelve, she started paying attention to the teasing of the children at Zachary Taylor Elementary School. They gossiped that Miss Ada was really Zorita's daddy. Not knowing what they meant by such a statement, she confronted her mama; Pearl told her to pay them no mind. But when she came home early and found Miss Ada and her mama in bed, she became ill and threw up in the kitchen sink.

CHAPTER 2

PREGNANT ZORITA

Zorita was constantly bragging about how happy she was to be so fair. Her bragging about the brightness of her skin made her dark-skinned cousin, Sally Mae, feel someone should teach Zorita a lesson. Sally Mae had long been disgusted with the nonsensical beliefs her cousin had about fancy possessions and the skin color of people. It was the main two things that dominated Zorita's psyche and her cousin couldn't stand it.

Zorita was fourteen and Sally Mae was sixteen when Kashif arrived in Macon to visit his grandmother, Miss Juanita. Sally Mae was the first to see him and she fell head over heels for the sixteen-year old visitor. When Zorita saw him, the first thing she noticed was his dark skin. Even though Kashif was tall and had a most handsome face, Zorita could not get past his coloring to see the attractiveness about him. When she caught up with Sally Mae, Zorita went on and on about how dark the boy from out of town was. She made fun of his complexion and told Sally Mae she could not figure out how somebody that dark-brown could have such a nice grade of hair. "Why I should have good hair with this pretty skin tone of mine," she conceitedly told Sally Mae.

Zorita was very unconscious of her attitude. It never entered her mind she was hurting Sally Mae's feelings. Revolted, Sally Mae said, "Zorita, nobody can help what color they are. Besides, it's not like you're white. You must think you're high and mighty or something. Did you forget I'm dark-skinned myself?"

"No girl, you know what I'm talking about. You're different, you're my cousin," Zorita justified.

"What's that suppose to mean? I'm still dark, far darker than you. Besides, I don't get why you're so hung up about that. We've got all kind of colors in our family. You happen to be the fairest."

"Goodness, Sally Mae Frazier. If I've hurt your feelings, I'm sorry. You know me, my tongue speeds up before my brain catches up. I guess, if I really think about it, color don't have a whole lot to do with anything."

Sally Mae challenged, "If you're so concerned about hurting my feelings and you're saying color doesn't matter, then I dare you to go out on a date with Miss Juanita's grandson. I wanted him for myself but he ain't interested in me. Yesterday he asked me if I thought you'd go to the church dance with him."

It thrilled Zorita that a guy would pass up her cousin. Because even though Sally Mae was dark-brown, she had a shape on her that wouldn't quit. Zorita's shape was big and round. It never caught any of the boys' attention. In fact, she never even had a boyfriend because of her weight. She suspiciously asked, "Why would he want to go to the dance with me? How come he doesn't want to go with you?"

"How do I know? He just does! Kashif likes you, at least that's what he told me."

"Kashif? Kashif? Aaw shoot, what kind of name is that? That's an ugly name."

"What kind of name is Zorita? Has anybody ever told you Zorita is a god-awful name?" Sally Mae asked without waiting for an answer. "You ought not to be so judgmental about people, girl. It's a real turn-off."

Even though Zorita and her mother did not go to the Baptist Church, she found herself wanting to attend the dance with the new visitor. She didn't dare have the teenager meet her at her home, so she enlisted the help of her cousin. Sally Mae knew how color-struck her Aunt Pearl and Miss Ada were. She always suspected it was the reason Zorita's mind was as twisted as it was. She readily agreed to go to Peachtree Park with Zorita to meet the boy. There, sitting on the bench was Kashif. He got up to greet the girls. It was the first time Zorita had seen him up close and she was in awe. Though he was very dark, he had beautiful jet black, soft, fine hair. As she was admiring his hair, she reached up and felt her course, hard curls. Once Sally Mae officially introduced Zorita to Kashif, it was as if magic had flowed into Zorita's life. She was impressed with the tall boy and found conversation with him easy and intriguing. When Zorita looked around she noticed Sally Mae had disappeared. The cousin had gone behind the line of trees and was at the pond feeding some of her potato chips to the ducks.

The night of the church dance Sally Mae went to Zorita's house to get her. They walked to the dance together. The whole time Zorita fretted about how nervous she felt going to the dance to meet Kashif. When she saw him standing by the punch bowl her fears melted. She walked over to him and he handed her a cup of the strawberry and kiwi punch. They were inseparable the whole evening. With the help of Sally Mae, they dated for the remaining summer behind her mama and Miss Ada's back. She found him to be funny and charming. He was so charismatic, she allowed him to sweet talk her out of her panties. Right before the summer came to an end, he left Macon to go back to his home.

The first time she missed her period she knew she was pregnant. She was devastated and rushed to Sally Mae's house. When her cousin came onto the wooden porch, Zorita blurted, "I'm pregnant and it's all your fault."

"My fault? How is your being pregnant my fault?" Sally Mae asked in a whisper. She tossed her head toward the opened screen door to remind Zorita her mama was watching her soap, *As the World Turns*. In the next moment Zorita grabbed Sally Mae's arm, jerked her off of the porch and walked her down the walkway. Sally Mae continued the conversation. "Zorita, how can you say I had something to do with this? I didn't tell you to do it with him, now did I?"

"No you didn't Miss Smarty-Pants. I just want you to know, you shouldn't have insisted I go to the dance with him. I wouldn't have let him french-kiss me and feel all over me. He was so nice; buying me stuff the whole summer and treating me special. Now I'm pregnant all because I let him kiss me."

"Kiss you? Zorita, you've got to give him some before you can get pregnant," Sally Mae laughed at her cousin's naivety. When she noticed the girl was not laughing with her, she suspiciously asked, "You didn't let him get to second base with you, did you?" Nothing came from Zorita's mouth and Sally Mae saw a tear rolling down her cousin's face. She preached, "Zorita, you mean you pulled your dress up and your drawers down for him? How could you be so stupid? That's your fault if you gave in to him. You can't go blaming me for a mistake you made?"

Zorita wiped the tear off her face and angrily said, "All I know is I'm pregnant. If you had minded your own business, I never would have gotten this way. I hate your guts Sally Mae, stay away from me." She rolled her eyes at her cousin, then quickly walked one street over towards her home. Sally Mae wanted to console the pregnant teen, but Zorita was mad. In fact, Zorita was so angry, she promised herself she would never speak to Sally Mae again.

Zorita didn't dare tell her mother she was pregnant. She tried concealing it with her excessive body weight. Within weeks of throwing up and refusing her favorite foods, her mother figured it out. She beat Zorita until the girl finally broke down and told who made her pregnant. When Zorita admitted it was the grandson of Miss Juanita, her mama told Miss Ada. The older woman went into a rage. Pearl withdrew her daughter from school under the pretense of sending her to live with her father in North Carolina. She and Miss Ada locked the girl away in the windowless basement, letting her up only to dump her slop jar. Whenever Pearl came into contact with her daughter, she was sure to berate her. Every chance she got she reminded Zorita how dumb she was to get knocked up by the blackest boy she could find. She angrily scolded her daughter, "You had *a bird in hand, why let it get in your bush*?" Pearl pointed out she had disappointed not only her, but Miss Ada as well.

Weeks later, Sally Mae got the nerve up to question her Aunt Pearl about the whereabouts of Zorita. She was suspicious of the story her aunt had spread around the community. When Pearl still insisted Zorita was in North Carolina with her father, Sally Mae asked the woman for the address and phone number. Pearl was full of excuses as to why she did not want her daughter to be distracted while she attended the non-existent school. The woman didn't know years earlier Zorita had confided in her cousin. Zorita told Sally Mae her mother admitted she didn't know who her father was, and she should be happy just to have been born. In Sally Mae's heart she knew her Aunt Pearl was lying. She suspected they had hidden the girl away somewhere within those small apartments. Try as she might, she could never make her way inside either of the two conniving women's homes to search for her missing cousin.

On June 3, 1960, Zorita's water broke. Miss Ada was right there in Pearl's basement to take charge. She forced gin down the girl's throat before delivering the child. When Miss Ada pulled the baby out, she never bothered to see if it was a boy or girl. She took the dark infant, wrapped it in a towel, and rushed out of the door with it. The big woman wobbled to Peachtree Park, drowned the newborn in the pond and covered the baby's body with a thicket of brush. When Miss Ada returned, she said to her lover, "That baby was as black as me. I know the hardships I'm goin' through. Thank God it won't have to go through the same mess. It was stillborn so I took care of disposing it. If Zorita ask about the baby, tell her the poor little thing was born dead."

Pearl moaned, "It was born dead? Oh Lord!"

Miss Ada slowly approached Pearl to console her. She said, "The Sweet Jesus knew to take that black child to save it from the oppression of the white society. Besides, you too young to be a grandma. Why you'd be up all hours of the day and night takin' care of that heifer's baby while she's rompin' off to school. Probably lookin' for the next black-ass boy to screw." She saw Pearl crying and it bothered her a little; after all it was Pearl's first grandchild. Not wanting to hear the little woman bellyache about the loss of the baby, she said, "Look, I'm powerful tired. Keep her hot-ass in the basement 'til I can figure out what to do. I'm goin' back over to my place to rest. Deliv'ring that dead child done took a lot outta me."

Pearl, still emotionally spent by the whole episode, warned her intoxicated daughter, "You learn from this here mistake, Zorita. Me and Miss Ada have helped you as much as we can, so you got yourself another chance. That damn brat you delivered was born dead; you better make the best of it and forget you ever got yourself knocked up."

She locked the door to Zorita's basement and went next door to Miss Ada's place. She said, "We need to get the hell out of this town. I'm tired of my brother, his wife and that nosey brat, Sally Mae, tryin' to figure out what's goin' on. They always hounding me, askin' where is Zorita, and what do I see in you. I done ran out of lies to tell them. There's too many tongues a-waggin' and I'm afraid eventually they gonna go to the cops."

Miss Ada yelled at the tiny woman, "So what if they do? Do you think them white policemens is gonna worry theyselves about a missing, hot-tailed heifer? Hell no! If you want to leave our happy home because of some nosey, busy-bodies, I can make that happen. Just understand, you gonna have to keep an eye on Zorita. Keep her locked in the basement whilst I go in search of a place for us to live."

Pearl continued to keep Zorita in the basement while Miss Ada went far away looking for a home in a different state for them to live. Three months later Miss Ada pulled up in the wee hours of the morning. She loaded up Pearl and Zorita in a beat-up Buick she'd borrowed from Slick Rick. It took fourteen hours to drive to Slick Rick's place. They arrived in Timberland, Pennsylvania on a brisk, September afternoon. Pearl and her daughter settled in the spare room Slick Rick gave them. Pearl warned Zorita, "Miss Ada told me that Slick Rick is lettin' us stay here free of charge. That is, 'til we get ourselves a place of our own. This is a new beginnin' for us. Don't you go messin' it up, and pissin' off Miss Ada again."

CHAPTER 3

TIMBERLAND, PENNSYLVANIA

Early September 1960, in the tiny town of Timberland, Pennsylvania, the leaves were already turning yellow and crimson. The bottom of the valley, which is where The Inn at Walnut Valley is located, was surrounded by a patchwork quilt of brilliance. Nearly everyone flocked to The Inn at Walnut Valley throughout the day and night. During the day, some housewives would hurry to finished their housework and rush to the inn for socialization and snippets of fun. Some of the men had their own little escape of shooting pool and talking jive amongst themselves. And they loved their cigarettes and alcohol while they played pool, or gambled in the side room with Jack. Many of the guys hung out at the marbled bar and talked about women, money and the chances of Senator John F. Kennedy winning the Presidency. The women generally sat at the tables and talked, laughed and discussed the activities of their men and children. During the nights, especially the weekend nights, the inn would jump and rock until one o'clock in the morning rolled around.

Timberland, one of the smallest towns in Pennsylvania, was surrounded by many hills and mountains. With the mountains cascading the town, the inhabitants of Timberland felt nestled in a cloak of security. When the early autumn rolled in, it caught the Timberlanders off guard. For some reason a coolness engulfed the valley and the early chill had a changing effect on the trees. Timberland now resembled a beautiful watercolor painting; and the mountain of trees stood majestically around the small town in a show of colorful serenity. Fall, early or not, was always welcomed by the inhabitants. They love witnessing the mountain's forestry radiate from leafy green to a brilliant yellow, orange and red tapestry. The township had a richness about it, be it winter, spring, summer, or fall. And that richness of brilliance also showed in the colorful people of Timberland.

Even though Timberland was a little town, in the inhabitants' minds their town was just as big and sophisticated as any city of the United States. The people didn't know enough about the outside world to even realize their town was at least a good twenty years behind time. Where the larger cities had their own private telephone lines, Timberland still had party-lines, and Old Maid Ruth Mullencamp patching through their telephone calls. Where other metropolitan cities had school buses taking the students to and from school, Timberland's students hiked to and from their place of education. While nearly every city in the nation had public transportation, Timberland only had Queen City Taxi. And where indoor bathrooms were prevalent throughout the country, some less fortunate residents still had outside toilets. Even so, the Timberlanders overall were a happy, contented bunch.

Timberland had a mixture of people, both white and colored. And though the town seemed to have escaped the deep-seated prejudices which ate away the foundation of most of the nation, Timberland still had some small pockets of quirkiness. Though the whites and the colored people got along in a fairly sensible manner, there was still underlying dissension within each of the races. Some of the wealthier Caucasians shunned the middle class whites who didn't have luxuries. Some average-income whites had problems with white people who struggled to make ends meet. Even the poor whites looked down on each other, debating amongst themselves which of them were the poorest. As for the Negroes, though their problems were just as drastic as the whites, nevertheless, they held the tension down as best they could. Timberland's colored inhabitants had a menagerie of social classes within its race; there were rich Negroes, poor Negroes, smart Negroes, and not so smart Negroes. The well-to-do colored people snubbed the poorer ones and the poorer Negroes snubbed them right back. All of the colored people's nonsense didn't mean a thing. Because when it was time to socialize, The Inn at Walnut Valley was where they all gathered, snobbishly rich or filthy poor. The inn was their common denominator. Even a few of the whites came there for a good time. And a good time they all had.

Teenaged Zorita was happy to be a resident of the new town. She felt Timberland was much more beautiful than where she came from. She loved the colorful trees which surrounded the town. And even though autumn was surely engulfing the meadow, the teenager loved the fact that the grass was still lush and green. It was a pleasant change from the red clay dirt and flat terrain of nothingness which she had come from. She often suffered from the humidity and sweltering heat around the Georgia land. The small town was a great change for her, and this time she would not screw it up. She had let Kashif—beautiful, dark skin, wavy, black hair and all—sweet talk her into having sex with him. As a consequence, she became pregnant and was forced to live in the basement for a long time. She didn't want to go through it again.

Miss Ada took over Zorita's life and whenever the people of Timberland saw Miss Ada, Zorita and Pearl together they assumed the big black woman was Zorita's mama. This was only surmised because both Miss Ada and Zorita were big gals and Pearl was so petite, she simply looked like a friend tagging along. Having people think she was Zorita's mama suited the older woman just fine. Zorita was now fifteen years old. Even though she had missed almost a whole year of school, Miss Ada went to Lincoln High and demanded they put her in the tenth grade, with or without the teenager's school transcript from her previous school. So Zorita started her new school in the tenth grade instead of the ninth, and did very well in her class. She was bigger than any of the girls in the colored school, but it didn't much bother her. She liked knowing they thought of her as a powerhouse and someone they should not mess with. Because even though she was new in town, she wasn't going let the other teenagers think they could take advantage of her. If someone even looked like they wanted to challenge her at anything, she would not back down. Some school mates whispered it was because she had no dad around that made her so standoffish. Some said it was the thick southern accent which set her apart from the Pennsylvania teenagers. Others whispered those were not the reasons at all. They felt Zorita was unreceptive to the students at Lincoln High clearly because she was treated like the outsider that she was.

CHAPTER 4

ZORITA'S ADMIRER

Albert Manning was a big, bulky teenager. He was unlike the other huge, teenage boys at Lincoln High who had lots of girlfriends because of their jock status. His dark-brown face was pitted and his wooly hair showed signs of a much needed haircut. He had noticed Zorita when she first attended Lincoln High. All through the tenth, eleventh and part of the twelfth grade Albert secretly pined for her. By the middle of the twelfth grade he got up the courage to ask her to help him with his studies and she did. He loved her, but she didn't know it.

One evening Albert stopped into Fast Eddie's Soul Food Diner to pick up an order his mother phoned in. He had paid for and received the order when he overheard Big Butch and Wild Man Milford talking about Zorita's butt. Big Butch said, "Man, have you seen Zorita's ass lately. I swear that thing's gettin' bigger every day." Their skinny girlfriends both burst into laughter. Wild Man Milford added, "Yeah, you sure are right. Man, you could put a big platter of turkey on it and still have room to pull up a chair and sit down and eat."

Albert was furious. He liked Zorita, and he would not tolerate any disrespect of her. He placed his package on the counter and walked over to the hulked men. "You got somethin' to say about my friend, Zorita. Why don't tell her them jokes to her face and see if she thinks they're funny?"

Both jocks stood up in a team effort to fend off Albert. Big Butch said, "Why don't you mind your damn business, we weren't talkin' to your stupid-ass anyway."

Albert said, "You makin' fun of my friend is my business." Wild Man Milford hauled off and gave Albert a quick, hard sucker-punch to the gut. Albert slugged him back and the fight was on. The girls left their food on the table and were screaming as they ran out of the restaurant. The three boys battled it out. Albert took a pounding from the jocks, but he felt it was worth it when it came to defending Zorita.

Word got back at Lincoln High of what happened. When Zorita heard about Albert standing up for her, she felt honored. She admired him, even liked him, but after the incident with Kashif she was reluctant to give her heart away. Even so, as the school year progressed, she would spend her study-hall time assisting him. She tried to emulate the role of a tutor. It didn't matter how professional she tried to be, because though they never officially announced to one another they were a couple, they somehow knew they were. After the incident at the restaurant no one ever made the mistake of saying anything about either one of the two whenever they were in their presence. They knew Zorita was just as brawny as Albert and suspected she could beat them down if she had to. Albert already proved he could, and would, take on tough football players when it came to standing up for Zorita.

Zorita's face was pretty, but the teenagers used her big body as a reason to laugh behind her back. She never had any true friends. She only trusted herself and Albert, in that order. She walked with an aura around her that permeated confidence. The pretty girls and handsome boys wondered how the big, stocky, country girl retained her uplifted attitude. They did all they could to show their rejection towards her. They didn't know Zorita figured if they could not accept her as a friend, then she would strive to be smarter than the unsociable teens. That's why her esteem never wavered. It was her way of commanding the respect she knew she deserved which her fellow students seemed unwilling to give her.

It was March 1963, two months before the end of school, and the seniors were all excited. The upcoming school's graduation would be held the last week of May. Zorita and Albert had become extremely close; she fell hard for him. One evening after tutoring Albert for the last of their exams, she gave herself to him. The month of April came and went and she was afraid she was pregnant again. Zorita paced the floor a week and a half wondering what she would do if she was carrying a baby inside her. She did not want to be sent to the basement again to live. When she finally received her period she was so thankful. She swore to God she would not have sex again unless she was married.

The night of graduation rehearsal Albert pulled Zorita behind the auditorium curtain and kissed her passionately. "Let's get married, My Beautiful Zorita," he beamed. All she could think of was the life lessons of her mother and Miss Ada. As much as she was in love with Albert, she put him off by telling him to wait a while. Secretly, she was afraid of how Miss Ada and her mother would react if dark-skinned Albert came to them and asked for her hand in marriage.

One week passed and Albert hadn't seen nor heard from his beloved Zorita. He inquired all over Timberland. People told him she had left town; and they were right. Zorita returned to Timberland riding in a light-blue convertible with a tall, skinny man at the wheel. Albert was crushed. When Zorita announced she was married to Randy Banks, a man she met while vacationing in Hershey, Pennsylvania, Albert locked himself in his room for a week and cried like a baby.

CHAPTER 5

ARMY

Eighteen year old Albert Manning was crushed. If he could not have his beautiful Zorita he figured he might as well join the army instead of waiting for the draft to get him. Without Zorita in his life he might as well be dead. When he got into boot camp, he knew he had made a serious screw up. His large frame couldn't keep up with the more physically fit men. His time in boot camp was extended by two extra weeks because he was big and slow. He finally made it through the regiment by the skin of his teeth. Even so, he wanted to be released from his contract. Directly after boot camp he took his leave. He returned to Timberland to visit his mother. Instead of going on to his post after his two-week leave, he went AWOL and hid out in Silver Spring, Maryland. When the MPs found him they drug him back and flung him in the stockade. A month later they shipped him off to Vietnam. What a mistake the army had been for him. Albert could barely do any of the details the officers commanded him to do. He simply wasn't soldier material. He had been rough and tough in Timberland, Pennsylvania, but he discovered he was nothing but a wimp in the military.

While on duty in the jungles of Vietnam, Albert decided he'd had enough of the army life. He thought of how most all the other soldiers received love letters and boxes filled with pre-sweetened Kool-Aid, Vienna sausages and potted meat. He hadn't so much as received a post card from his mother since being in the military. PFC Albert Manning fell into a deep depression and wanted out of the war. He figured he would pay one of his comrades to shoot him in the foot. He found that wayward soldier in SP4 Jim Bo Johnson and paid the soldier a healthy sum. Within hours the medivac airlifted him out of the war zone. When the officer in charge investigated why the so-called accident happened, he found out about Albert's plot. He went straight to the hospital to question the soldier. It was Albert's fault the officer was two men short. Because not only was Albert removed from the line of action, but Specialist Johnson was brought up on charges and tossed in the stockade. The officer told Albert he was damn lucky the army hadn't considered throwing him in the stockade right along with Johnson. The officials in power refused to lock up Albert again. They knew he did not want to be in the army and they wanted to be rid of him as well. It was a unanimous decision; since Albert Manning was a lousy soldier, the military should waste no more of the taxpayers' money by keeping him. The man proved to be dead weight. However, Specialist Johnson would do his time and continue on with his military career. All Albert could do was lay in his hospital bed, with his foot in the hoist, and take the barrage of insults the officer hurled his way. When he found out he would be released from the army with a dishonorable discharge he did not care. Once he was back in the states, and dishonorably discharged, he took a flight to Pittsburg then caught the Greyhound Bus which would take him to Oaktown.

On May 7, 1964, Isaac saw Albert get off the Greyhound Bus. Isaac Wright, better known as Mouth, talks nonstop and knows nothing about everything. Mouth was at the Greyhound Bus Depot in Oaktown dropping off his aunt. When he spotted Albert he rushed over and vigorously shook the man's hand. He said, "Hey Al, man I didn't know you was comin' back here. Why, we thought you was gonna get yo' fool self killed over there in Vietnam." He looked at Albert and noticed something strange about Albert Manning; the ex-army man was using a cane to aid himself, and he didn't have his uniform on. Mouth asked, "Man, where's yo' uniform? And what's with this here cane, Al?"

Ignoring the first question entirely, Albert answered the second one immediately. "I got shot Mouth, that's why I got the cane. I got shot."

"You got shot. Them gottdamn enemies. I shoulda been over there. I woulda watched out for you man. You know me and you always did look out for one another at Lincoln High, remember?" It was an exaggeration on his part. When Albert was at Lincoln, no one except the two football jocks he'd fought, Zorita, and a handful of teachers even knew he existed. He was the big, black, pit-faced teenager no one wasted any time to get to know.

While Albert stood waiting to retrieve his duffel bag from the belly of the bus, Mouth stood around anxious to hear all about his friend's wartime experiences, but no stories came. Albert painfully bent to get his bag and Mouth gently pulled him aside. "Is this yo' bag? Don't worry my man, I got it." He swooped up the bag and shouldered it as though he'd personally returned from the war. Albert lifted his hand to hail a cab and Mouth shouted, "Aaw, hell naw! Man, is you for real? I ain't gonna let no war hero take a cab home. It's my honor to take you myself." On the ten-mile journey to Timberland, to take Albert to his mama's house, the know-it-all pumped the discharged soldier for information. "Man you know I always wanted to go into the army, but these here bad eyes of mine kept me out." Albert glanced at Mouth and saw the man jiggled his thick glasses up and down to prove his point. "Hell, I woulda been right there with you, my man, fightin' side by side and kickin' them damn Koreans' asses." he proudly added.

"They're Vietnamese, Mouth. That's who they are. Not Koreans. That's the Korean War you're thinkin' of."

Mouth continued, "Oh shit Al, you know what the hell I mean, Koreans, Germans, Vit-meeses they all the gottdamn same. I woulda kilt them all. Naw sir, your black ass wouldn't of got shot out of that damn helicopter if I'dda been there."

"No Mouth, I didn't get shot out of a helicopter. I said, I was ridin' in a chopper the VC was shootin' at."

"What you say?! Man, I coulda swore you said you was shot out of one of them whirlybirds. Umph, my mistake. Shit, I'm so glad to see you again. Like I said, if I'dda been over there that damn war woulda been over a long time ago." When Mouth pulled up to Albert's house he hopped out of the car and grabbed Albert's duffel bag. While walking Albert to his door, he said, "Man, when your leg that them . . . , what you call 'em . . . , Vit-Meeses, shot you in, anyways, when it heal, I'll come pick you up and we can go party over at Jacka Diamond's place. You's some kind of hero in my book. You ain't no baby-killer like they been sayin' on television. Hey, if I'dda been over there, I would not only have been a baby-killer, but a mama-killer and daddy-killer too. I'dda killed 'em all," he bragged. Albert could not get a word in at all to shut the man up. When Mrs. Manning came to the door and saw her son leaning on the cane and Mouth proudly shouldering the wounded man's duffel bag, she ran out to hug her son and welcome him home.

"Miss Mannin', take good care of my man here. He done got shot up pretty bad. All through his body. They did a number on him over there. He's back home now, safe and sound; and I done bought him to you."

The widowed woman looked over at Mouth, "Thank you for givin' my Albert a lift. I didn't even know he was comin' home on leave. You only been in the army for eleven months. Why did they let you come home again so soon, son?"

"Naw, Miss Mannin' he's home for good. Got wounded, and he told me he's discharged too. How 'bout that? Hey, let me take this here bag in the house for our hero." With that, the woman opened the screen door. Mouth walked into the living room and tossed the duffle bag onto the green, tweed sofa. Mrs. Manning and Albert followed him into the house. Mouth walked over, slapped Albert's shoulder and said, "Hey man, I'll catch up with you later." He walked out of the house with a pep in his step and headed towards his car. He spoke into the air, "Them bastards is lucky I wasn't over there. I woulda killed all them Chinese bastards."

Before the sun went down, most everyone Mouth ran into learned about Albert Manning's return. He told them how the man had taken bullets throughout his body, even one close to his heart. Mouth collected over one-hundred dollars for the Manning family from the community. He spent fifty dollars of it for himself. *Hell, if it wasn't for me, he wouldn't even have the fifty*, he justified.

No one knew the particulars of Albert's return from the war. The town welcomed him with much jubilance because he had returned from a hell of a conflict. They knew they were lucky to have their Timberland son back, even with a limp. He had been injured in Vietnam so naturally the townsfolk declared him as a war hero. And with the accolades he basked in the glory. He had wanted to be a fearless man, but deep down inside, he knew he was fraudulently portraying himself as a courageous soldier. Even so, he stayed in his mother's house and marveled at the advantages of being a hero. She waited on him hand and foot, and she loved it. Why her son was a very brave man. With him being such a great guy, it made the people look at Mrs. Manning as a super mama who raised a wonderful, war veteran. The town of Timberland had never received any national attention and this could be one sure way of getting Timberland, Pennsylvania on the map. At least that's what they all thought and Albert Manning would say nothing to let them think otherwise. Because, although he knew he was no hero, thanks to Mouth's exaggeration, everyone in Timberland now looked upon him as a man of valor. At this point, the man was too embarrassed to tell the truth about himself. The truth? He was a coward, who wanted out of the Vietnam War; and he did whatever he had to do to make it happen.

CHAPTER 6

RANDY

Zorita loved Albert, and that scared her. She remembered the first teenage boy to pay her any attention, Kashif. A man's love confused her, but on the other hand, it was something she longed for. She had no father to tell her she the apple of his eye. She wished she knew who her daddy was, but doubt she'd ever know. She was once pregnant by Kashif because she fell for his handsome features and smooth line. Now, though she would never admit it, she was in love with Albert and panic set in. So, on June 1, 1963, when shy Mary Ann asked Zorita to accompany her to Hershey Park to celebrate their May graduation, she knew it would be a great break from Albert's pressure of marriage. When Zorita asked Miss Ada if she could go celebrate with her friend, to her surprise, the old woman said yes. That was where Zorita met a total stranger named Randy Banks. She married him. Randy told Zorita he was very wealthy, but when she returned home with him, she discovered he had to take a job at Timberland Steel Mill.

Miss Ada was not pleased at all about the extra mouth to feed. She hated the thought of filling a man's gut, no matter how much food there was in the house. Every time Randy sat at the table and devoured the food Pearl and Zorita prepared, Miss Ada would roll her eyes and suck her teeth. She endured the displeasure of having the man share their table for many, many months. Often she would slap her fat, open palms hard upon the table and leave the kitchen table in total disgust. One evening, as she was giving Randy the evil eye, he threw an unfinished pork chop hard onto his plate. "What the fuck is the matter with you, Ada? You have been givin' me them dirty looks for almost a year now."

Zorita stopped chewing and looked at the woman; Pearl blocked out Miss Ada's anger altogether. Miss Ada snarled, "How many times am I gonna have to tell you it's not Ada. It's Miss Ada to you, boy. I ain't gonna . . ."

He injected, "Miss Ada! Miss Ada! I ain't no boy, just like you ain't no Miss. In fact, who the hell is you callin' boy anyway? I ain't never been nobody's boy?" I wasn't a boy when I was a boy." He continued, "I'm a man. I'm a gottdamn man, and don't your big ass forget it." He beat on his chest with both fist.

Her eyes bugged out and she spit saliva as she shouted, "You's a boy as far as I'm concern. You come in here from that smelly steel mill, takin' over the television and drinkin' up all me and Pearl's beer. You don't pick up after yourself, and you got my Zorita runnin' all over the place for you like she's your slave."

"She's my wife, you crazy bitch. A wife is supposed to do things for her man."

Zorita said nothing, she simply sat there. Long ago Pearl learned to let Miss Ada handle all problems. She removed herself from the table and start cleaning up the kitchen. Miss Ada stood up, placed her hands flat on the table and stared at Zorita. "Can I see you in private?"

Randy glanced over at his wife, then at Miss Ada and shook his head. *"What a fuckin' lunatic,"* he mumbled to himself.

Zorita followed Miss Ada onto the front porch. "Does this here porch symbolize anything to you?" Zorita couldn't think of a thing it should remind her of. She looked blankly around the area and scanned the yard. Frustrated, Miss Ada said, "Your life lessons on the porch in Macon, Georgia. Remember?"

"Oh yeah," Zorita said, "Yeah, but why did you bring me out here to tell me that?"

"Child, 'cause I think you done lost your fool mind. That's why. Me and your mama sent you away on that Hershey trip as a graduation present and you come back with a husband. A damn ugly, black one at that. I think all we done taught you on the porch in Macon went straight up there in outer-space. What was you thinkin', comin' back home with him?"

"But, Miss Ada, I was goin' there with Mary Ann like I said; at the last minute she got sick. She couldn't make it so I went without her. The second day I got there I was a little lonesome and Randy came up and . . ." It suddenly dawned on her. She wasn't twelve or thirteen years old anymore. She was a grown woman; a married woman who did not owe Miss Ada any explanation whatsoever. In a show of fortitude, Zorita roared, "So what, we're married! You're gonna have to accept that. He likes me and I kind of like him too. Besides, he wants to settled down and start a family."

The fact was, Zorita hadn't used an ounce of logic in her marriage to Randy. He pulled up in his big, fancy car and told her how fine her wide hips were. Before the week was over he whipped out his credit card, flew her to Las Vegas and they married in a quickie wedding chapel. With Randy, there was no asking her mother or Miss Ada for her hand in marriage. Besides, marrying Albert scared her. She wasn't supposed to feel love for any poor man, according to Pearl. On the other hand, Miss Ada told her she wasn't to love any man, period. Yet, Zorita felt she needed a man in her life. Consequently, she married Randy Banks a man she didn't love, but gave the impression he had money; in order to keep from marrying the man she really loved, who was poorer than the Georgia dirt she had come from.

In the months her husband had been living with the women, the house turned into a dump. Miss Ada complained to Pearl. "He drinks all of our beer and leaves them bottles scattered about. Why Pearl you've seen how he leaves his filthy work clothes strewed all over the place." She shook her finger in Pearl's face, "Remember all them times you and Zorita done tripped over his work boots. And don't forget 'bout his piss splattering all over the bathroom floor; and how that bastard never puts that damn seat down."

Sick of everything about Zorita's husband, Miss Ada called upon her old buddy, Slick Rick. Slick Rick's real name was Rachael Jarvison, but she looked, dressed, and sound just like a natural man. Miss Ada asked her friend to investigate and find out all she could about Randy. Slick Rick managed to track down a person who once knew Randy and the skinny lesbian got the whole scoop. The mannish-woman telephoned Miss Ada. She reported, "I done talked to my pal in Hershey, Pennsylvania and he told me the man named Randy Banks is dead. He was killed by some hoodlum named Samuel Lynch. Anyways, who you got in your place is really Samuel Lynch, not Randy Banks. He murdered the real Randy Banks and stole the man's wallet. That son-of-a-bitch is an imposter. He's using the dead man's credit cards, license and social security card to get jobs and stuff. He's a felon, so he can't get nothin' under his own name."

A day later Miss Ada and Pearl met at Slick Rick's place. The tall, thin, black woman laid the complete saga on the line about Sam Lynch. "That bastard's got a record longer than my arm. Even spent a coupla years in prison. Right now he's wanted for bank robbery, wanted for assault, wanted for parole violation, plus he's a suspect in two or three murders. Apparently, he did away with this Banks person so he could hide away from the law, without havin' to hide; if you know what I mean. Randy Banks was a young kid, only twenty-one, when he got his fool self done in." Slick Rick's facial expression was contorted with anger. She continued, "Look like your Zorita picked a real charmer with this here guy, 'cause he ain't twenty-one years old like he been tellin' y'all. He's Samuel Lynch, a twenty-nine year old convict. He been using the name of the man he murdered to lead a better life. Maybe he figure by marryin' your Zorita, no law would ever suspect who he really is; especially livin' in a small place like Timberland."

Miss Ada said, "You're right. Sounds like he done picked my Zorita to make his-self look like an ordinary person." In a rage, she said to Pearl and Slick Rick, "I'm gonna get that gottdamn bastard out of our house. He has got to go."

Pearl regretted getting mixed up with Miss Ada many years ago. She had once been a pretty, young girl; but because she was lazy, she settled for a life with Miss Ada calling the shots. The stress of living with the old woman was slowly diminishing her vibrant beauty. Months after the three of them moved to Timberland, Miss Ada told Pearl that Slick Rick wanted her in the worst way. It would be payment for when Slick Rick lent Miss Ada the old Buick to go back to Macon and get her and Zorita. When Pearl refused, Miss Ada slaps the small lady around until she agreed to bed not only Slick Rick, but Miss Ada at the same time. When Zorita graduated from Lincoln High, Miss Ada told Pearl when the girl returned from the Hershey trip, they could start including her in on their fun with Slick Rick. Pearl realized she was afraid of Miss Ada. Though she did not want Zorita forced into their sordid relationship, she was too scared to deny the big woman. Zorita hadn't known it, but when she returned home with a husband she had thrown a glitch into Miss Ada's sexual plot. Now Miss Ada was talking about getting the man out of their house and this worried Pearl.

Pearl said, "You can't run him off. He's Zorita's husband." Pearl never complained about Randy being in the house. She had long ago missed being in the company of men. There were times when men had shown a desired for Pearl. The small woman noticed a week or so later when she ran across them in the town, they'd pull their hats low and walk pass her. Zorita's husband might have been a louse; but he was Zorita's louse, and Pearl didn't want Miss Ada chasing him off. She reiterated her concerns, "Miss Ada that's Zorita's husband, please don't send him away."

Miss Ada turned and stared directly into Pearl's eyes. There was not a trace of empathy in the big woman's heart. She shouted right in Pearl's face, "You stupid bitch. Didn't you hear what Slick said? His name ain't Randy Banks, it's Samuel Lynch. And fool, he's done killed the real Randy Banks, plus some more mens; so technically Zorita ain't even married to the piece of slime."

Miss Ada didn't care about the man being Zorita's phony husband; she only knew she wanted to be rid of him. She gave Pearl a wild stare; a look Pearl had seen often during the man's stay at their home. Pearl knew from the older woman's character, that Miss Ada had no plans of letting Randy hang around. She could feel her face getting hot and her eyes tearing. She turned and ran out the door, slamming it behind her.

Slick Rick went over and placed her bony, black hand on Miss Ada's shoulder. She leaned in and whispered in Miss Ada's ear, "I've got good news for you. He's got Zorita as benefi'cheery on his life insurance policy at Timberland Steel. Thirty-thousand dollars." They looked at one another and a smile came across both their faces. "You go on home and figure out if you really want to chase him away or if you want to do him away." Miss Ada covered her mouth and gave a muzzled laugh. She hugged Slick Rick and gave her a kiss on the lips, then ran onto the porch where Pearl stood crying. She rubbed her lover on the back. "Pearl, don't worry," she said, "Everything's gonna work out real fine."

CHAPTER 7

ROCKY BLUFF

Zorita kept pressuring her husband about finding a place of their own. But Samuel Lynch had no desire to relocate. Samuel Lynch was accustomed to women hiding him out and taking care of him. The thought of him getting an apartment for him and Zorita never entered his mind. With his new identity he felt very comfortable living a regular life with his new family. He even liked working at the steel mill. At the factory he could hang with the guys and talk the bull that men talked when they are out of the presence of ladies. He figured it was a way for him to stay clear of the law. The man may have changed his unlawful activities for the moment, but he never changed his mind-set of using women to make life easier of himself. Even with the women fussing about picking up after him, he still felt at ease. He'd been around a lot of women and they all complained about him being so messy. He wondered what made Miss Ada and her crew think they should be treated any differently? He did what he damn-well pleased around the ladies. If they had a problem with him, it was their problem, not his. He didn't care how they felt; his own comfort was his only concern.

A few days after Miss Ada's conversation with Slick Rick, Zorita's husband came home from work with a quart of Colt 45 Malt Liquor beer for himself. He also had two bulldog puppies he'd purchased from a co-worker. It took Miss Ada all she had to keep her cool. Through the grit of her teeth, she said, "You think them bulldogs gonna be layin' 'round here, eatin' and leavin' muddles of piss and shit for Pearl and Zorita to be cleanin' up?"

He opened his beer and took a long gulp. In a sardonic voice, he said, "I ain't worryin' 'bout no bulldogs. It a bulldyke that's got me worryin'.'" No sooner than he finish the sentence Miss Ada grabbed a skillet from the stove, swung her arm back and hit him on the side of his head as hard as she could. He lurched, and the table tilted as he fell onto the floor. The Colt 45 Malt Liquor bottle toppled and rolled off, spilling the liquid as it traveled across the linoleum. The two puppies whimpered and sniffed around their semi-conscience master.

"See what you done made me do?" she said him. She bent down to see if he was breathing. As she put her hand on his chest to feel for a heartbeat, in a surge of survival, he grabbed onto her arm and sent her big rump tumbling onto the floor with him. He reached for her neck, and with both hands he began choking her. She gasped and struggled, she discovered the small man had super strength and he had somehow overpowered her. Pure rage of adrenalin took over and with all her might she pried his hands off of her neck. She had an awful feeling the man might be taking her out instead of the other way around. As they wrestled, Miss Ada eyed the partially emptied quart bottle. She strained and stretched to get her fingers at the neck of the bottle. When her fingertip touched the bottleneck, it rolled away. Angered at the small man's ability to get the best of her in the tussle, she chomped on the first spot of flesh that came close to her false teeth. He screamed profanities. He immediately released the woman and grabbed hold of the wounded area. Miss Ada got up and ran from the man, but he chased her down and cornered her in the living room. With unbent arms he strangled her again. She kneed him with her fat knee and he let go, hollering in agony. Her only resource was a bat, meant for intruders, which was propped in the corner. She grabbed the bat and swung it at his head, like Jackie Robinson swinging for a home run. He went down with a thud. She knew by the way his head hit the corner of the coffee table she'd killed him. Miss Ada stood looking at him. She became raving mad when she saw the two puppies whining around their dead master's body. They had been the reason she was forced to murder him prematurely. As she glared at them sniffing and licking at the body she instantly went berserk. Furiously, she raised the bat then beat and pummeled the two puppies. She stomped upon both their heads and could feel the bones of their skulls crushing beneath the heel of her shoe; then she beat them some more with the bat. As she clubbed them, the crunching and cracking of their tiny bones never bothered the big, burly woman. Their small, contorted corpses were mangled and deformed. After she had bludgeoned the helpless, little animals to death she snatched one, then the other from the floor. She could feel their crumpled, crushed bones crunching within the palms of her hands. Angrily, she hurled the pulverized puppies into the garbage pail. She returned to the living room and took a quick surveillance of the disarrayed rooms. Miss Ada shook her head in disapproval. To the dead man on the floor, she said, "Look at this mess. I was gonna get rid of you in a less violent way, like poisonin' your ass. But noooo! Thanks to your smart ass, I done had to go tearin' up my house fightin' with you for makin' that nasty remark. I gotta get your dead ass out of here before . . . ," she heard footsteps on the front porch and then the squeak of the front door opening.

"Miss Ada, you should have seen Zorita tryin' on them clothes. Couldn't get her big butt in half of . . ." Pearl's eye caught sight of the body on the floor. "What's done happened here?" she asked. Her small frame tried to shield Zorita from seeing her dead spouse. It was too late, Zorita spotted the body. She pushed her mother aside and ran to her husband. She plopped down onto the floor and cradled his head. Zorita rocked him back and forth praying he was not gone. He had expired, and no amount of praying or rocking would bring him back. Pearl poked her fingers into Miss Ada's shoulder, "What are you gonna do now? You wasn't satisfied just lettin' him be. You gonna have a hard time gettin' yourself out of this jam. I sure hope you know a good lawyer?"

"I don't need me no lawyer. We gonna haul him the hell outta here, and as far as anybody is concerned he just took off. We're movin' his body, that's what we gonna do," she snapped back at Pearl.

"What do you mean *we*? Me and Zorita ain't had nothin' to do with no murder and we don't want to get ourselves involved," Pearl protested.

Even so, Miss Ada waited until all of Timberland was sleeping peacefully. She helped Pearl and Zorita prop up the dead man on the passenger side of the blue convertible. She informed Zorita to drive the man's body to the remote side of Rocky Bluff, while Miss Ada and Pearl followed in their car. Even though Zorita's husband had taught her how to drive the car, he never showed her how to rise and lower the convertible's top. As she drove with the top down, she prayed she would not get stopped by a cop. When Zorita started out, the dead man was in a sitting position, with a cap slightly covering his closed eyelids. As soon as she made the first sharp turn, the body fell over onto the seat, toppling the cap onto the floor. "Oh my goodness," Zorita cried into the darkness. "Oh Lord, please let me hurry up and get to Rocky Bluff. That damn Miss Ada, why did she have to kill him?"

When the two cars finally pulled onto the far side of the bluff, she was relieved. She stumbled out of the convertible, falling to the ground in shock. Delivering the corpse to Rocky Bluff had been too much for her. Miss Ada pulled up behind the convertible. She could see the young woman in the headlights of her car. Miss Ada said to Pearl, "Look at that stupid bitch, fallin' on the ground." She quickly put her car in park and she and Pearl got out. She went over to the girl and yelled at her, "Get up Zorita, get your big ass up and help me and Pearl push this car over the cliff."

Zorita got up, angrily looked at Miss Ada, and spit in her face. "Push it over your damn selves." She climbed into the back seat of Miss Ada's car and waited. Miss Ada decided she'd take care of Zorita later; right now she had something more critical to oversee. She wiped the runny saliva off her cheek and made Pearl help her reposition the man's body behind the wheel. Miss Ada put it in drive and she and Pearl pushed it over the cliff. By the car's headlights Zorita witnessed her parents cover up the murder.

There was no way Miss Ada could force Zorita to report her husband missing, so she did it herself. It took a missing-person report from Miss Ada, and an anonymous phone call reporting a car toppling over Rocky Bluff, from Slick Rick, before the phony Randy Banks was officially declared as dead. No one bothered to check the true identity of the man, so on Monday, May 11, 1964 the insurance money came rolling in. Miss Ada was all in Zorita's face when the check arrived by special delivery. "Ain't you gonna split that with us?" she asked, when she notice Zorita folding the check and stuffing it in her big bosom.

"What do you mean?" the widow asked.

"Where's me and Pearl's cut? If it wasn't for us makin' it look like an accident, you wouldn't have gotten double indem-nee from the insurance company."

Once again, Zorita stood face to face with the big woman. This time she wanted to plow her fist into Miss Ada's jaw, but she knew it would only make it worse for her child-like mother. Instead, she spurted, "Are you kidding me? Let me get this shit straight. I come home from shopping with mama to find my husband dead as a doorknob after you've bashed his head in. You won't let me call the police, but force me and mama to get involved by removing Randy's body. Are you telling me I've got to split this with the both of you?"

"Yeah," Miss Ada abruptly answered, "That's exactly what I'm sayin'. Me and Pearl want our share of that money. Pearl gets twenty-thousand and I sure want my twenty-grand."

The following day, when Zorita cashed the check and received the satchel of large bills, she gave Miss Ada the amount requested for both women. After turning the money over to them, she warned Miss Ada, "Stay the hell away from me. If you see me on the street, don't you so much as speak to me."

That evening Zorita found a cute, rent-to-own house three blocks from where her mama and Miss Ada lived. She had had so many hopes and plans made with her husband. A home with him, children with him, trips to Disney World with their little family. Her dreams were now destroyed. Thanks to Miss Ada, her husband was dead. In her eighteenth year she found herself graduated, married, and widowed. She decided to let the women do and live as they choose.

Their way of life was not for her. No more would she have to listen to Miss Ada's ramblings of getting all you can get out of people and of not associating with dark-skinned people. Besides, the woman was near-black herself. Zorita could not understand Miss Ada's logic. Her obsession of Pearl's honey complexion, and her fixation with Zorita's very bright tone now seemed totally obnoxious to Zorita. It caused her to fall into a trap of judging friends, relatives, and people she didn't even know. It was upon meeting and loving Kashif, she realized the fallacy of the old woman's belief. She had tired of it. And now she had experience the ultimate pain of losing her husband at the hands of Miss Ada. Zorita knew she would avoid the two women as much as she could. Her life with them had been different, at best. She witnessed her mama become brain-washed by Miss Ada. Zorita was determined her life would not go that way. When she was a child she witnessed her mama become more and more subdued. As the years rolled pass, her real mama, Pearl, seemed to have disappeared from her role as Zorita's mother and Miss Ada seemed to have taken over the position. Zorita was now grown and on her own; no longer a child in need of Miss Ada or her mother. Finally, she was free. She wanted to be around people she liked. She wanted to treat people right, and to have them do the same by her. Zorita looked around her new, furnished apartment and was very pleased. She felt as though she had walked straight out of a hellhole and right smack into a haven of peace.

CHAPTER 8

DISPATCHER

Max Salerno was the owner of Queen City Taxicab Company. He was a short, stocky man of forty-one years of age. His thinning hair was made quite noticeable by the way he combed the longer strands of hair towards the bald front of his head. His belly girth was extra large, extending into his groin area, thus making him look very uncomfortable in his clothes. On Friday, June 5, 1964, his cousin, Andy, quit the dispatching job. A week after Max posted the help-wanted ad in the Timberland Times, Zorita walked into his office wearing her best dress, a new pair of nylons and a brand new pair of heels. Her brown hair was curled under with a thick bang. She wore only a touch of lip gloss, a little bit of blush and eye liner.

Having no previous job experience to include on her resume, she did the next best thing; Zorita listed the marketable skills she had learned in school. She also included all of her positive attributes as well. On her resume she indicated that she was reliable, trustworthy, professional, a quick learner, and would be easy to work with if given to the opportunity. She attached to her resume a copy of her school transcript, which verified her high-academic average and one-hundred percent school attendance with zero tardiness.

Max studied her impressive resume and school transcript. After going over it thoroughly, with her sitting across from him, he put the resume down on his desk. He looked at Zorita, then looked at her documents. Max, using both hands, pointed his two index fingers down towards her resume; he said, "I like what I see," then pointed both fingers towards her, "I like what I see." Then matter-of-factly asked, "When can you start?" She never had to say a word, the job was hers.

Being a dispatcher for Queen City Taxi suited Zorita. She was happy with her job. Initially, the drivers were quite flirty once they discovered a woman's pretty voice instead of Andy or Max's gruff tones over the dispatch radio. What a surprise they got when they stopped by the terminal to check out the lady with the sensual voice. Some of the men openly showed their disappointment when they met the two-hundred and ten pound woman, who stood only five feet, four inches tall. The next time they gave their pick-up information, the flirtation in their voice had disappeared. Zorita took it in stride. She knew she was larger than most men were accustomed to. And that was okay with her.

~ ~ ~

Five years later, Zorita was still dispatching for Max. She had adapted to dating sporadically. It was 1969 and Zorita was twenty-four years old. After the murder of her husband, she secretly pined for Albert's attention. Whenever she spotted him walking through the town she'd slow her car down and look his way, but he would always busy himself by intentionally looking straight ahead. She still hoped Albert would come around and propose marriage to her once again. Her hope was fruitless because Albert continued to ignore her. Zorita figured she had blown her opportunity of being his wife. When she finally accepted the fact the man would not pursue her, she continued dating. But going out with different men had worn thin. When the fellows got what they wanted, she found herself once again watching television during her time off. She decided to concentrate on her work and give up the dating scene for a while. And to take her mind off of her loneliness she purchased her rent-to-own house and excitedly remodeled and decorated the small home. She found a sense of pride and happiness in taking ownership of the little house.

One day Percy Thurman walked into the office and Max gave him a job as an evening driver. When he heard Zorita's voice over the radio, he went to the office to meet the lady behind the alluring voice. He introduced himself, but Zorita took it with a grain of salt, telling him how nice it was to meet him. Often the man would stop in and sit his butt on the corner of her desk and chat on his breaks. She observed his conversations becoming a little more sweeter with each visit but put it off as just another lonely man on the prowl for sex. Zorita never thought of Percy as anything but a nice, friendly cab driver. The new driver shocked her three months later when he asked what were her thoughts on marriage. At first, she figured he was messing with her head to get into her panties. As the months went by she noticed the look of love, not lust, in his eyes. She sensed he was very much in love with her. On a cold, winter night at the end of their shift, she allowed him to follow her home. There, they made passionate love. She knew it would happen because Percy was persistent, bringing her chocolates and magazines to read so she could fill in the slow periods at the office. He was a tall, thin man and as dark as Kashif. Though he was not as good looking as her first love, she knew with his soft, gentle ways she would fall in love with him. For years she waited for Albert to come around. The man's pride was too bruised after she ran off and married the man she knew as Randy Banks. Zorita could no longer wait for Albert; she felt her life was slowly slipping by.

On Sunday, March 22, 1970 Percy proposed to her at a romantic restaurant. She accepted his proposal. The two lovebirds had a plain wedding ceremony at the court house. When the word got around they were married, Pearl showed up on Zorita's doorstep. "Miss Ada ain't too pleased about this you know," she said in a foreboding voice.

Zorita looked at her mother as if the woman had lost it. She hadn't spoken to either of the women since she stormed out of their home in 1964. She told her mother, "I don't care about Miss Ada. Is that the only reason you marched over here, because if it is, you can march right out of my house."

"Child, you know Miss Ada ain't been right since you done up and moved out. She ain't been the same. Zorita it's been nothin' but lonesome ever since you've been gone." She gently ran her soft fingers up and down Zorita's bare arm. A weird feeling crawled down the young woman's spine and she snatched her arm away. Zorita long ago learned not to trust her mama. Too many years of seeing Pearl become Miss Ada's marionette made her realize Pearl mentally was unable to be a responsible mother. She knew she could never be comfortable around the woman again; and her trust in her mother was gone.

Pearl looked around Zorita's house. She could see signs of Percy living there. She noticed some of his personal papers strewed about the end table. Clothes that Zorita had pressed for Percy hung on a rope strung from end to end of the small kitchen. She even noticed the man's large, fancy shoes. This infuriated Pearl. She hadn't had a man in so long and she was wild with envy. She had long ago tired of lying up with Miss Ada and Slick Rick. It angered her to know her daughter was freely having sex with a man while she had to fake organisms with the two older women. When Zorita wasn't looking, Pearl tucked one of the many romantic cards that was displayed on the end table into her pocket. It was a card Percy had signed, *I love you Mrs. Zorita Thurman, more than you will ever know. Your husband, Mr. Percy Thurman.*

For a few years Zorita and Percy were happy. Percy kept Zorita anchored. They ate, drank, slept, loved, and laughed together. He escorted her to most all the town functions, and he especially loved taking his woman to Holy Baptist Church of Christ. He always looked sharp in his three piece suits, Florsheim shoes and fancy fedora; and boy could he sport that fedora. And how elegant she looked in the tailored dresses, high-heels, matching purse and stylish, brim hats, which Percy bought for her to wear when he took her to church. Every Sunday they went to service because Percy did not believe in drinking, smoking or cursing; he was a God-fearing man. Another thing about Percy, he never seemed embarrassed by the weight Zorita put on. If his wife mentioned she needed to lose a dress size or two, he would flash his big, beautiful smile and tell her he was just thinking she needed to put some more meat on her bones. Life was good for Zorita and Percy. The couple decided earlier in their marriage to have a big family. Percy was quite virulent, and made love to his wife every chance he got. They even did it in every position imaginable. As time passed Percy began to feel very bad that he could not impregnate his wife. He suggested they adopt a little boy and girl; and so they began their search for a reputable adoption agency.

~ ~ ~

It was a cold, winter's night in 1973 that Zorita got a call on the dispatch radio from a taxi driver named Hank. He said in a rushed voice, "Zorita call the police, Percy's been shot."

"Percy's shot?" she spoke loud into the mike. "Who shot him?"

"Don't know, but you got to get off of this radio and call the cops. I'm over here on Central Street near the Regal Theater with him. Hurry up and make that call. I don't want to be a sitting duck out here and get my tail shot off. Girl, call the cops now! Now, for goodness sake!"

Zorita put in the call to the police and anxiously waited for Hank's voice on the radio again. She didn't trust herself to drive over to Central Street and check on her husband. Minutes seemed like hours, and a sick feeling made a home in her stomach. Twenty minutes later she saw one of the taxi drivers pull up. By the street lights she could tell it was Hank's cab, and then Benny pull up behind Hank. She grabbed her jacket and ran out into the cold, night air towards Benny's car. Hank was out of his cab and walking back towards Benny's vehicle. It was Benny who gave her the bad news. Percy had sat in his cab waiting for a fare that flagged him down, then disappeared into a building. As he waited for the person, a man came up and shot him. That's what a witness said. When asked who it was that hailed Percy's cab, the witness said it was too dark to see the face and it was the same situation with the shooter. Zorita fainted and the two cabbies struggled to get the large woman out of the cold weather and into her dispatch office. She was unconscious for almost five minutes. When she came to she laughed as she told them she just had the worst nightmare. The cab drivers let her know it wasn't a nightmare. After they told her the complete episode again, Zorita sat at her desk shocked and heartbroken.

Max was saddened about Zorita's loss. Not only had Percy been a good husband to his dispatcher but Max had come to regard the man as a dependable cab driver. Max gave Zorita two weeks off for her bereavement. Even though she didn't want to be away from work for so long, Max made her take the time anyway. He convinced his brother, Ed, to fill in on the evening shift until Zorita returned.

It was about a week and a half later that Zorita noticed Miss Ada and her mama riding around in a brand new Lincoln Continental. Through the car windows she could see them both dressed in furs with matching hats. It was strange to see the two women flaunting such extravagance and Zorita was sure there was something underhanded about the whole situation. The following day she drove to Miss Ada and Pearl's place. She knocked on the door, Pearl yelled for her to come in. Zorita was taken aback when she walked into the house. New furniture was in the living room and a brand new dinette set graced the kitchen. They even had new drapes and carpet. Zorita looked at Pearl who was sitting as close she could sit next to Miss Ada. Miss Ada ran her fingers through Pearl's long, tinted hair. "Zorita, just look at my baby. Ain't she beautiful." Pearl smiled at her daughter. Miss Ada continued, "You can have some of what we got if you come 'round our way. Why Slick Rick's done had her eye on you for years. Ain't that right, Pearl?"

"Yeah Miss Ada, that's right," she agreed. Pearl gave her daughter the once over, turned to Miss Ada and said, "Miss Ada, you know what they say, *You can lead a horse to water, but you can't always make them be thirsty.*" Pearl seemed to mess up any proverb she tried to use as she shared her infinite wisdom. In front of her daughter, she turned her head towards Miss Ada and kissed the old woman passionately in the mouth. Pearl turned back to see the bewildered look on Zorita's face. She gave a sexy smile to her daughter. "Zorita, Slick Rick will give you anything you want like

Miss Ada done gave me." Pearl's eyes looked lovingly around the newly-decorated living room. In a dreamy voice she added, "Don't this place look wonderful?"

Zorita could feel her stomach getting queasy. The bacon, eggs and grits she'd eaten that morning were coming up and ready to explode from her mouth. She remembered long ago, when she caught her mama and Miss Ada having sex in Macon, Georgia. She could feel the gritty texture on her tongue. She tried to rush to the bathroom, but the vomit gushed onto the new carpet. Miss Ada threw Pearl aside, jumped up and shouted, "You simple-ass cow. We just got this carpet put in yesterday." Pearl looked at her daughter in disgust. It was a mess she knew Miss Ada would make her clean up. Pearl hadn't had to clean anyone else's filth since Miss Ada killed Randy and Zorita moved out.

Zorita went to the bathroom and got herself together. While she was in the back area of the house something told her to look into their bedroom. It too had new furniture. On the dresser was a picture of the two women holding one another like lovers do. She quickly went back to the living room where the two unhappy women were. With the taste of coarse vomit still in her mouth, Zorita said to both women, "Don't be thinking I'm gonna have me a woman to be my man." She looked hatefully at Miss Ada. She accused, "I know you had a hand in killing my Percy." She looked around at the newly-furnished house. "I want to know how you got him to sign over an insurance policy so you could get the money to pay for all this stuff."

Miss Ada walked over and stood breast to breast with Zorita. She hated when the girl challenged her. In fact, she wasn't so sure if she even liked the high-yellow ingrate anymore. She said, "Looka here bitch, you is mine. I'm the reason your fat ass is even here on this earth. If you don't watch yourself, you is libel to be pushin' up daisies with them two dead husbands of yours."

She took her titties and grinded them as hard as she could next to Zorita's breast. With her big, man-like hands she grabbed Zorita's face and forced her tongue into the woman's pukey mouth. When Zorita finally pulled free from Miss Ada, she hauled off and slapped her as hard as she could and left the house. Miss Ada went over to Pearl and grabbed her up from the carpet she was scrubbing and start beating the small woman. She screamed at Pearl, "Did you tell her what we did? Did you?" Pearl tried desperately to convince Miss Ada she hadn't said a word to Zorita concerning the man's death. She hadn't said anything, because she hadn't known anything about it.

Zorita was right to be suspicious. After Pearl stole one of the cards Percy had given his wife, she hid it away in her drawer. Often the tiny woman would take it out and admire it, pretending it was meant for her. She loved looking at it, touching it, kissing it and reading it over and over. She convinced herself that her imaginary man-friend had lovingly given her the card. Unfortunately, Miss Ada found it, and the big woman came up with a great plan. It didn't take long for the scheming woman to talk Slick Rick, who was tall and skinny like Percy, to practice the man's signature. Slick Rick not only perfected Percy's signature, but she even rode in the man's cab so she could fine-tune her impersonation of him. When she and Miss Ada were convinced Slick Rick's mannerisms, dress, and attitude were similar to Percy's they called East and South Insurance Company and took a policy out on Percy Thurman, making Miss Ada the beneficiary. When the insurance man gave Slick Rick, whom he thought was Percy, the pen to sign the contract, Slick Rick forged the man's signature with ease. They patiently waited years later for the appropriate time to murder Percy. The odd couple felt with the span of time the two of them would not be suspected. True to their calculation, the law never looked their way.

PART TWO

CHAPTER 9

THE INN—OWNER,
JACK OF DIAMOND

Upon returning from the Korean War in January of 1955 Jack Phillip grasped a bargain of a lifetime. That was when Jack purchased his precious inn from Theodore Burton. Teddy Burton was a seventy-two year old man who no longer had the energy to keep the place going. The old man knew he could not get top dollar for it so he let it go for five-thousand dollars. It was easily worth twenty-grand. There were many violations against the inn, but the violations were of no concern to Jack. Over time he knew he would take care of the infractions. He managed to leave the navy with a chunk of money and was looking for something in which to invest. The inn would be that something. It had eight rooms total on the second and third floors and other amenities to go with it. For years the place had simply been known as The Inn. It was an easy name for the bar and lounge. Whenever someone had to give directions, they'd simply say, *You go pass The Inn* or *It's not too far from The Inn;* because people all knew and loved the big, boxy, brick building in the middle of the colored neighborhood. It was the only such building in Timberland. Not even in the well-off white section of town was there a building of such grandeur. It took Jack less than three months to get The Inn up and running. He decided it would be best to get his barroom, lounge and billiards room remodeled before he made improvements on the upstairs rental rooms. The pool room was a cinch. The pool table and all of its equipment was already there. He let the guys shoot pool for twenty-five cents a game. Since there was a quarter coin-slot attached to the table, he didn't have to worry about being around to collect the coins. The bar was a different story. The old man had taken all of the bottles of booze with him when he sold the place to Jack. Jack borrowed one-thousand dollars from his brother, who lived in Buffalo, New York, to get the bar stocked. There was a little bit of money left over. With that, he purchased walnut trees from a vendor trying to unload his end-of-the-season inventory. Jack planted the walnut trees on the sides and all along the back of the inn. He purchased thrift shop furnishings for the eight rooms. When he felt the rooms were completed, he began renting the rooms out. He rented them by one, two and three hour room-rates, by a nightly-rate and weekly-rate.

There are four ways of getting to the inn's upstairs rooms. You can walk up the beautiful, mahogany stairway, which was in the center of the inn. You can take the elevator, which is located at the back of the inn. Then there is the rickety, constricted stairway next to the elevator. But few people even know about the hidden, narrow stairwell because it is located behind a closet-like door. And finally, the last way to get upstairs is the steel staircase on the outside of the building. Lovers happily paid the money and would sneak away to the outside stairs to get to their rendezvous rooms. Out of town guest stayed at his inn, even husbands who found themselves thrown out, by angry wives, had a place to stay at Jack's inn. By the end of 1955 The Inn had a new name and so did Jack. Because of the walnut trees he planted and the location of the building, which was in the deepest part of the valley, Jack renamed it, The Inn at Walnut Valley. With all of the fancy diamond rings he sported on his fingers and his love of the game of poker, his customers nicknamed him Jack of Diamond.

Ten Years Later

In the spring of 1965 Jack of Diamond threw a tenth anniversary party to celebrate a decade of service to the community. The innkeeper was proud to have been in business for ten years. People dressed up for the occasion. Even the poor people, who sometimes didn't have enough money for their rent, saved enough money to buy a fashionable outfit for the ten-year gala. Jack of Diamond, who had once did a big favor for Wilson Pickett, convinced the singer to come and put on a show at the inn. The evening of the party the place was really jamming. Wilson Pickett belted out *Mustang Sally* and *Midnight Hour* with bravado. He had the crowd partying the night away. The soul singer brought down the house and Jack of Diamond laughed like a crazed hyena as he raked in all the money.

~ ~ ~

Jack ran through cooks like he ran through women, plentiful and unfulfilling. He consistently had bad luck with each cook throughout owning his inn. The inn owner got rid of the first cook when he caught him blowing and picking his nose as he fixed the food. The second cook had warrants for his arrest and was taken away by the Timberland cops. The third cook came and went on his own accord. The fourth cook spotted his girlfriend slow dancing and trading saliva with the town's Romeo. The lover-boy turned up stabbed to death with one of Jack's butcher knife, and the cook fled Timberland. The fifth one was a lady cook; she fell for the drummer. The lady turned in her cooking utensils for a baby in her belly and a wedding band on her finger. Number six was a big guy who weighed a good three-hundred and twenty pounds. When Jack discovered the cook ate up almost everything he prepared, Jack had to let him go. By 1970, Jack of Diamond fired the seventh cook for pilfering pork chops and chickens to feed his hungry kids.

It was Thursday, August 6, 1970, two weeks after Jack had fired the seventh cook, when Nick walked into The Inn at Walnut Valley. Jack of Diamond had never seen the guy before. He wondered what wind had blown him into the little, dinky town. When the stranger asked if he could see a menu, Jack's ridiculous laugh exploded, "Har, har, har." He laughed so hard the stranger wondered why the man was laughing so outlandishly.

Jack stifled his laugher. He said, "You want to see a menu? Sure, I can show you a menu, my man. Unless you gonna eat the damn thing, that's about the only way you'll get anything off of it. You see my brotha, the damn cook quit," he lied. He didn't want to let the stranger know he was slow enough to let somebody steal food from him.

The man said, "You need a cook? I can cook; I can fix anythang you want. Besides, I needs me a job."

"Yeah, that's what my last cook said. He up and quit on me," Jack embellished the lie. "This ain't no way to run this here inn. Shit, I might as well be outta business."

"I told you I can cook, man. If you need a cook, hire me. I need a job and I'm a damn good chef."

"Chef? I don't need no chef. What I needs me is a cook." Jack continued with his silly laugh, "Har, har, har! Just messin' with you. Com'on, my man, let me show you my kitchen." Nick tagged along with the innkeeper. "This inn is my pride and joy. Here's my kitchen, now if you say you can cook, fix me somethin'." He pointed towards the stove, indicating to the stranger to get busy with his craft. Jack left the kitchen and Nick began to work his magic. He worked extra fast whipping together macaroni and cheese, mashed potatoes, fried chicken, seasoned green beans, skillet cornbread and walnut pound cake. When he was done he went out to the lounge area where Jack was preparing for the evening's crowd. He motioned for Jack to return to the kitchen. The small table in the corner was transformed into a magnificent table for two. It had a white tablecloth and a small vase containing red, white and purple petunias to enhance the atmosphere. On the countertop there was a delicious buffet waiting to be consumed. The aroma of macaroni and cheese danced around the kitchen and swelled into Jack's flared nostrils. He hadn't had cornbread in such a long time, his mouth watered at the sight of it. Nick's fried chicken looked crispier than any Jack had ever seen. He grabbed one of the plates on the counter, and his utensils which were wrapped in a napkin. As he piled the food onto his plate, he said, "Go ahead, get a plate and fix you some of this good food. You ain't afraid to eat yo' own cookin' is you? Har, har, har." He placed his plate of steaming, hot food on the table. The innkeeper sat down and rubbed his hands quickly together in anticipation of enjoying the meal. Nick was still at the buffet fixing his plate. Jack of Diamond took the opportunity to turn the rings on his fingers around so only the gold bands showed. Seconds later Nick joined him at the table. Jack stuffed a hunk of hot, buttered cornbread into his mouth and chewed. Then he took a big bite out of the drumstick and stuffed a forkful of buttered, mashed potatoes into his mouth. While chewing and wiping his mouth with the paper napkin, Jack of Diamond said, "Man, this here is some good shit."

Nick dove right into the macaroni and cheese, then attacked the chicken breast. Nick joked with Jack, "I see you is a leg man." He held his bitten piece of chicken breast up, pointed at it, and said, "I'm a breast man myself."

Jack looked at Nick's chicken breast then glanced at his drumstick and burst into that goofy laugh, "Har, har, har. That's pretty good man, you's a real funny dude."

"I tried to tell you I could cook, my man," Nick said as he put the forkful of macaroni and cheese in his mouth and practically swallowed it whole.

"Jack," he said, as an introduction, "My name's Jack; friends call me Jack of Diamond." As an afterthought, Jack lied, "They call me that 'cause I like playin' bid wiz."

"Nick, Nick Hutchinson," the man extended his hand but Jack did not shake it. Nick nonchalantly removed his hand that Jack hadn't acknowledged. He plowed a forkful of string beans in his mouth and as he chewed, said, "Nice to meet you Jacka Diamond. Hey, what do you think? Can I cook, or can I cook?" A big broad smile flashed across his face followed by a hardy chuckle.

Jack nodded, "Right-On! Shit yeah, you can cook. You is hired Nick Hutchinson. Man, you is definitely hired. Hey, I'll be payin' you under the table, if that's alright with you. I mean, it ain't like the gov'ment's gonna miss them little coins. Know what I'm sayin'?"

"Well like I was tellin' you Jacka Diamond, I'm a chef. Cooked on the USS Forrestal from 1964 to 1966." Nick added, "I got off of that ship a year before that thang caught fire."

"Umph," Jack commented. "Yeah man, I heard about that damn fire. Set off some explosions, too. Heard over a hundred and thirty sailors died in that fire." He shook his head in pity. "Damn shame!" He got up from the table and went to the buffet. Jack of Diamond grabbed the other drumstick and another piece of cornbread and returned to his seat. He chuckled, "So you's a swabbie! Gottdamn, ain't that somethin'. I'm a navy man myself. The Lord musta sailed yo' ass right over here boy 'cause He knew I needed a good mess-hall cook. Welcome to my galley. Har, har, har." The proprietor gobbled his food, then took a long swig of the root beer. He complimented, "Wooooo! That was some meal, Nick. Shit, that hit the spot." He eyed the walnut pound cake, went to the countertop and cut three healthy slices of it. Each hunk of cake he put on a napkin. "Here man, have a piece of yo' cake." When Jack of Diamond bit into the warm, moist pound cake, he chewed pleasurably slow. "Dammnn, this is good, my man! You mean to tell me I get a baker out of this deal, too?"

The new cook grabbed his slice of cake. He responded, "Hope you don't mind, but I noticed them walnut trees. Figured you must have some shelled walnuts around here somewhere. Found some in the cupboard."

Jack of Diamond took another big plug out of the cake. As he was chewing, he suggested, "Gottdamn Nick, we can make a fortune with you baking walnut pound cakes like this."

Nick finished off the slice. He confessed, "Hey brotha, that's my secret recipe. Got a secret recipe fo' my cookies, coffee cake and homemade ice cream, too. With them walnut trees, I know I can keep a steady stream of sweet-tooth customers happy."

After chomping down most of the second slice of the pound cake, Jack of Diamond added, "The hell with the customers. Just make sure I get at least one of these bad boys a week." He chewed the last of the walnut pound cake in double time, grabbed the napkin and wiped his hands and mouth.

Nick reared back in his chair. He was pleased to know he had a job, but he knew that was half his battle. He said, "All I need is a place to stay."

"You need a room? Shit man, you can stay here. Hell, I own this big-ass building." He proudly offered, "Let me give you a grand tour of *The Inn at Walnut Valley.*" He pronounced the name of the establishment with such an elegance of pride. "You're already familiar with my kitchen, oops; I mean my galley. That's the navy terminology, right? Har, har, har. I see you found my pantry, stove and 'frigerator with no problem." Jack walked towards the left into the fairly, large dining room, Nick followed. The room had an antique buffet and dining table with eight chairs. Jack pointed, "This is the dining room. Nothin' fancy, just a place fo' the tenants to sit and have one of them scrumptious meals you'll be fixin'." Then Jack of Diamond walked towards the front of the place. "This is where the party jumps off." He smiled, "Hey man, Ev'rythang's—Ev'rythang!" He swung his arms around in a level motion. "Man, we have big fun up in here; a downright funky, good time. All kind of pretty chicks and fancy cats be struttin' they stuff. Know what I'm sayin'? Har, har, har." He gave Nick a hard slap on his back. Jack pointed out his jukebox and the stage where different bands hooked up their instruments. He showed Nick the parquet dance floor. "Check it out." He did a cool slide on the smooth, wooden floor, then added some James Brown fancy footwork to prove, for an old guy, he still had it. When he was finish showing off, he exclaimed, "Man, ain't this a fantastic floor? Shit man, a whole lot of ass-shakin' goes on here. Hey, some fine-ass ladies be on this dance floor, I must say so, myself." He stood momentarily and stared at Nick from head to toe. He took note of Nick's narrow waistline, his fine, wavy hair, his golden-skin tone and hazel eyes. He added, "Humm, you ain't a bad lookin' rascal. Let's get one thing straight, Mr. Nick Hutchinson. Loretta, Beverly and that Yellow Jell-O chick, they's mine."

"Yellow Jell-O?" Nick questioned.

A wide smile came across Jack of Diamond's face, exposing the gap in his teeth. He answered, "Yeah, my man. Yellow Jell-O!

> That would be Isabello;
> With skin so yellow.
> Ass shakes like Jell-O . . .
> Off-limits, my fellow!

You get it? So like I was sayin', Loretta, Beverly and Isabello, they's mine. That makes all the other unattached ladies fair game for you. Understood?" Jack of Diamond once again checked out Nick's head of hair. It was neatly tied in a pony-tail at the base of his head. It hung a little past his shoulders. "Yeah, you is one of them wavy hair, pretty-eyed mens. Probably got a real good rap for the ladies too, don't you? Umph! I see I'm gonna have to keep my women on a real tight leash with you around. Better yet, you make sure you stay yo' ass in the kitchen." He gave Nick a gentle back-hand slap on his chest, then continued on with the tour. "Oh, I forgot to show you this." He doubled back in the direction which they'd come from, a little pass the gated-elevator. He pointed into the billiard room, "You shoot pool? If you do, in yo' free time you can join the boys in a friendly game." He walked towards the main part of the inn to get to the mahogany stairwell. "C'mon, let me show you the second and third floor," he said, as they were about to start up the mahogany stairs.

When Nick discovered they were taking the steps, he pointed out to his new boss, "Hey Jacka Diamond, man we could've taken the elevator up to the second floor when we were back there by the kitchen and pool hall." Nick glanced towards the gated-elevator at the end of the long lounge area.

"Shit man, that damn thing broke down yesterday. Remind me to put an out-of-order sign on it. Until then, it's hikin' the stairs, so let's get to hikin'. Har, har, har." With a wave of his hand he coaxed Nick to take the lead up the stairs. Nick smiled at the man's cool attitude as he started up the stairwell. The stranger was pleased to know he would be working for a boss with a great sense of humor. As Jack of Diamond walked behind Nick, he removed all of his rings from his fingers and slipped them into his pocket. He sped up and caught up with Nick on the wide stairs. They came to a landing, and proceeded up the second set of stairs to get to the second floor. Jack said, "Floor two has four rooms and so does floor three. This here is my room," he pointed to room number one on the right-hand side that had a big brass numeric number one on it. I got two weekly renters on the second floor; Harry, he's in and out, mostly out. Then there's Paulette, she's a widow, 'bout fifty-five years old. She mostly stay in her room, but her son comes over ev'ry now and then to visit with her."

At that moment the widow poked her head out the door. "I thought I heard somebody out here. Who's this young man, Jack?" Jack of Diamond briefly introduced the new cook and Paulette went on and on about how she was looking forward to finally getting a decent meal. When the innkeeper warned Nick that Paulette would talk him to death, the widow woman laughed and shook her head. "Aww now, I ain't that bad," she kidded; and her head disappeared behind her door.

"Up on the third floor is Fred," he pointed upwards. "He's up there by his-self." Jack put his hand on Nick's shoulder, and added, "Good thing for us 'cause he don't like to wash his funky ass or brush his yellow teef. Whew! Take yo' gottdamn breath away. Speakin' of which, the bathroom's at the end of the hall on both floors, complete with tub and shower. It's way down there by the elevator."

"The elevator that don't work, right?" Nick injected.

"Har, har, har. You catch on fast, my brotha! Har, har, har," Jack allowed himself to laugh at his new cook's quick wit. He continued, "So look, I got four vacant rooms. Pick any one of them and you can stay rent-free for as long as you cook for the inn." He was quick to add, "Look dude, if you take that deal, I won't be payin' you a cent. Yo' free room and board will be yo' pay. It ain't much, 'cause the rent's only ten dollars a week. I ain't never raised it since I bought this place fifteen years ago, just ain't had the heart. Now, that's the best I can do, brotha." A change of attitude engulfed his mild disposition, and his facial expression showed an edge of firmness. He cautioned, "Keep your hands off of my property, and my ladies, and we'll get along just fine." There was no har, har, har, laughter after his warning.

With an offer like that, Nick knew he could not pass it up. He jumped at the proposal and sealed the deal with a handshake. Jack would wait to see how Nick worked out before he felt comfortable enough to sport his many diamond rings in the new cook's presence.

CHAPTER 10

DISPATCHER DATES

The time was going by excruciatingly slow for Zorita's bereavement leave. She was pleased when the two weeks were up. The first day she returned to work she felt relieved. Hearing the fellows' voices over the dispatch radio was music to her ears. A week after she was back at work, Pearl delivered a package to Zorita. She placed it in her daughter's hands with no explanation, then drove back to she and Miss Ada's house. When Zorita opened it she discovered ten-thousand dollars in it. *Blood money* she thought. *They're paying me off to keep my mouth shut.* Even though she didn't know how they had managed it, she was sure they were involved in murdering her second husband. She figured Pearl was too mousy to shoot anyone in the head so Zorita felt it was between Miss Ada and Slick Rick. It troubled her that the women felt she would be a threat to them, enough to give her a box of money. What would she do, go to the Timberland Police Station and say, *S'cuse me, but I think my mama's lesbian lover and Slick Rick killed my husband.* She would never be able to prove a thing. She felt down on her luck; here she was twenty-eight and already widowed twice. Zorita hid the box of money with the remainder of the money from her first dead husband in the junked-up basement of her home.

As the years passed Albert Manning secretly kept track of Zorita. For nine years he'd see her driving the streets of Timberland but he never pursued her. He wished the inflated, heroic sagas that Mouth had spread would die down; but they lay dormant. Albert always had the weight of losing Zorita, and the deceit of his heroic adventure in Vietnam hidden in his soul. He knew he could not change the cowardly action he displayed in the war, but maybe he could be brave enough to let Zorita know his love for her had never waned. Though his heart told him he could win her back, his brain lacked the courage; so he did nothing.

Zorita long ago gave up the thought of ever being with Albert. Besides, she came to the realization that as long as she stayed in the tiny city she could not marry another man with Miss Ada and Pearl keeping tabs on her. And as bad as she wanted a husband and family, she knew she may end up having neither. For so long she wanted to live a normal life; but she wasn't so sure she knew what normal really was. If she listened to Pearl and Miss Ada, normal was what they had going on for themselves and everyone else was out of sync. If she looked at everyone else's life, normal presented itself in many different forms. Zorita came to think of normal as an individual concept. And simply being alive gave each individual the right to live life the way they saw fit.

She had hidden the twenty-thousand dollars from Randy's death in the corner of the basement. It had remained there all through her marriage with Percy. How could she possibly tell her second husband the money came from Miss Ada killing her first husband? Unfortunately, in trying to forget about her past connection with the women, she felt it best to keep the money a secret. She now believed it may not have been a good idea. Maybe if she had told Percy the whole story he would be alive today. For many months she felt sorry for herself and Max noticed things were not right with her. He even asked her if she needed more time off when he heard she was making mistakes in fares; but she promised she would get herself together. She even started having nightmares about the two women killing the next husband she married. She knew it was a premonition of what would happen if she chose another spouse. There was no way she would ever take a chance on a third marriage.

As the months rolled on, the woman slowly got over her second husband's murder. She dated a lot of men and had sex with them; secretly hoping to at least get a baby out of the deal. Her priorities shifted; now she wanted a child more than anything. If she couldn't have a husband because the two women seemed destined to rule her life, she would at least have a baby. They could not stop her from doing that.

Around the fall of 1975, two years after Percy's death, someone called the office for a cab. Before Zorita could hang up and dispatch the cab, the voice on the other end said, "Oh, you don't recognize me anymore, huh girl? Have you erased me totally from your mind to the point that I'm just another customer on the phone, My Beautiful Zorita?" It was the way he said her name that made her realize her high-school sweetheart, Albert Manning, was on the other end of the phone.

For over a decade, Albert put off calling Queen City Taxi for a cab because he knew Zorita was the dispatcher. He always paid Mouth to chauffeur him around town for a small fee. The fear of being rejected, and the horrid thought of the true Vietnam story being exposed, were the main reasons he never approached her. After eleven years of being out of the military, he was sure it was now all behind him. He tried to conceal his excitement as he spoke to her. He had heard her voice many times on the phone. On occasions he would call to hear her pleasant voice; he did this a few times a year. She always mistook the hang-ups as a customer who changed their mind about needing a cab and never suspected a thing.

Albert moved out of his mother's house after the first year of returning from the military. Being around his mama's constant praise wore him down. He moved to several different apartments over the course of time. Many years later he found solace in the room he rented at Jack of Diamond's place.

In a controlled voice he asked, "How are you doin', Zorita?"

"I'm okay, Albert," she nervously said. Absent-mindedly she added, "You know I've lost two husbands."

"Yeah, I heard about both losses. That's a shame; it really is."

"Thank you," she said. "That's very nice of you, Albert."

He thought about telling her how sorry he was for her loss, but he knew he was not. Instead, Albert inquired, "Zorita, how would you feel about goin' out with me," then hated himself after the words flowed from his mouth so freely.

She felt as though butterflies would flutter her heart away, "I would love to Albert. I really would."

Albert inquired, "What time do you get off from work?"

"Eleven," she eagerly answered.

"You know, The Inn at Walnut Valley will be partying pretty good 'bout that time. You think you might wanna go there with me?"

"Sure. Fact is, I live about a block and a half away from the place." To let him to know she was not a regular patron of the establishment, she added, "I've never been inside. I'd love to go with you."

He was relieved she said yes. He replied, "Fine. Only thing is, I don't have a car, so I can't pick you up and take you there. Can you meet me at the place?"

"Of course I can. I'll meet you there at eleven-thirty," she confirmed.

He was happy. Zorita told him she would dispatch his cab immediately. He said, with a smile in his voice, "Cancel the cab. It was you that I needed all along."

She laughed, "Okay, Albert. I will see you soon." She hung the phone up and smiled with elation.

He knew about the first husband and second husband. The death of her first husband happened shortly after his return from the war. He was living with his mama. The old woman kept him abreast of everything she heard around the neighborhood. Another thing Mrs. Manning did was repeat the stories as they came from Mouth. His mom's much loved story was how Albert saved his whole platoon, and any day her son would receive a The Medal of Honor for his valor. Albert listened to the tales as the people told them. When each account would supersede the previous legend, he found himself too afraid to say anything to differ. Albert was a war hero in everyone's eyes. Mrs. Manning even thought about having the Timberland Times write a feature article, sparing no adjectives, to praise Albert's heroism. Her pride was so exuberant that Albert was tired of hearing all of the fabrications. The lies were like a runaway snowball tumbling down a snowy mountain slope. The more stories told, the bigger it got. The bigger it got, the more he dread the day it would burst apart, and the real truth would finally unleash the avalanche of lies all over the town of Timberland.

After Zorita received Albert's phone call, the evening lagged. She was anxious to meet with him. She never expected to hear from Albert ever again because he'd been so successful in avoiding her. She had always loved Albert; but feelings had been hurt and years had passed. What would she say to him? Would he treat her badly for hurting him, or would he let bygones be bygones. Zorita knew the only way she would find out how he really felt, would be by spending an evening with him at The Inn at Walnut Valley. She passed the place many times, yet she'd never step foot inside. When she was married to the convict, who passed himself off as Randy Banks, he stayed away from the inn. Zorita now felt it was because he was trying to lay low. And her second husband, Percy, preferred the church over a bar scene. She was excited. Tonight she couldn't wait to get inside of the building.

CHAPTER 11

LOVE

Albert still had a slight limp but could easily get around without the aid of a cane. His friend, Mouth, talked him into the continual use of the walking stick. Mouth even insisted he use a fancy-looking carved stick which Mouth had special made one evening at the Downtown Friday-After-Four Festival. Mouth told Albert the cane would enforce the fact that even though he was a disabled veteran he was still cool. When the craftsman said the price would be twenty dollars, Mouth even paid for it. The know-it-all did a lot for Albert, and the ex-military man always felt he was forever in Mouth's debt. That is why he allowed Mouth to continue the exploitation.

Once, when Mouth picked up Albert for a night at The Inn at Walnut Valley, he noticed Albert did not have his elaborate cane. He said, "Man, go get the walkin' stick I bought for you." When Albert insisted he'd be okay without it, Mouth told him, "Like hell. Man, that's what people look for, a hero. You is our hero and people buy heroes, *and heroes' friends*, drinks. Shit, I ain't bought but a few drinks for myself since I been goin' to the club with you. Go get that stick, it's savin' us lotsa money."

Albert remembered one night when an out-of-towner, named Jasper, came into the bar. He was a friendly fellow who met no strangers. He mingled with the customers at the inn. Even though he was passing through town, the people in the club took to him very well. When the guy stopped by Mouth and Albert's table to make small talk, Mouth told the stranger he'd fought in Vietnam in the same unit with his pal, Albert. He lied about how the two of them single-handedly captured four Vietnamese and killed them. After he told the tall-tale, Jasper was so impressed he purchased a round of drinks for his new, brave friends. "Brotha, I tell you any man that's been to Vietnam and made it back here in one piece deserves a medal. The least I can do is buy drinks for you guys. He paid the bill when the drinks were delivered, picked his glass up to toast them. "Here's to some real brave soldiers." The three men sat there and drank and drank, each round being paid for by the man with the big bank roll. The more Mouth drank, the more war stories he created to impress the out-of-towner.

When the man bid Mouth and Albert good evening and left the bar, Albert challenged, "Man, why did you have to tell Jasper that you were in the military?" Albert shook his head negatively, indicating his displeasure. He continued, "I mean, I know you use me to hustle drinks, but why tell somebody that don't even know you that you were in 'Nam. Lotta men died over there. Believe me you might not have made it out alive if you had really been over there."

Good ol' Mouth played it off like it was all in fun. Laughingly, he said, "Aww man. Shit, it ain't like I'm gonna ever see the fool again. He don't live here. Spendin' the night at the inn and takin' off tomorrow mornin'. That's what the joker told us. Rememba?" He slapped his friend on the shoulder, "Hey, it got us each four free drinks, didn't it? Al, don't worry 'bout it, man. Besides, it ain't like he couldn't afford it. Did you see the wad of cash that clown pulled outta his pocket?"

Albert appeased Mouth for many years by allowing him to fool the public with the hero-rouse. Long ago he had wish Mouth hadn't generated the stories about his military experience. Tonight he wanted to impress Zorita. He did not want the praises which he knew he didn't deserve. He did not want free drinks, and he did not want to be anyone's hero. Tonight would be different. Tonight he would meet his beautiful Zorita at The Inn at Walnut Valley.

He found a nice, cozy, out-of-the-way table. When he spotted her at the door, he went over and led her to it. He seated her, excused himself and went to the bar and ordered a Crown Royal for himself, and the Gin and Tonic Zorita requested. She didn't even know what it tasted like; she knew years ago she'd seen Miss Ada and Pearl drink the concoction. She took a big swig, the bitterness of the drink made her gag. Albert chuckled, "You don't even drink, do you?"

"No. I don't know why I didn't just order a cola. It seems so strange ordering a pop at a bar instead of an alcoholic beverage," she admitted.

"It's alright Zorita. No sense in drinkin' liquor if you don't drink. I'll be right back." When he walked away from the table she noticed his limp and she wished she'd gone to the bar to get the soda herself. When he returned he had a glass of Pepsi-Cola and another Crown Royal on the rocks. "Compliments from Jacka Diamond," he said. Even eleven years after Albert's return, occasionally, Jack would give him a free drink. The innkeeper looked upon Albert as not only a fellow military man, but a great warrior as well. He even discounted Albert's room rate by two dollars a week.

Albert sat down, happy to be sitting across from Zorita. He looked at her and she looked at him. No words were exchanged; the two of them sat staring at one another. Zorita, a woman who always held her own, felt uneasy as Albert stared into her eyes. Unable to take it any longer, she bent the straw towards her lips to take a sip of her soda. As her stomach quivered with excitement, she kept her eyes on the glass of Pepsi, then she glanced over her straw and looked at him. He was still staring. She released the straw from her lips and began poking it up and down between the chips of ice. Gradually she looked pleadingly into Albert's eyes, as if to beg for forgiveness. Finally, Albert touched her hand; he gently spoke, "Why'd you do that to me? You knew I loved you and you loved me, but you took off and married somebody you didn't even know." He quickly thought, then asked, "Did you know him?"

"No Albert. No I didn't," she confessed. "I got nervous 'cause I loved you so much and I was afraid." She wasn't going to explain the irrational porch lessons the two women felt necessary to instill upon her when she was a child.

Albert took a drink of Crown Royal, he folded the swizzle stick in half and squeezed it back and forth between his thumb and finger. He thought it was the dumbest thing he'd ever heard, not wanting to marry him because she was afraid of being in love with him. He scowled, then said, "I wish you hadn't done that Zorita. I gave up hope that I'd ever have you in my life again, so I joined the army. I didn't really need to be in the military. I loved you. If you weren't ready to marry, I would have been patient and waited. You didn't have to marry a stranger to keep from becoming my wife."

Zorita found herself feeling bad about what she had done to Albert. Because of her, Randy and Percy were murdered and Albert, the love of her life, wounded in the war. She couldn't do anything about her two dead husbands, but since Albert had come back to her she was determined not lose him to Miss Ada's hit squad.

She wanted to make things right by him. She said, "I know I did you wrong. I hope you can forgive me." There was a sparkle in her eyes. When her fingers touched his hand he felt as though there was a chance the two of them would be able to become lovers once again.

Within days Zorita and Albert were feeling like two teenagers in love again. Even though they felt so amorous, Zorita knew she would not marry Albert if he asked her. And Albert was determined he would not lose his beautiful Zorita a second time. When Zorita explained to Albert that she loved him so much and would always love him, he was happy. He confessed his undying love to her. When he did ask her to marry him, she gently turned him down. Once again he was crushed, yet still he came to her office and kept her company while she worked at Queen City Taxi. Sometimes he would call her and keep her company when the evenings were slow. Never did he ask her to marry him again.

Zorita finally explained to him she believed she had an aura of a curse surrounding her soul, because two of her husbands were dead. She admitted though she wasn't superstitious, she felt for some reason it wasn't in the cards for her to be married. Albert, sadden to hear how hard her life had been, said in a solemn voice, "It's a shame we can't just pledge our love for one another. Not legally get married, but spiritually. No one will ever have to know."

Zorita was pleased at his sensitive nature. She said, "Why Albert, that's a wonderful idea, and no one will be none the wiser. We'll be husband and wife in our hearts, and we will live together like husbands and wives do. To outsiders it'll look like we're living together. Only you and me will know we're man and wife by the way we love and respect one another. We can even start a family. We don't have to be legally married to do that." Albert smiled at the suggestion. He wanted children with his Zorita. He didn't care if they weren't married in the eyes of the law. A baby with Zorita meant he could finally start his life with her. He felt God was smiling down on him. His life had taken a turn for the better now that Zorita was back in his arms. They celebrated their eternal love for one another before God and themselves. In their mind, heart, and soul they felt married. Though Zorita legally kept her second husband's last name; spiritually she placed Albert's surname wrapped lovingly in her heart.

That night Zorita drove Albert over to The Inn at Walnut Valley. She waited in the car while he checked out of his rented room. On the way out Jack asked him why he was moving after living at the inn for so many years. "Got me a woman now; gonna move in with her," he said with a grin.

"She must be some kinda woman for you to be movin' into her place," Jack of Diamond said, as he dust and straighten up his liquor bottles.

"She is. It's Zorita, my main-squeeze. You know, that pretty, light-skinned girl I been datin' fo' a while?"

"Well, that sounds like a celebration. You is shackin' up with Zorita. Man, I didn't know she was yo' ol' lady. Why, that's great Al. Since I can't give you a weddin' gift, how 'bout I give you a shackin'-up gift. Har, har, har." He reached beneath the bar and pulled a bottle of champagne from his mini-frig, then left the bar and returned with a new bottle of Crown Royal.

That night Albert lay in bed with Zorita. And though both their bodies were large, they managed to make love in the double bed.

During the early morning, Zorita awoke and did not find Albert in their bed. In a frenzy of a panic she ran from the room to search for him. When she went into the darkened kitchen she saw her spiritual husband's silhouette by the moonlit window. He was sitting at the table in his boxer shorts and the bottle of Crown Royal up to his lips. He spotted his woman standing in the room and tried to hide the bottle. It was too late, she had seen it. She turned the light on and he covered his eyes with one hand to avoid the harsh light. When his eyes became adjusted to the brightness, he slowly removed his hand, "Zorita I love you. I got so much love for you in my heart and I don't even deserve you." She went over to him and held his worried head against her big belly. She comforted Albert and told him not to concern himself, because she was sure she didn't deserve him either.

CHAPTER 12

CURTIS MAYFIELD

Jack of Diamond heard that Curtis Mayfield was playing at the Move and Groove Club in Pittsburgh for their Thanksgiving matinee. He decided to drive over and meet with the singer. He wanted to convince Curtis Mayfield to help a brother out by singing at his inn for a Christmas 1975 celebration. When the singer agreed, he posted flyers in his window that the musician was coming to town. Everybody wanted to be there to see and hear the soul singer.

Most all who patronized the club did not want to miss the special event. For weeks the customers were excited. *Are you going to the inn to see Curtis Mayfield? What are you wearing? Who are you taking? You know he ain't with The Impressions anymore; that cat went solo back in 1970. Can you believe he's comin' to Timberland?* Everyone who had planned on going was extremely excited, including Albert and Zorita.

It snowed the night Curtis Mayfield and the musicians arrived to put the show on. As the people flocked into The Inn at Walnut Valley they headed straight for the bar to warm their systems up. Albert and Zorita had arrived an hour early to ensure prime seating, but so had everyone else. Consequently, they sat three tables away from the stage. When Curtis Mayfield came onto the platform to sing, Albert and Zorita made themselves nice and comfortable. Curtis brought two guys with him. One was on bass while the other guy funked out the right notes on the inn's old, beat-up piano. Most everyone had a drink in their hand and cigarettes propped between their fingers, or hanging from their lips. Jack of Diamond had decorated his marbled bar with blinking Christmas lights. Behind the bar, at one end of the shelf, sat an illuminated Santa carrying a bagful of toys, and at the opposite shelf end was an illuminated snowman, complete with carrot nose, coal eyes and smile. Earlier in the week, Jack asked Nick to help him hang paper snowflakes from the ceiling so the bar and lounge could resemble a winter wonderland on the inside as well as the outside. The place was festive and it made Albert happy he and Zorita were there to celebrate the holiday amongst the town folk. Albert pulled Zorita close to him and had his arm draped around her shoulder when the trio played *I'm So Proud* and *The Woman's Got Soul* for all the romantics in the club. Zorita squeezed Albert's thigh as they watched the lovers on the floor dancing to the music.

Jack spent the whole evening walking around with a red and white Santa hat on his head. He was laughing and having a great time hanging out with the patrons, dancing and cajoling with everyone. He especially mingled with Curtis Mayfield and the musicians when they came down from the stage for their twenty-minute break. Albert noticed the guy who had been pounding out the keys on the piano. He wasn't sure, but he thought he'd seen the man before. He took a gulp from his drink then looked a little harder at the individual as they all stood around the decorated bar talking and laughing. The man sported a beard which was cropped close to his face. Albert strained to get a better glimpse at the piano player. He could have sworn the man's eyes were similar to his old army buddy, Jim Bo. Could it be? He stared intensely, trying to imagine the man without the beard. He thought it was probably somebody who looked like Jim Bo. When he heard the man's thunderous laughter, he knew it was his buddy who had helped him get out of the army. It was Jim Bo Johnson, the soldier he paid to shoot him in the foot. For a moment, all of the lies he let Mouth spread around town about him being a hero began to swarm in his head. He felt sweaty and when he saw Jim Bo looking his way he panicked and wanted to disappear from the lounge. He heard the men all talking loudly about the military.

When Jack began telling the guys of his experience in the Korean War, Albert's heart beat fast. He wished he and Zorita hadn't come to the lounge to hear Curtis Mayfield play. He start reaching for his coat which hung over his chair. Before he could grab it he heard Jim Bo's big, booming voice, "Yeah man, I knew this dude when I was in Vietnam; shit, he paid me a lot of money to shoot him in the foot. Hey, that got him the hell out of 'Nam, and quick. Man, I think that cat came from a small place like this here town, Timberwood, Timbertown, something like that. Anyway they threw my ass in the stockade, and I heard they gave him a dishonorable discharge."

As Jim Bo was telling the story the crowd around him was laughing. In Albert's heart he knew they were laughing about him. Albert was trying to hide his face so Jim Bo would not spot him. Nervously he asked Zorita, "Look sweetheart, you ready to go?" When his companion objected to leaving so early, he said, "Zorita, I ain't feelin' too good. If you want to stay, go ahead and stay. I can use the pay phone over there and call me a cab."

Zorita tried to convince Albert not to leave but he insisted. She was disappointed. With a heavy huff she said, "Alright Al, let's go."

He tried to shield himself from Jim Bo. But when he and Zorita got up to leave amongst the seated customers, Jim Bo spotted him moving about through the smoked-filled room. He shouted out, "Hey, there he is. Man, what a small world. I can't believe this shit. There's the guy I was tellin' y'all about." He yelled, "Hey Manning! How the hell have you been? Man, come on over and meet the group." Zorita was impressed that a member of the trio knew her Albert. Jim Bo continued waving for the former soldier to join them. "Come here man, come and meet Curtis Mayfield and Teddy Schaffer." Reluctantly, Albert walked towards Jim Bo with Zorita by his side. Jim Bo put his arm around the disgraced man. "Hey man! What it is, my brotha?!! Man, I ain't seen you in over a decade." Then he told Albert, "Manning, I was just tellin' Curtis and these fellows how you paid me to shoot you in the foot. Hell! That was one way to get out of that damn war. Shit man, how the hell you been?" He went on like it was common knowledge that

Albert Manning had been smart enough to find a way to get himself discharged.

Jack of Diamond said, "Naw Jimmy, you got it all wrong. This here is the town's hero. He returned from Vietnam wounded. He's our hero. He's even got a purple heart and everything."

"Yeah?" Jim Bo replied in disbelief. "Is that what you told everybody, Manning? Purple heart, huh?" He looked Albert dead in the eyes; it was then Jim Bo knew he had blown his friend's cover. At that instant he felt like a fool. What was he thinking? Who would tell the truth about being a coward? What better way to conceal a wounded foot by simply letting everyone believe it was a war injury? Trying to patch things up, he looked at Jack of Diamond, then let out a vigorous laugh. He kidded, "Man I got yo' asses. Fooled all of you didn't I?" He burst out laughing as though the humor was killing him. He even managed to wipe some laugh-tears from his eyes. "Whew, shit man. I really had yo' asses goin'."

Jack of Diamond turned to Curtis Mayfield, and said in a smug tone of disgust, "Your piano man's got a weird sense of humor. Why everybody knows Albert's a war hero."

Curtis said, "Yeah Jack, ol' Jim Bo is a real prankster here. Anyway man, you know you can't believe everything you hear, 'specially from Jim Bo's ass. He got me a coupla times just like he got you."

"Jack shook it off; with a wide grin on his face, he said, "Son-of-a-bitch. Har, har, har." He slapped Jim Bo on the back, "Man, you had me goin' for a while. Har, har, har, son-of-a-bitch," he repeated, totally flabbergasted. He noticed Albert and Zorita with their coats on. "Hey! Where you guys goin'? Curtis and these cats got a couple more sets to do."

Zorita heard the whole conversation. She thought it was odd for the piano man to say one thing about Albert, then switch to another. Though she didn't say a word, she suspected the man told the truth with the first tale. She figured the piano man tried to pull the whole thing off as a joke when he realized no one really knew what had happened to Albert's foot. Even though Jim Bo tried to clean up the mess, Albert knew the man had exposed him as the true coward he'd been in the Vietnam War. Zorita clung onto Albert's arm. She leaned over and whispered in his ear, "Look Al, if you're not feeling good then let's get out of here."

Jim Bo extended his hand, he said, "Nice to see you again, Manning. Good to shake a hero's hand."

Albert simply nodded and said, "Take care Johnson." He gave a generic goodnight to the cluster of men. He and Zorita steadfastly walked towards the door.

When Zorita awoke the next morning she searched throughout the house for Albert. He was nowhere in their home. Albert had packed his few possessions and disappeared. For a week she looked all around Timberland. Zorita asked everyone she knew if they had seen Albert Manning. No one had.

PART THREE

CHAPTER 13

THE INN—OWNER, ZORITA

On February 22, 1976 Zorita turned thirty-one. It was a lonesome birthday for her. She had hoped to celebrate this birthday with the love of her life, Albert. She had even thought about having a little party for herself. But now Albert was gone and there was no happy birthday for her. She was sad and was beginning to realize she might even be depressed.

Zorita had been married twice; widowed twice, and her spiritual husband had run away. She decided to never marry or shack-up again. She felt very defeated. Her life experiences made the townsfolk look upon her with mistrust. The people knew of the deaths of her two husbands, they knew of their town hero shacking up with her, now he had disappeared. Some wondered, would he mysteriously turn up dead or did Albert manage to leave before the twice-widowed woman managed to become a widow for the third time. A few of the residents warned, *"Man, don't date her. You might end up dead or disappearing too."*

Some people said they liked Zorita and some admitted they didn't much care for her at all. She had a handful of acquaintances, but even those she found hard to trust. Because of all of the tragedies in her life, over the years her skin toughened. She knew Miss Ada and her mother, Pearl, were behind the rocky road of her life. She attributed Albert's disappearance to the two women. They were the ones who had contaminated her thinking, thus forcing her to pass up Albert's marriage proposal when she was younger. She was sure if she and Albert had married they would have moved far away from the women; and Samuel Lynch and Percy Thurman would be alive today.

Zorita was a fair woman and would try to do things to help the few people she cared for. Even so, some still talked negatively about her. The handful of people who claimed to be Zorita's friends swore you only had to get to know the woman. According to them she had a heart of gold. It would be your own stupid fault if you were dumb enough to cross her. Because, cross her if you dared, you were sure to end up licking your wounds and crawling away with your tail between your legs.

Zorita had been to the inn numerous times with Albert. It was a place where she had smiled and laughed with him. It was a place where he held her close and kissed her ear as they enjoyed the music. At that club Albert taught her how to drink Crown Royal, an alcohol her system could tolerate. Ever since Albert left, without so much as confiding in her, it set Zorita into a deep slump. She shied away from the inn, visiting it only once in a while. She wanted desperately to talk to someone, but she did not trust any woman. The only guy friends she had were Max and the taxi drivers and there was no way Zorita would spill her guts to the guys she worked with. They always thought of her as a tough-as-nails kind of broad. She certainly did not want to tarnish their concept of her.

~ ~ ~

Over the years, as owner of The Inn at Walnut Valley, Jack of Diamond gambled hard. His game of chance started out as a minor hobby. He played poker on a weekly basis in the inn's side room. As time went on his gambling hobby became a full-blown addiction. Now he owed twelve-thousand dollars, an amount impossible for him to pay.

Tuesday morning, March 16, 1976, Zorita was feeling very low. She felt the need to be surrounded by something that reminded her of Albert so she went to the inn. She was nursing her drink when she noticed two roughed-looking men at the bar with Jack. The larger man was speaking to Jack in a low voice. By his stance and mannerism Zorita could tell Jack of Diamond was being threatened. The other man simply stood quietly by with his hand in his pocket. She saw the big man reach over the bar and jerked Jack by his shirt collar. As he was nose to nose with Jack he spoke, then thrust him quickly aside. He and his partner walked out of the place in slow, deliberate strides. Zorita sensed something was seriously wrong. She waited a few moments before going over to Jack of Diamond, who was now sitting on his bar stool with his head bent down. She said, "Jacka Diamond, you alright, man? What the hell was that all about?" Zorita could see the large, brown, bald spot in the center of his afro as he held his head low in worry. He slowly got off of the stool. She could tell by the expression on his face the dangerous-looking men had spooked him. He looked desperate. She had known what it was like to be desperate because she'd been at her wits ends many times. However, Jack's desperation was sheer fear, while her desperation was of anger.

Jack of Diamond said, "The trip I took to visit my brother up there in Buff'lo, New York, was supposed to be a vacation. You know, gettin' a rest from work and all."

Zorita was the only customer in the bar and lounge area. She seated herself on a stool at the bar with her unfinished drink. Jack put two glasses on the counter and poured her a Crown Royal on the rocks and a Cutty Sark for himself; he left both bottles on the counter. She killed her drink, pushed the empty glass aside and moved the newly-poured drink closer. Zorita said, "I know. Everybody was surprised to see you close the place up and take a vacation this past summer." Trying to lighten the atmosphere, she added, "Hell, I thought you was married to this inn." The attempt at humor did not work. Jack of Diamond still looked worried. He downed the scotch and poured himself another and downed it too.

He sadly said, "My brother have these friends, you know. Anyway, he said he played a lot of poker with them so he invited me to get in on the action."

"What happened, you win or lose?"

Jack said, "I was winning, and winning good the first coupla days. I won over two-thousand dollars. Man, I was thrilled to pieces. I thought for sure it was me and my brother takin' them fools with our hustle."

Zorita shook her head, grabbed the Crown Royal bottle and poured another shot for herself. "Geez, I can't believe you won so much. Did you go there especially to gamble?" she asked him.

"Well, I went there to have a visit with my brother, besides I ain't had me no vacation since I bought this place way back in 1955. Anyway, Billy remembered how much I liked poker so he told me he knew a coupla big games him and me could probably take. I thought, what the hell, it's been decades since me and Billy's been together. I figured it would be fun to be playing with him again."

"Did your brother know these guys?"

"He said he did. Said they had big money, just ripe for the pluckin'. Damned if I didn't spot Billy all hemmed up in a corner talkin' real serious to one of them. Shit, I didn't pay no mind to it, thought it was part of the thing we had going. Maybe I should've, because instead of us ripping' them off, I think they all ripped me off. I lost the two-grand I won, plus four-thousand of my own. After I ran out of money, I got deeper and deeper in debt trying to win my four-grand back." He shook his head in disappointment. "Twelve-grand in the hole, Lord! Anyway, these men don't look like nobody to be messin' around with. If my brother did set me up, I will take care of him later. Right now I got to get somebody to loan me twelve-grand so I can get this thing off my back."

"Damn, Jacka Diamond. All these years I've known you, I didn't even know you had a brother. What kind of brother do you have that would set you up like that? Did he have it in for you?"

Jack shook his head and poured another drink. He knew Zorita was right. It was foolish for him to think he could trust his brother. Since buying the inn, he gambled in the side room with the men of the community. He hustled his friends, but nothing very big. Thirty bucks here and there; fifty buck if his hustle was really good. Even still, his friends didn't know Jack of Diamond had duped them, because they thought their money was lost by honest wager. His mind drifted back to episodes with his brother. He wondered why he had ever thought he could patch things up with Billy. They were close in their younger years, now they were old. Years, distance, money, and Jack of Diamond had even suspected, jealousy when he purchased the inn, weakened their brotherhood. He hoped there was a chance for them to bury the hatchet. So when his brother invited him to come for a visit, he agreed to go. The end result of the visit was the fact that he was twelve-thousand dollars in debt to his brother's crooked friends.

Zorita saw Jack's dilemma as an opportunity for him and her. She could get Jack out of the enormous debt and become owner of The Inn at Walnut Valley at the same time. Owning the inn would surely keep her from thinking about how her life had spiraled downhill. She would have less time to ponder the murders of two husbands, and Albert's disappearance. She decided she would buy it from Jack of Diamond who needed money desperately to pay off the huge gambling debt. Zorita had lots of money hidden away inside her small house because she did not trust the banks. It was a bad habit she'd picked up from Miss Ada, hoarding money within the confines of her home. The purchase of The Inn at Walnut Valley would be a great investment opportunity.

Zorita said, "Jacka Diamond, I tell you what, I got me a little nest egg set aside. I can help you out of your problem. How about you selling me The Inn at Walnut Valley? How much did you say your debt was for?"

The old man suspiciously eyed her. He start fiddling with the wet bar towel, then threw it aside. He took a big gulp of his scotch. With the glass hovering below his lips, he said, "Twelve-thousand dollars, that's what I said I need. Do you think I'm gonna sell you my establishment for a measly twelve-thousand dollars? You must be crazy." He finished the remainder of the scotch and placed the glass on the marbled counter. "Look girl, this place is worth at least sixty-grand. I tell you what, how 'bout if you go into one-fifth partnership with me?"

"Partnership? Jack, I don't go into partnership with nobody when it comes to business," Zorita snapped "Hey, it's your lights they want to snuff out, not mine, so you can go ahead and risk your life with the thugs. It don't matter to me." Even though she despised Miss Ada, she could not deny over the years she'd picked up a few of the woman's worse traits. Zorita hadn't intentionally wanted to emulate her. It just happened as a subliminal defense mechanism against people who thought she was an easy mark.

She grabbed the Crown Royal bottle to refresh her drink; but Jack of Diamond clamped down on it before she could pour another shot. "What you think you're doin'?" he said in a harsh voice.

"I'm getting me another drink." she tersely answered.

Jack was pissed with the big, young woman. He wondered what kind of fool she had mistaken him for. His eyes narrowed to slits. He said to her, "You want another drink, you pay for it."

She gave him a cold, hard stare. She pulled a money clip from her big bosom, pried apart a five-dollar bill and hurled it onto the counter. "Here, buy some drinks for yourself on me. They might be the last drinks anybody buys you before those goons return. Here's my number in case you change your mind." She rambled around in her large dress pocket and pulled out the stubby pencil she'd picked off of her floor earlier that morning. She jotted her telephone number onto a bar napkin, then pushed the napkin towards him and left the inn.

Jack felt his heart tightening. For a brief moment he thought about returning to Buffalo with his thirty-eight to kill his brother; then remembered he would have the two goons to contend with. He could use the money of Zorita's, but he didn't want to sell her his place. He scoffed. He was a sixty-two year old entrepreneur, and here a woman half his age had enough money to clear his debt. He wondered how someone so young had possession of so much money. He was very angry she had such a bundle; and even angrier at himself for being in such a bind.

The following day he went to Timberland Savings and Loan to borrow the money. He couldn't get a dime from the loan officer, not even if he put his inn up as collateral. Even though the bank official didn't come right out and say it, Jack knew the bank was not interested in an inn located in the heart of the black neighborhood.

Nick saw Jack sulking about and asked his boss what could possibly have him looking so down and out. When the troubled man told him, the cook shook his head and said, "Man, I'm sorry to hear you is got such troubles. I would give you the money if I had it. You know I would." The innkeeper knew people always said they would help you if they could. It was only condolence talk; that's all it was. Zorita had the money, but she wasn't talking about loaning it to him. She was looking to make more money with the money she already had. She was a smart lady. Jack knew if such an opportunity presented itself to him, he certainly would not loan the money to the person who was desperate for it. He'd make just the deal which Zorita was offering him. Who in their right mind would loan such a large sum? Why, even a person with the best intention might default on repaying the money. In his heart he knew he was over a barrel; and if he did not take Zorita up on her offer, he might wind up dead.

He shook his head in defeat. He humbled himself and called Zorita, begging the sharp woman to come back. Over the telephone he explained, "I hate partin' with this place. My whole life is here." If he thought Zorita would soften and would offer to loan him the money, or would give in and invest twelve-thousand dollars to become one-fifth his partner, he was surly mistaken. She drove to the inn as quickly as she could. When she walked in the door, Jack of Diamond motioned for her to step into his gambling room. Once she was inside the opened door, he said, "Look, I'll sell you this place for thirty-thousand dollars; that's half its market value. Take it or leave it."

She stared long and hard at the man. Out of nowhere, a guttural laugh emerged from her. She sarcastically asked, "Did you count them?"

Confused, Jack scratched his head and asked, "Count what?"

She replied, "The number of times some fool clobbered you upside your head and rattled your brain. 'Cause you must be nuts if you think I'm gonna pay thirty-grand for this run-down dump." She did a panoramic sweep with her outstretched arm, then haughtily folded her massive arms across her belly. She continued to stare at Jack. She wished he would accept it; she was his only way out. Already a few of the regulars were milling around outside of the gambling room. That was all she needed, somebody else to hear their conversation through the opened door. What if someone else was willing to loan him the money; or worst yet, purchase the inn right from under her nose for the thirty-thousand dollars he had proposed. She didn't know if any of the other customers had money like that. She did know she didn't want her great opportunity to slip through her fingers.

It had not gone as Jack hoped it would. He knew the big gal had him behind the eight ball. Even so, he could not see selling his place for such an asinine amount of money. He was caught up in a lethal mess, but still he thought he could manipulate her to agree on his pricing term. Dragging his heels, he said, "I gotta think about it some more. Can you come back a little later in the day?"

Disgusted with the stall tactic, she told him, "Look Jacka Diamond there's things I've got to do. I don't have time to waste going back and forth like this with you. I see you ain't sure what it is you want. Look, I'll be back at midnight with the twelve-thousand bucks with me. That's all I'm bringing. If you're serious, we can swap my money for the deed to this place. If not, no harm done; least not to me!"

A little before midnight, Zorita was at the inn with the money inside a valise and her first dead husband's gun in the pocket of her jacket. Jack had the deed in his hand and a pitiful look on his face. He let Zorita into the building then relocked the door. Jack of Diamond stood staring at the lady as though he was in a horror movie and she was the villain. Her big, solid frame seemed overpowering to him and for an instant he felt intimidated by the woman. "Well?" she said. "How long are you going to put this thing off; you want to sell this place to me or not?"

"Yeah, yeah, I do. It's just . . ."

"I know. You hate giving up this inn."

"That's right. I hate knowin' you might change the name of the inn. And I hate thinkin' 'bout you cuttin' down them walnut trees around it." He looked hard into Zorita's eyes. "Just do me a favor, Zorita."

She was getting anxious to close the deal and Jack's hesitation was getting on her nerves. She asked in an aggravated tone, "What kind of favor, Jack?"

He wiped the beads of sweat off of his forehead. His voice cracked as he said, "Just don't go changin' the name of the place and don't cut down the walnut trees. Those trees are my heart. Planted each one of them myself over twenty years ago, right here at the bottom of this valley. Please don't touch them. Oh yeah, and promise me you'll let Nick work here for free room and board as long as he wants. He's a real good cook and I did tell him as long as he cooked here he would have free room and board."

Zorita thrust the case toward him and he took it. With Zorita right on his heels, he went into his gambling room to count the money. She stared at the man and felt a surge of empathy for him. With a little touch of compassion, Zorita said, "Look here Jacka Diamond, I ain't going to change the name of your precious inn. And having those walnut trees taken out would cost me a lot of money. And as for your last request, it ain't no problem with Nick staying and eating for free as long as he's cooking for the inn." She was anxious, so out of frustration to finalize the agreement she blurted, "Look man, you got my money so hand over the deed to this inn." She discreetly touched her jacket pocket with the side of her arm to feel the steel piece. He gave her the deed to his adored inn. He had taken care of all the documents earlier in the day. Zorita would have to finish up the paperwork as soon as she could. He sadly extended his hand and she shook it. The deal was sealed. He slowly walked out of the gambling room with the case of money and Zorita followed with the deed in her hand. The Inn at Walnut Valley had been a strong part of the man's life for twenty-one years. He purchased it when he returned home from the Korean War in 1955 from old Teddy Burton. His misfortune of gambling with the wrong men forced him to sell it at a give-away price to the young Zorita Thurman. He glanced at the very first dollar bill he had earned at the inn. It was in a wooden frame which he made himself, hanging right above the antique cash register. He once thought about changing the push button cash register to an updated one. However, each time the bell rang and the cash drawer flew opened he knew he could not trade it in for a newer model. Jack noticed the photographs on the wall behind the bar. They were pictures of celebrities who managed to find their way to The Inn at Walnut Valley; Scatman Crothers, Redd Foxx, Louie Armstrong, and his four most favorites, Otis Redding, Marvin Gaye, Wilson Pickett, and Curtis Mayfield. He wanted to go behind the bar and take the photos from the wall, but that would have been too final. Instead, he simply stood still and studied them long and hard. They, just as the old-fashioned cash register, were history of the inn. He left them there upon the wall. The Inn at Walnut Valley was no longer his; it was now Zorita's. He looked at the woman and shook his head. Jack of Diamond slowly walked out of, what used to be his cherished inn, The Inn at Walnut Valley.

CHAPTER 14

NEW OWNER, NEW CROWD

For the first time in quite a while, Zorita was feeling so much happier. With the purchase of the inn she sensed she was getting back on track. She felt as though 1976 was going to be her year, and she planned on making the most of it. She felt she made the best deal for twelve-grand by obtaining the inn *and* a brand new life.

In the beginning Nick was not happy about having a new boss. However, once he discovered Zorita shook Jack of Diamond's hand on his job and his free room and board he was beginning to think the big woman an alright lady. Wanting desperately to show Zorita he could handle the inn while she worked the cabstand, he gave her the low-down on how Jack operated the place when he owned it. Nick told her of the one, two and three-hour room rates Jack offered for the rendezvous couples. He informed the new boss of the illegal gambling of cards, dice, three and four-way numbers and bets on pool games which had gone on. And Nick especially put a bug in the woman's ear about the bartender lining his pockets. With all of the details Nick had given Zorita, she knew her first job was to fire the bartender and have Nick fill in temporarily.

She tried to manage the newly acquired inn as she lived in her home. She even kept her job at Max's cabstand. Max switched shifts with her, working nights while she worked days. That freed up her evenings so she could tend to The Inn at Walnut Valley's night crowd. After two weeks of trying to work the inn, work at the cab company, and maintain her house, she realized it would be an impossible routine to maintain. She told Max she had to let her dispatching job go and devote all of her time to the inn. The new entrepreneur put her small house up for sale. She moved into the best room of the big building, which believe it or not, had been Jack of Diamond's old room. She discovered it was much easier for her to run the inn herself instead of having Nick oversee the place. It eliminated a lot of unnecessary worry of who she could, and could not trust. Because though Nick seemed like a good man, she didn't want to chance him being caretaker of her place on a long-term basis.

Zorita loved being the proprietor of the inn. Even though it took the customers weeks to get use to her taking over the place they still came around. The people who did not particular care for Zorita still came only to see what the new owner was all about. Sometimes she'd notice them talking in low whispers to Nick. Zorita was no fool; she knew they were feeling her out by questioning Nick. She didn't care. She was a wise woman. The lady knew the people had no other place to go where they could be comfortable and put their worries aside for a few hours. To let her patrons know she had their best interest at heart she spent the second month of ownership offering drinks at half-price. And the customers found themselves actually liking the hefty woman. In no time they were engaging in conversations with Zorita and telling her some of their innermost secrets, same way as they had done with Jack of Diamond when he owned the place. In their interactions with Zorita they came to realize she had a great sense of humor. When she laughed you couldn't help but laugh along with her. At first it shocked her customers to hear Zorita cracking her sides when someone told her something funny. Since owning the inn she softened to the point of becoming an easy-going person when it came to her customers. But the woman was no pushover. If a patron made the mistake of thinking they could take advantage of her or cause a ruckus in her establishment, she was quick to throw them out. She knew she would make the place work. Though she loved her customers, she would not sat idly by and let any of them destroy her only livelihood. She concentrated on The Inn at Walnut Valley so much, she almost forgot the many pains of her life. The only time she thought of Albert was when one of her customers would absent-mindedly call her Mrs. Manning. It was a name the people tried to give her when they first heard she and Albert were shacking up. Whenever that happened, she would quickly tell them to call her Zorita because she and Albert had never married.

Zorita was happy to find most of Jack's regulars were still coming to the inn. She lost a few, but she figured if they were not comfortable coming around because she owned the place it was well and good by her.

When Zorita purchased the inn, never in her wildest dreams did she think it would be more successful then when Jack of Diamond had its ownership. As the months passed she made many improvements to the place. She paid Nick, and two of the cook's buddies, to paint the interior of the inn. Zorita removed all of Jack's memorabilia from behind the bar. She designated a special wall to display the pictures of the celebrities who visited the inn when Jack owned the place. His framed dollar bill and antique cash register she placed on a shelf beneath the bar. The now-bare wall behind the bar was redecorated with large mirror panels; and she purchased a state-of-the-art, digital cash register.

She hired Betty Morgan to work her decorative magic on the lounge. The woman made new tablecloths and matching cloth napkins for all of the tables. The talented grandmother even made globed candles for each of the tables in the lounge. Betty Morgan was a tall, thin, fifty-something year old woman who was very agile. She was tan in color with freckles all over her face. Her hair was course brown and she wore it in a flip style with a thick bang. Though Zorita rarely trusted any woman, for some reason she found herself liking Betty's pleasant personality.

A cleaning crew cleaned the windows of the inn and the innkeeper had a new neon sign made to grace the front of her building. Slow but sure, The Inn at Walnut Valley was emerging from the 1950's and entering the mid 1970's with its décor. The rooms which Jack once rented out by the hours and nights had been revamped; Zorita only rented the rooms to individuals by the day, week or month. There was no longer a billiards room. The new innkeeper donated the pool table to Timberland's Fire Department's recreation room. Zorita made sure her clientele knew that even though The Inn at Walnut Valley's name hadn't changed its reputation of being Timberland's flop house and illegal gambling establishment no longer existed. With the many improved changes the place attracted new customers. She had a willingness to give the young, local musicians, both black and white, an opportunity to play at her place. With that, the members of the groups invited their friends, and those new people became patrons as well.

Once Zorita felt the lounge and bar areas were completely revamped, she worked her way towards the kitchen. She checked with Nick to see what was needed in his area. When she approached him, he said, "Shit, gurl, it's been so busy in here with the word out about drinks being half-price and all. It looks like with everybody drinking more, they is eatin' more. The only thang I might need is more food for the galley; and to wish there was two of me so I could work twice as fast to get them fools fed. Know what I'm sayin'? I got to take they orders, go and fix the food; then deliver it, then take they money when they pay fo' the food, sometimes even bring they change back. And when they is done I got to clean off they table." Nick made his job sound more complicated than it really was because he liked feeling important to his new boss. Zorita told him she would let him purchase what he needed for the kitchen, plus get him hired help. The proud cook told her he would take her up on the restocking of the food, but he didn't need her to hire another hand to help him in his galley. The new innkeeper would not hear of it. She liked Betty because the tall woman was fast and friendly. The moment Zorita asked Betty if she could use some extra dough by helping Nick on busy nights, the woman jumped at the opportunity. Nick reluctantly accepted the help. He wished he had not embellished his task of being an overworked chef so vividly.

PART FOUR

CHAPTER 15

OLIVIA & JENNIFER

John Q. Adams High School was in the heart of the white community of Timberland. The white students of the school enjoyed the freedom of being amongst themselves. They loved the school's amenities, updated school books, the latest equipment for physical education, modern home economics classes, the most well-equipped woodshop and auto body classes, not to mention classrooms which were not overcrowded.

Lincoln High School was bustling with the energy of Timberland's black youth in the thicket of their black neighborhood. There was a joy about the school as the teens went through the best years of their lives. Even though they had old tattered football uniforms, no budget for updated books, and a surmountable list of items which the school desperately needed, the black students worked with what they had the best they could.

When the candidate for school superintendent, Gene Hickman, promised the people he would improve the town's school system, they were happy. Both schools were expecting better conditions and greater education for the children. When the man was voted in, Superintendent Hickman went right to work. He ordered mandatory integration for the elementary and junior high schools and voluntary integration for the high schools. If he could not get enough high school students to participate, he would randomly assign a percentage of students from each school to switch over. He also appointed fifty percent of the white and black teachers to switch schools. So not only was the student body integrated, but the teaching staff as well. In previous years most of the school funding went to the white schools; this time it would be split in half. The whole process created a dissention for some of the parents of Timberland. The uproar was mostly amongst the white parents. The angered white adults squabbled behind closed door, over clotheslines and at their gatherings. They did not want to be perceived as prejudice; they simply wanted to keep in tack their perception of equality. They mingled with the blacks many times. They even liked them, but they did not understand why the new school superintendent thought it necessary to take such harsh steps. It wasn't as though the Timberlanders were like the rebels and the Klansmen in the Deep South, or the protesters and rioters from the other northern states. They couldn't see anything wrong with the way things had been for the many decades the school system had been in existence. It angered the white parents when the school superintendent made vast improvements to the black schools, then decided the schools were even-keeled enough to start equally dividing the balance of the funds between all schools. The black families always knew of the inadequacies of the school system. They simply dealt with making the best of the lopsided situation. When the new superintendent proved his campaign promises were more than lip-service, the black families were thrilled to see the changes come. The first day some of the black students approached the steps of John Q. Adams High School they were accosted by belligerent white parents and students who stood hand in hand blocking the doors of the school. The angry parents were all hauled off to jail. They were fined, released and warned to stay away from the school. The students were given a three-day suspension. Seeing the black faces in their children's school was more than they could tolerate. All of a sudden their perception of the purity of their school had been forever tarnished. They had gone to the all-white school decades ago. Why couldn't their children enjoy the same privilege as they once had? Besides, the way they figured, it was an entitlement which their children had inherited. The Separate But Equal system worked for the people for decades; so what was the problem?

In 1975 Olivia started the twelfth grade. She announced to her mother, Sharon Burns, she and a group of her friends were transferring to Lincoln High. Her mother was shocked by the disruptive news. She didn't mind speaking her piece about keeping Olivia out of the black school system. She told her daughter under no circumstance would she be allowed to attend the black school.

Sharon and her husband agreed with the other aggressive, white parents, that black people had a different way of looking at things. They felt the superintendent made a big mistake using their precious white children to diversify all of the schools. They began to hate voting Gene Hickman into office.

What they hadn't known, was the fact that the federal government was involved with the integration of the schools. It was only through oversight the schools of the tiny town of Timberland, Pennsylvania had not been integrated. Years after Brown verses The Board of Education the nation had tried to ensure proper and equal education for all children. Timberland, however, fell between the cracks. It didn't matter whether Gene Hickman won the votes of the people, or Joe Schmoe. The word had been given to the town of Timberland if the schools did not soon integrate, all federal funding and grants could desist. There was also a possibility the town's failure to comply could be taken to the Supreme Court. The political powers of Timberland knew this would cause an uproar and did not want to take any chance of their town being stormed by the National Guards.

Olivia was an attractive, petite teen and quite popular at John Q. Adams. She wore her beautiful blonde hair with a full bang and a long ponytail. Her blue eyes and dazzling smile could melt butter when she needed a favor. She stood five-feet, six inches and had the cutest little shape. She talked her girlfriend, Jennifer Nesbaum, into transferring with her to Lincoln High. Her popularity convinced seventy-nine other high school students to join her and Jennifer to make Lincoln High their high school choice. And just as many students from the tenth, eleventh, and twelfth grade of

Lincoln High switched over to John Q. Adams also; some with the approval of their parents and some in defiance. And true to School Superintendent Hickman's word, pupils were randomly chosen to balance the government's lawful percentage at both schools.

Jennifer Nesbaum had never tired of her friends at John Q. Adams High School. She liked hanging around Heather and Amy in study hall and typing class. But Olivia was her very best friend. Even though she wasn't particularly interested in making local history by transferring over to the black school, Jennifer decided to at least give it a try. It was quite a social shock for the reluctant girl to be with the new teenagers. The difference in culture was stressful on her sheltered life. On the other hand her friend, Olivia, flourished around the new students. Jennifer found herself getting jealous when she'd see Olivia hanging out with the black girls and boys. They seemed to always be laughing and having a good time together. Olivia found something unique about the teens at Lincoln High, they had style and a sense of savvy. They seemed more hip than her friends at John Q. Adams.

When the school superintendent was forced into integrating the school system, it set off a chain reaction. Black students would go to various restaurants they'd normally pass up. They would meet their white teenage friends at those fancy eateries or go by themselves. They even start shopping at stores which were considered too costly for them or their parents. The white students would check out different restaurants too; and soon they found themselves sharing a grape soda with their black friends at Fast Eddie's Soul Food Diner, or splitting a submarine sandwich from Dolly's Sub and Soup.

Not too many of the black parents had problems with the new generation's attitude. In fact, they were happy about the change. It only confirmed what they had already known, that whites and blacks could openly socialize together. The white race had been mingling with the black population for decades; they kept it hidden behind closed doors. Deep down inside, they knew that most of them were liking the blacks and an abundance of the blacks were liking them right back. And not just cordially, but sexually as well. God knows there were enough different shades within the black race as substantiated proof.

Sharon Burns hated her daughter's choice. She wanted Olivia to return to John Q. Adams. She tried to get her husband to talk some sense into his stepdaughter, but he backed down. Olivia was no longer that scared little girl he had once controlled and repeatedly raped whenever he felt the urge. The last time her stepfather tried to force himself on her, she was fifteen. She told him if he touched her again she would go straight to the cops and tell them how he'd been raping her since she was a little girl. She even informed the man she'd let them know he murdered her brother, and it was not an accidental death as he'd claimed. The man tried hard to keep his power over the blonde teenager but she was older now and his threats no longer frightened her. She became too difficult for him to handle. He did not know who she'd been talking to because she had become less tolerable whenever he tried to rub against her. If she went to the authorities he could very well end up in prison and raped himself. The notion of being sent to the pen scared him so he thought long and hard about ever bothering the teenager again. Afraid Olivia would tell his filthy secret, he let the girl do and say whatever she pleased, and presented no confrontation whenever he felt she was disobedient. She was now a threat to him.

Olivia's mother noticed a drastic change in her daughter. The girl had her own mind and would not listen to anything she said. The teen often showed little respect and this made Sharon furious. She accused Olivia of intentionally wanting to humiliate her and she would not stand for it. The mother even noticed that Olivia talked like the cool, black teens. Even when the teen dressed, she would wear the sharpest looking clothes and fanciest shoes, instead of the shirts and jeans that the kids at John Q. Adams sported. Often Sharon sat quietly by and eavesdrops as Olivia made plans on the telephone to meet with some of the black teenagers of Timberland. When she could no longer stand it, she said to Olivia, "Why do you have to go visit with those people." Olivia told her mother she liked being around the black teens because they made her feel like family. This annoyed her mother so much that she jumped from her chair and slapped the girl.

Months later, Sharon realized it wasn't going to be easy to get her daughter to stop going to the black part of town. She wanted the girl to return to John Q. Adams High School. Through the embarrassment of her neighbors gossiping behind her back, she decided it was time to take desperate measures. She warned Olivia she'd better put things back to normal, or move out of the house. Out of fear of having no place to go, Olivia explained to her mother that getting back into John Q. was not possible once she had transferred to Lincoln High. If it would make her happy, she agreed to give up socializing with the black teens. Having no choice, Sharon said that would be fine. If her daughter couldn't get back into John Q. Adams, she would settle for the girl's promise to stop venturing into the black neighborhood.

One evening, when Sharon Burns was coming from Tammy's Hair Salon, she spotted Olivia riding in the car of a black man. When she confronted Olivia, the teenager explained it was her teacher and he was taking her to the school to pick up some books she needed. That night Sharon kicked Olivia out of the house. Olivia sweet-talked her best friend's mother and father into taking her in. "My mom is being so unfair," she explained to them. "My English teacher was trying to help me out. Mother never even gave me a chance to really explain."

Olivia stood before Marilyn and David Nesbaum like a baby finch with a broken wing. She explained how she was unfairly forced from her home. Mrs. Nesbaum looked at her husband for guidance. She said, "I don't know. I'm not too sure we should do this, David."

Olivia, who was standing next to her friend, discreetly poked Jennifer in the side to prod her into saying something in her defense. Jennifer spoke up. "Like, wow Dad. It's only until graduation, then Olivia and me will get a job and everything. Like, it'll be so cool 'cause we'll be out on our own. Like, come on Mom and Dad. We can't let her go to a homeless shelter, can we?"

David Nesbaum looked at the two girls, glancing first at his daughter, then at Olivia. He had a puzzled look about his face. He shook his head as if it was a hard decision. Jennifer clasped her hands together as if in prayer. "Please, please, please Father. Geez Father and Mother like please say she can stay. Like wow, she need our help!" she begged.

"I see you two are ganging up on us." He glanced at his wife, "Marilyn, let's give the girl a chance. We are a Christian family, you know. God would not want us turning our back on this child in her time of need. The Christian thing to do is help her. She's got no place to go. Besides honey, this is Jennifer's friend; for Pete's sake, they've been friends since grade school. Surely, we can help her for such a short time."

It took a little coaxing, but Mr. Nesbaum convinced his wife they should take Olivia in for the remaining months of the school year.

Olivia's moving into the Nesbaum household was fun for Jennifer. She was an only child and having her best friend live with her made Jennifer happy. It seemed like a party amongst the two best friends. And like, wow, how cool was that?

CHAPTER 16

OLIVIA'S MANIPULATION

Jennifer knew about her friend's obsession with older men. When they both went to John Q. Adams High School the students whispered amongst themselves about the crush Olivia had on their science teacher, Mr. Ladowski. Often a student would pick up on the sultry stares she gave to the bachelor teacher. And though they never saw him outwardly looking at her in anything but a teacher-pupil manner, most of them were suspicious. Olivia proudly told Jennifer about her escapades with the science teacher. Whenever Jennifer tried to preach to Olivia about the evils of fornication, Olivia merely told her they were hurting no one. It was one of the reasons Jennifer agreed to transfer to Lincoln High with Olivia. She felt if she and her friend changed schools, Olivia would no longer be around the science teacher and the affair would have a great chance of fizzling out.

When the white teenagers transferred to Lincoln High, the black students welcomed them more eagerly than anyone had anticipated. Olivia became just as well liked with the students at Lincoln High School as she had been as with her friends at John Q. Adams. Even though Olivia's new friendships were hard for Jennifer to take, she still dedicated herself to her friend and hung in there. When the black seniors gave Olivia more and more attention, Jennifer could not take it any longer. She knew she was out of luck because there was no transferring back to original schools. She managed to convince one of her favorite teachers of John Q. Adams to pull strings. Without explanation Jennifer was sent back to her old school. She still liked her friend but was strangely unsettled with Olivia's popularity with the new teenagers. And then there was Olivia's sexual interest in their black English teacher, Mr. Elliot, which she just could not understand.

Mr. Elliot was one of the most popular teachers at Lincoln High. He was affectionately noticed by the female faculty and the young female students as well. It made no difference to Mr. Elliot that he had an obligation to his wife and adorable twin boys. It was the young, tender, attractive students which mainly caught his attention. He had many flings with the hot teenagers at Lincoln High School. He loved being admired, especially by the high school girls in their tight cashmere sweaters. The young girls that were interested let him know they could be had, so he flirted back with them. It didn't take much for the pretty teenage girls to accept his flirting as something special he saw in each one of them; so he took advantage of their naivety. When the integration of the high schools brought forth the white boys and girls, his taste for the young girls expanded to blondes, redheads and brunettes. He took his approach to them phase by phase. Complimenting the white teens on their style of dress or telling them how nice they looked was phase one. If that went well he would go into phase two, touching. It would start out with casually touching their hands or arms as he gave them after-school assistance. Some gave him dirty looks and others boldly told him not to touch them, less they would tell their parents. Olivia was one of the few white girls who never moved her arm away when the teacher explained something to her; he knew she was primed for phase three.

The first time Olivia had sex with Mr. Elliot was in the back corner of the locked classroom. She loved sex with the black teacher, and the sex was good for him as well. Somewhere she'd heard black men were great in bed. Even though she only did it with Mr. Elliot while bending over a desk she felt the rumor was true. His manhood proved to be humongous compared to any of the other men she'd experienced.

Olivia hadn't had sex with her English teacher for over two weeks. They found it harder and harder to steal kisses and to fondle one another between class and after school. The principal, Mr. Bryant, had been suspicious of Mr. Elliot from prior years. Rumors and accusations from other teachers had reached his desk. Though he had an inkling the teacher was overstepping his boundaries with the black teenage girls, he could never catch the man doing anything inappropriate. Since his school was now integrated, the principal knew he must step up his surveillance on the teacher. He could not take a chance of the man seducing a white student. This is what made it so hard for Mr. Elliot to take advantage of his new pupil, Olivia.

Olivia missed Mr. Elliot's touch. Hours after Jennifer was fast asleep she'd lie in bed caressing her body. During those hours she'd hear Mr. Nesbaum rushing to the bathroom. Since she needed a man to fulfill Mr. Elliot's void, out of desperation she fantasized that Mr. Nesbaum was on top of her.

Early one morning, as regular as clockwork, he sleepily walked into the bathroom. Half asleep he fumbled around in the darkened bathroom. When he discovered he was not alone, he became startled. "Oh s'cuse me, I didn't know anyone was in here," he said to Olivia, as he turned to walk out of the bathroom.

She reached out and gently touched his arm. Nervously she whispered, "It's okay Mr. Nesbaum, I pretty much know your night time bathroom schedule."

"What?" he said quietly to the teen.

Hoping he would not reject her, she said, "That's right, I've been trying to get your attention for a while, couldn't you tell?" She didn't wait for him to answer as she took his hand and lead it beneath her nightgown. His heart and soul told him to leave the girl in the bathroom, and run as fast as he could. His flesh was weak, so he fondled her and let the young girl suck him off. When she was done she bent over, held onto the sink, and let him have his way with her. That moment of satisfaction made the remaining night restless for him. He played the episode over and over in his mind. He wondered how he could have so easily betrayed his God, his wife, his family. Though he felt disgusted with himself, he knew he could not send the girl away without giving his wife and daughter an explanation. He decided the only thing to do was pray, so pray is what he did. In his heart he knew God would forgive him. The following Sunday when the Nesbaum family went to church, David Nesbaum prayed long and hard that God would give him the strength to yield not to temptation ever again.

Mr. Nesbaum was good, but he held not a candle to her lover, Mr. Elliot. She found herself always looking for her next opportunity to be with the teacher. She constantly thought of him inside of her. She loved the contrast of his black skin upon her milky, white complexion. She always wanted to be with him. When she found her teacher putting the brakes on their relationship for the sake of not being exposed, she would look elsewhere to fulfill her sensational, sexual appetite. She would give herself freely to other men, white or black. Still, she could find no one to satisfy her the way the teacher did.

When she would demand Mr. Elliot see her on days which he had family obligations, he'd remind her they must keep it low-keyed. He told her not to forget he was married, and more important, he was a black teacher and she was his white student. If they were ever caught together there would be hell to pay.

Bernard Elliot knew of a motel in Oaktown which he and Olivia could secretly meet. He informed her to take the city bus to a particular street and he would meet her there then drive her to the motel. This way, few Timberlanders would have a chance of catching them together. She explained her absence to the Nesbaum family by telling them she had to visit a sick friend. While at the motel she pressured Bernard Elliot into making her his permanent lady. He said, "Look Livvy, you're an attractive girl and you mean everything to me; but people won't take too kindly if they know I'm messin' with you. Besides Livvy, I've told you I'm not divorcing Annie, you've known that from the start. I got two kids with that woman. What good would I be to you broke. 'Cause that's what I'll be, broke by the time I get finish paying alimony and child support through the nose."

"I don't care about money," she protested. "I just want to be with you." A tear flowed down her face; her hand quivered as she wiped it away.

Bernard pulled her close to him and stroked her silky hair. He put his hands on her shoulders and gently leaned backwards from her so he could look into her blue eyes. Tears now stained both sides of her face. He softly said, "Livvy, you say that now, that money don't matter, but if we ever lived openly as man and wife things might not be so good for either of us. Does that sound like something you're ready to take on in your young life?" Olivia knew he was right. She never brought the subject up for the rest of the school year.

The remainder of the months she found Mr. Elliot could only accommodate her sparingly. She made it her business to meet Mr. Nesbaum in the wee hours for sexual gratification whenever they could steal the sinful moments together. David Nesbaum would ask God to forgive him many more times. The day after graduation, Olivia and Jennifer were hired by Kroger Supermarket. They rented a small house on Grandview Road. Though Mr. Nesbaum was very sad to see Olivia go, he was extremely relieved he had not been caught with her. The following Sunday he prayed to God that he could get the girl out of his system.

CHAPTER 17

GRADUATION PARTY

Zorita was approached by the two class presidents, Willie Smith, of John Q. Adams High and Chester Lieberman, of Lincoln High. The two seniors class presidents wanted to inquire if their Classes of '76 could jointly have their graduation party at her place of business. "Why, of course you can. I would be happy to have you young folk celebrate here. I tell you what, I'll have the inn opened exclusively for your party. You young people won't have to worry about the older crowd being at your celebration; I'm gonna post flyers to notify everyone that on Saturday, May 29th the inn will be opened to graduates only." The innkeeper got excited knowing the young people would be partying at her inn. She added, "I won't be charging an admission fee for your Class of '76 Celebration. All I request is that you young people purchase your food and drinks from my establishment." She gave both of the class presidents a stern look, "None of that BYOB crap, either. I can't afford to lose my liquor license because somebody might think it's a Bring Your Own Bottle affair. So if you can agree with those terms I'll be happy to let you use my place of business. Shoot, I'll even find a band from somewhere. I would love to host your party."

As soon as the class presidents left Zorita ran into the kitchen and told Nick of the future business they would be having at the club. "Why my goodness, I have no idea what I'm going to do for a band. I told them I'd try to find some musicians for them, but I just remembered the few bands in Timberland will probably be booked for graduation parties around town."

Nick, always wanting to impress Zorita, said, "You ain't gonna believe this gurl, but my buddy Roscoe is real good friends with them Ohio Player cats. Why shit gurl, I bet he could get them to come here to play fo' them kids."

This excited the innkeeper and when she left the kitchen she got on the phone and called Betty and told her the news. "Betty, we got to really decorate this place for those seniors. They're coming here and I want to make sure they feel right at home."

The excitement spread through the telephone lines and Betty was just as thrilled. "Zorita, I got a great idea for decorating the place. I'm gonna roll up some white napkins and wrap them in gold ribbons so they can look like diplomas." She shrieked with pleasure, then asked, "Hey, what do you say if I paint little caps and gowns on the candle globes? You know I'm real artistic. I can use some washable paint and write Class of '76 Celebration on those big fancy windows of the inn."

The day of the party Zorita, Nick and Betty were busy with last minute touches of decorations in preparation for the evening's crowd. Everything was in place; Betty had adorned the inn in the welcoming colors of both schools. Blue and white, for John Q. Adams High and purple and gold for Lincoln High. CLASS OF '76—JOHN Q. ADAMS boldly arched one of the inn's large glass pane and CLASS OF '76—LINCOLN boldly arched the other inn's window.

The graduated seniors start piling into the inn around eight-thirty. The mood was festive and the music was loud. Nick's friend pulled off getting not only the Ohio Players to come to town, but The Righteous Brothers as well. And when they were taking their session breaks the graduates enjoyed dancing to the tunes on the jukebox. That night, Nick was swamped with orders of chicken wings, catfish, cheeseburgers, french fries, and his house specialty, walnut pound cake. Nick and Betty were so busy with filling and delivering orders that Betty called home and ask her husband to come lend a hand.

The inn was packed with both white and black seniors; and everyone was having a good time. While the jukebox was playing the latest record, someone from the crowed party hollered, "It's Soul Train!" and immediately there was a soul train line formed and the young people were showing off their best dance moves down the dance line. It was a real pleasure for Zorita to see the black and white graduates laughing, talking, dancing and enjoying their evening; and she was proud to be a part of their event.

As the weeks passed, most of the graduates still continued to patronize The Inn at Walnut Valley. Nick, who had never been fond of the Caucasian race, was sure things would go back to normal after the night of the graduation party. He could not understand why a lot of the young whites continued to socialize at Zorita's place. But truth be told, they liked the excitement, the people, the food, the music, and they especially liked Zorita.

One evening Betty had to take a quick break and was unable to deliver a large order of chicken wings and french fries. Before the assistant left, she pointed out the table in which Nick was to deliver the tray of food. It was the table where Olivia and a group of her white and black friends sat. When he delivered the food, Olivia smiled and said, "Why thank you, sir."

Nick looked at her coldly and said nothing. He wondered, was she trying to be smart, or condescending. *Why thank you, sir,* he mimicked to himself. He silently thought, *Does she think I'm they personal servant?* He wasn't sure what she was trying to convey. He did know he was uncomfortable around the young, white people. *Traitors,* he thought, as he noticed the young blacks talking and laughing amongst the crowd at the table. After delivering the order he abruptly returned to the kitchen.

Zorita noticed the influx of white graduates patronizing the club annoyed Nick. She knew her cook had a great sense of humor. She decided to nip the problem with a touch of wit to get him to change his attitude. An hour after witnessing Nick's behavior, Zorita felt the need to let him know his insensitiveness could not be tolerated. The innkeeper secured the bar and went into the kitchen's storage room to retrieve a new bottle of Canadian Club. Nick asked, "Zorita, why is all them white kids still comin' here? They graduation party is been over for weeks now."

Zorita was smiling from ear to ear, she said, "Nick, we gotta change with the times. They need a place to party, same as we do. Why those kids have probably seen their ol' parents partying all stiff and boring. They only want to add some fun to their lives. I can't too much say I blame them." She went into the storage room to get what she needed. On the way back to the bar, she said to Nick, "Besides man, the more people, the more business. They might be white, but their money is green enough for me."

Betty added her two cents in, "You damn straight on that. And Nick, the inn can sho'nuf use more money. Ain't that right Zorita?"

"You're right, Betty." The innkeeper laughed and said, "Now get to frying those french fries and that catfish fool; we got hungry black *and white* customers to feed." Both Betty and Zorita chuckled as the cook mumbled, tossed the catfish in the cornmeal mixture then placed them into the rolling, hot grease. Nick never again approached Zorita about her new customers and made sure he kept his opinions about them to himself.

CHAPTER 18

SURPRISING OLIVIA

David Nesbaum now found himself in the position he promised God he would never be in. Earlier in his life he promised God if he sent him a good woman to marry he would treasure her forever. But after having sex with Olivia, the Christian man wanted the young girl all of the time, more than he wanted his wife. When his daughter and her friend moved out of his home, he was sure he could forget about Olivia. Even attending church and praying for God's forgiveness didn't seem to cleanse his soul. He felt his life was tainted and there was no turning back. Trying to analyze why this awful thing ruined his Christian family's well being, he began blaming the complete situation on Olivia's mother. It was her fault for splitting up with her husband and not being a better parent to her children. It was her fault for marrying that jerk of a man, Jim Burns. If she hadn't kicked the girl out of her home, he and his wife would not have been forced to take Olivia in. How could the cold woman be so selfish? It was up to her to care for her daughter, and make sure she finished school. He had ruined his life by having sex with the teenager, now he was hopelessly in love with her. The man was even thinking about giving up his wife and daughter to be with the girl. A week after she moved from their home he sought her out. He convinced Olivia to meet with him. When Olivia got into his car he excitedly drove to a secluded area and parked. Mr.

Nesbaum and Olivia passionately kissed. Their hands were all over one another's body. Olivia suggested they get into the back seat and they did. They made passionate love and Olivia made sure his erotic desires had been completely satisfied. When she was sure she had fulfilled him completely, she gently kissed him and informed him it would be the last time they'd see one another.

Mr. Nesbaum was in love with Olivia. He was sure the young lady was not serious about their love affair ending. So when his daughter was out of town at a training seminar, he waited until the wee hours of the morning and slipped out of his house to be with her. He saw the lights on through the living room drapes and was happy to know she was still awake at that time in the morning. He used the spare key his daughter had given him and let himself in. When he opened the door, he was shocked to see Olivia lying beneath a black man on the living room sofa. It was Bernard Elliot, her ex-English teacher. He angrily slammed the door shut and in a fit of rage charged the naked couple. Quick as lightening, Bernard grabbed his pistol from the end table and shot him in the chest.

Shocked by what had happened, Olivia shouted, "Oh Lord, what am I going to do? What am I going to do? Gottdamn it Bernie! Did you have to shoot him? Did you?!"

"What the hell you think Livvy? What do you think would have happen to me if he had got his hands on my ass? I thought you had the door lock!"

"I did Bernie, honest I did. That's my roommate's father and he has a key to our apartment," Olivia explained to him.

"Your roommate's dad? What the hell is he doing walking in here unannounced, key or no key?"

"How do I know? He has never pulled a stunt like this. Jennifer gave him the key for emergencies only."

Mr. Nesbaum's being there surprised her as much as it had surprised Bernard Elliot. When she had the last fling with him in his car, she told him it was over. The fact was, she no longer needed sex from Mr. Nesbaum anymore. She had graduated from high school and Bernard Elliot continued to want her as badly as she wanted him. After all, she was eighteen and no longer his student. If people happened to see them together during any of their rendezvouses he could not be accused of seducing a student and in jeopardy of losing his job. At the most, all they could do was whisper about him having an affair with a gorgeous, young, white lady.

Having the white girl as Bernard Elliot's lover was indeed a fascination he was proud of. The fact that he had a very attractive Caucasian lady made him feel more superior to the other black man in his town. Surely none of them could claim such an accomplishment. The few black men who dated white women had the scruffiest looking hags they could find. Too fat or too bony, missing teeth, stringy hair, uneducated and desperate for any man, white or black. Bernard Elliot knew he had something special in Olivia and it pleased him. But right now, there was a dead man in the house and Bernard wanted to know why he had come to Olivia's place.

Olivia continued the fabrication, "He's probably came to check on Jennifer. She was sick yesterday." Blood was oozing out of David Nesbaum's chest and Olivia began to panic as she saw Bernard rushing to get into his clothes. "Where the hell do you think you're going?" she yelled at him. "We've got to call the cops."

"Livvy, I just shot a man." He had a look of bewilderment as he moved around trying to get his stuff together after he clumsily threw his clothes on.

"Bernard, can't you say it was in self-defense?" she yelled as he zipped up his slacks. She moved around with him as he dressed, swinging her arms about, trying to emphasize the urgency of calling the law.

"The man does not have a damn weapon, how can I claim self-defense Livvy? Think girl, think. My god, I can see my ass getting sent to prison if we don't cover this shit up."

"Well Bernie, what are you going to do?" Olivia went over and looked at the dead man. His eyes were wide open and his fixed, cold pupils stared into space. Her lover stopped in his tracks. He knew she was right. He couldn't leave the death of the man on her hands. He could see Olivia telling the cops he was raping her and shot the man who came to her rescue. He wouldn't put anything pass the white girl when it came to saving her own neck. He reached in the dead man's pocket and removed his wallet and car keys. "What are you doing, robbing him?" she asked in disbelief.

"No, I'm making it look like robbery. We've got to drag his ass out of here and put him in his car. That way the law won't even know he's been inside your place. It'll look like a robbery gone bad."

"Look like robbery?"

"Yeah," the English teacher said.

"Oh goodness, oh god, how did this ever happen? How?" she starred at the body on the floor.

"Olivia!" he sharply said. "Pull yourself together, girl! Go turn the light off," he ordered. She rushed over and flipped the switch off. Bernard put the man's wallet in his own pants pocket, picked the body up beneath the dead man's armpits and ordered her to grab his legs. The two of them managed to get the body out of the front door and into the nearby car. Fortunately, the man's car door was unlocked. It was a struggle positioning the body behind the wheel of the car, but they did it. He wiped away his fingerprints and rolled down the driver's window. He scattered the contents of the wallet all over the body, and tossed the emptied wallet on the floor of the car. He stuffed the thirteen dollars in his pocket, reached passed the body and inserted the wiped-down key into the ignition.

Olivia ran back into her house. In the apartment she was coming undone. What would she do when Jennifer returned home and found her father dead? She turned the lights back on and cleaned up every trace of the teacher's visit; wiping down everything she remembered he touched. She remembered the blood flowing on Mr. Nesbaum's chest, but she could not remember if any rolled down onto the carpet. She got on her hands and knees to see if she could find blood on the brown carpet. Everything looked normal. She tried to calm herself but could not. Bernard Elliot rushed back into the apartment. "Look Livvy, when you wake up in the morning, you will *discover* the body so call the authorities. Got it?"

"No Bernie, no, I don't, I can't do this by myself," Olivia cried, "I just can't."

"Well you don't have much of a choice," he roared. "I have too much to lose here and I'm not tossing away everything I've accomplished over this bullshit." Bernard stormed out of the back door. He cut through the wooded area to get to his car which he parked in K-Mart's parking lot. Olivia cleaned her face, brushed her teeth and put her pajamas on right after he left. She couldn't sleep at all so she paced her bedroom floor, peeped out of her window, paced the floor some more, and peeped out the window at Mr. Nesbaum's car more times than she could count. About the twenty-seventh time that she had stole another quick look out of the window, she saw Jennifer pulling up. Her roommate parked the car she had borrowed from her boyfriend not far from her father's car. From the darkened room Olivia strained her eyes to see what Jennifer would do. Her heart dropped as she saw Jennifer walking towards her dad's car. When she saw her roommate quickly heading for their door she slid into her bed and pretended to be asleep. As soon as the distraught lady entered the house she flipped the light switch on. She shouted, "Olivia! Wake up Olivia, somebody's killed my father. I've got to call the police." She rambled, "I just had that feeling that something was wrong. I just had that feeling."

Olivia got out of bed. She walked into the living room, rubbing her eyes as though she'd awaken from a deep sleep. "What, what did you say?" she faked concern.

Jennifer was on the phone, and in a panicked voice she said, "Can you send the cops over here? My dad has been shot." There was a pause, "Oh sorry. Jennifer, Jennifer Nesbaum. Yeah, it's my father, David Nesbaum. I'm pretty sure he's dead." More pause, "Okay, it's 3158 Grandview Road. Yes, thank you. Bye." She slammed the phone receiver into the cradle. Olivia did not know how to react, so she just stood there. When Jennifer saw her roommate's color completely drained from her face, she said, "Olivia, are you okay. You look pale, sit down." Jennifer tried to coax her friend to have a seat on the flowered sofa, but Olivia remembered the shock on David's Nesbaum's face when he saw her making love to the school teacher on that couch. Olivia stood firm. "Come on Olivia, the cops are on their way. There's nothing we can do so you might as well have a seat while I wait at the door for them." She paused, then asked, "Did you see anything, and didn't you even know my father was out there?"

"Why no, uuh, no. I didn't see or hear anything. I took a pain pill and went to bed early this evening. I've been really sick."

"You do look bad. Sit yourself down," Jennifer insisted

I can't sit down, I feel so . . .", she wanted to say, *bad about Bernard killing your dad,* but instead, she said, "I feel so afraid. Who could have done this to Mr. Nesbaum?" Olivia continued to stand. She noticed the more worked up she got over the crisis, the more it seemed like she had nothing to do with it. She wished it hadn't happened; the whole thing seemed surreal. She gave her friend a hug. Jennifer thought Olivia was hugging her to console her loss, but Olivia was only trying to make herself feel better. No matter how much she tried to force herself to believe she had nothing to do with Mr. Nesbaum's death, deep inside, she knew she did.

"Where are those officers? My dad never hurt a soul." Tears flowed down Jennifer's face. "Why? Why did this have to happen to my dad? He was a wonderful Christian man. For goodness sakes, he would have given the person who murdered him anything they wanted. Who could have killed him?"

Olivia gently hugged her again. She truly felt horrible about Mr. Nesbaum's death and she sound full of empathy when she said, "I don't know, Jennifer. I just don't know. You'll probably never find out why this happened." And Olivia secretly hoped Jennifer never would.

After Mr. Nesbaum's death she could no longer face Jennifer. Guilt robbed her of their friendship. They both still worked at Kroger Supermarket, but when Olivia's conscience got the best of her, she knew she had to move out of their place. Olivia found a small apartment on the other side of Timberland, closer to the black neighborhood. She even transferred to the second shift at Kroger so she would no longer have to face her former friend. Jennifer had all but become a distant memory in Olivia's mind. It seemed to Olivia the two of them had been best friends in some other lifetime. Even so, she could never erase the memory of Mr. Nesbaum's cold, dead eyes staring up at nothingness.

CHAPTER 19

MONEY PROBLEMS

The day after Mr. Nesbaum's death Olivia began to see things in a different light. Witnessing Bernard kill Mr. Nesbaum had changed her perception of the teacher. Olivia no longer wanted the wedding ring and white picket fence from him. The death of her friend's father had given her insight as to the type of man she was really involved with. It had worried her when she'd seen him with the gun a week before Mr. Nesbaum's death. When she questioned Bernard about it, he told her he always carried protection; he simply hadn't shown it to her.

A few days after Mr. Nesbaum's death Olivia carefully explained to Bernard she was breaking it off; he didn't believe her. When he'd call her and she would not answer the phone, he became irate. He came over to her place and asked why she hadn't returned his phone calls. "It's over Bernie. I can't keep on like this. There's no future for us, so please don't call me anymore," she warned him. He called her vulgar names then left in a huff.

Many evenings she sat alone in her apartment wondering how things had become so bad. She tried to analyze her mother's refusal to love her, her brother's death and her father's suicide. It made no sense to her as to why Jim Burns would take her innocence away. And Mr. Nesbaum's death deeply troubled her. She was only eighteen and so much turbulence had shaken her young world. In order to pull herself out of the rut, she hung out at the inn even more.

Bernard Elliot didn't want to let the young lady go. It angered him to see her happy and to be getting on with her life. He wanted to keep Olivia close to him for two reasons. The first reason, control; the second reason, murder. He wanted to make sure she kept the Nesbaum murder their little secret. He knew with her leaving him, there was a chance she could reveal the dark secret. Bernard was angry and paranoid; he called her from a pay phone. In a hostile voice he threatened, "Just don't go getting remorseful and start spilling your damn guts. Because bitch, if you're thinking about telling the authorities about that incident a couple of weeks ago, remember this, nobody will believe a nymphomaniac over a school teacher." He rattled on, "You think I don't know the man I shot had been screwin' you too, along with a whole lot of others around this town? How dumb do you think I am? Listen carefully to what I say, if I were you, I'd make sure I kept my mouth closed." He slammed the phone down in her ear. She was stunned. How did Bernard know about Mr. Nesbaum and the others? Had he figured it out, had he guessed, or was he bluffing. She had never even considered informing the cops. She knew she would be in serious trouble for being an accessory to the crime. Since she'd broken off with him he had become a scared man. She knew she would have to watch her back, but she was determined not to fear him. Working at Kroger and partying at The Inn at Walnut Valley made Bernard's threats meaningless to her. After Olivia called it quits, Bernard stalked her. When she spotted the man she would get nervous, but most always shook it off. Her saving grace was The Inn at Walnut Valley. All of the times she'd gone there she had never seen Bernard Elliot in the place. Once she asked him to meet her there, but he told her he didn't lose anything at the inn. Olivia discovered why Bernard never went there. Many of the fathers of the black girls which Bernard had seduced were regular customers of the establishment. There was gossip about an angry father cornering the teacher inside the inn. He threatened to castrate him if he ever had sex with his daughter again. Olivia figured it had been the catalyst which made the teacher start carrying a gun; the fear of some enraged fathers seeking revenge.

When payday came, she was ready to hit the lounge. Some of her white and black friends she'd graduated with hung out at Zorita's place with her. When they were busy with other things she went by herself. Tonight she was alone.

Earl Richardson, whose nickname was Popeye, noticed the white girl weeks ago when she ventured into the club. Though he really wanted to get to know her better, he shied away. He was thirty, a dozen years older than Olivia, but she had his nose wide open. He earned the nickname, Popeye, because of a thyroid problem which caused his eyes to bulge. As if that wasn't bad enough, every once in a while his eyes would cross whenever the pressure was on. He was six feet, one inch tall, dark-chocolate in color and sported a short afro. Although he could deal with the darkness of his skin, he could not stand the awful protrusion of his large, bulging eyes.

This evening Popeye became concerned as he watched the young lady sit in the corner of the lounge by herself. Whenever she came into the inn she was always smiling and so full of life. But tonight Popeye wondered what was troubling her. He had never before seen her in such a state. He walked towards her table with her favorite drink, a Tom Collins. Popeye had witnessed many black men acting like damn fools trying to get Olivia to notice them. Even some of the young, white men, who braved the sea of black faces at the inn, tried to hit on her. The pretty blonde only smiled and talked briefly with them and that was the extent of it. He knew she was a friendly person because she talked and laughed with nearly anyone who struck up a conversation with her. This evening was different and it worried him to see her looking so distressed. His heart raced as he neared her table. There was an anxiousness about him and his palms began to sweat. She glanced at him and nervousness engulfed him. He shook it off, and recouped his courage. "Are you okay?" he asked. Popeye continued to stand, but he placed the Tom Collins in front of her as she sipped on the drink she already had.

She looked up and gave him a solemn smile. "Thanks," she motioned for him to have a seat. He sat down and pulled his hat forward, using the brim to shadow his eyes. He tried to steady his voice because he felt his looks were against him. A lot of ladies came into the inn but he never paid much attention to them. It had only been Olivia who had touched his heart. Each time he saw her he felt something special when she casually smiled or said an occasional hello to him. It made him think he was almost a regular-looking guy instead of cursed with awful eyes. She grabbed the new drink he had purchased for her. From beneath the brim he saw her looking at him. It was the closest he had ever been to her for any length of time. She said, "I have something on my mind, that's all." It had been a two weeks since Olivia called it quits with the teacher. She had lost Bernard's weekly stipend, and last week her hours were cut. Heaviest on her mind was finding a way to get to and from work. Her co-worker, Veronica, had not only given her a ride to and from work but had taken the young girl under her wing as well. She even let Olivia use her car to take her driving test. But now the thirty-six year old, mother of three, had to move. Her husband had landed a good-paying job in Rochester, New York. Olivia had no one else upon whom she could depend for a ride and this presented a problem. "I'm okay, really I am," she said. She talked to him, she actually spoke to him. His heart pound so hard, he hoped she could not detect his anxiety. "I've got a whole lot on my mind, bills and all. And to make things worse, I'll soon have no transportation to work." She took a sip of the drink which Popeye had purchase for her. "I don't know why I can't manage my money to pay my bills. It keeps disappearing." Popeye looked at her; she was very well dressed from her beautiful hair to the tip of her expensive heels. That's how Bernard had groomed her. And though she was rid of the teacher, she still had a taste for the fine clothes and accessories he'd taught her to appreciate.

Money! Almost everyone Popeye knew had money problems. He had some money in his savings account. But he had been stiffed once before by a pretty face and there was no way he would let it happen a second time. Though he felt bad for the young girl, he did not feel bad enough to help her with her debt. He did know he could alleviate her transportation issue. He simply did not know how to tell her the piece of news without it sounding like a come-on. He carefully said, "I know you'll find this ironic, but I've got an old automobile I can let you borrow. It's been sittin' in the driveway for a few of months."

Olivia looked at him, but as soon as he could feel her eyes searching beneath his brim, he lowered his head even more. Her soft, white hand touched his and he could feel himself becoming hard. He tried to shake it off, but at the same time it felt too good for him to suppress. "That's so nice of you, but I can't do that. Besides, how can I take you up on such a generous offer? I don't even know your name."

He smiled at her, "Oh, I'm sorry. My name's Earl, Earl Richardson. Everybody calls me Popeye." She extended her hand to shake his. And though he felt uncomfortable touching her small hand, he gently shook it anyway.

"Nice to meet you Earl Richardson; I'm Olivia Territino." In total curiosity she asked, "How did you get a nickname like Popeye, with such an imperial name as Earl?"

Popeye casually removed his hat as the young lady looked at him with concern. His eyes had the usual bulge to them. The protrusion was enough to send the average lady into a frantic gasp; but Olivia was not average by a long shot. She looked at Popeye's face. She studied it hard, from his short afro to his forehead, to his eyebrows, to his big, bulging eyes, to his cheekbones, to his thin nose, to his strong jaw line, to his well-shaped lips and then to his chin. She looked sincerely into the man's eyes and said five words to him, "You've got nice features, Earl." Popeye was shocked to receive such kind words. It was the first time anyone ever said something so nice about his looks.

"Thanks," was all he could say. He put his hat back on his head, but Olivia reached over, took it off and placed it on the table.

She gave him a kind-hearted smile and said, "You have such a gorgeous head of hair. No need to put this hat back on." She placed the straw between her lips and sipped. "Look, I realize you're only trying to help me but I don't think it's a good idea."

Popeye could see the link of the car, connecting the two of them, slipping away. He wanted her to take him up on the use of the spare car because he would have a chance of seeing her again. Not being the type of man who forced himself upon any woman, he indicated with a nod that he understood. He picked up his hat and rose from the table. In a soft voice, Popeye said, "If you change your mind, let me know." He casually disappeared amongst the partying crowd.

It was Tuesday, June 22, 1976, when Popeye heard the Timberland Steel Mill office paging him because he had a visitor at the outside guardhouse. Thinking it was his father he pulled his goggles off, and rushed into the noontime sunlight towards the guardhouse. He was surprised to see Olivia. She was wearing a yellow, sleeveless dress with white, polka dots. Her long, blonde hair was curled under and hung passed her shoulders. She wore sunglasses to shade her eyes. Her blush and lipstick were so perfect you would have thought she was doing a photo-shoot for a magazine cover. There stood Popeye in his work clothes with no hat brim to camouflage his popped eyes. He wondered how she found him, how she even knew where he worked. It didn't matter. It didn't matter at all, because every swinging dick, standing near the picnic table had their eyes on Olivia, and then him. His peripheral vision allowed him to see the men on their lunch break whispering amongst themselves. They were obviously trying to figure out who was the lady, and why was she talking to, of all people, Popeye. Gaining his composure, he said, "Hello Olivia."

Olivia felt the guard staring at her through the large window. As she greeted Popeye she walked towards a small patch of grass away from the guardhouse. Popeye walked with her. While they walked, she said, "Earl, I'm sorry to bother you at work but . . ."

"Don't apologize, it's alright." He wanted to look around to see how many co-workers were still eyeing them, but he did not. "What is it Olivia?"

Fidgeting with the handle on her purse, she stalled. In a sugary voice, she asked, "The car? Is your offer still good? I mean you weren't saying you had a car I could borrow just to be saying it, were you?"

Gently he replied, "Of course not. I would not do that to you or anybody else. I'm a man of my word." He knew loaning the young lady the car would help her out and that made him happy.

"Good. I was wondering if it would be okay if I use the car. You can charge me by the week. You know, like the rent-a-car places do. I can rent it from you instead of you simply letting me use it."

"No, I can't do that. I can't charge you to use somethin' that's takin' up space in the driveway." He smiled, wiped the sweat from his forehead with the palm of his hand and continued on, "I want you to know it ain't much to look at, but it will get you back and forth. You're more than welcome to use it."

"Thank you," she said. "That's so kind of you. When can I pick it up?" She looked at Popeye with a nervous smile on her face. "I mean, I don't want to put a rush on things if it's not convenient for you. But my co-worker was giving me a ride to work; now she's moving to New York next week."

"It's no problem. Tomorrow evening, at six o'clock, will be fine. Can you get somebody to bring you to my house so you can pick it up?"

"Are you serious? Sure I can," she eagerly agreed. "What's your address?" When he gave her the information she said, "Perfect. See you then." She left, and Popeye took a deep breath and walked towards the building to go back to work. As the sun shone on his face, it dawned on him that Olivia hadn't flinched or acted repulsed from the sight of his bulging eyes. He had a wide, proud smile as he passed the men standing by the picnic table. By their smug expressions, he could tell they resented the fact that he had been the one talking to the beautiful lady, and not any of them. As he walked pass the steel mill workers they stared at him with resentment and ebbs of envy in their hearts.

CHAPTER 20

CAR

Popeye's mama died when he was three years old. He never knew the love of a mother, only the brutality of his drunken father, Kenneth Richardson.

He was the eleventh and last kid to be born in his family. His brothers and sisters were scattered throughout all corners of the continent. Very few of his siblings came back home to see how their drunken father was doing. They were too busy living their lives and hoping they could live in peace. The few times they did visit he'd extract money from them to buy his booze; and he was famous for pitting one sibling against the other. They not only didn't trust their father, but they didn't trust one another as well. One by one they left the small town for a better life. When the old man would fall upon hard times he'd call any one of them and place a guilt-trip upon them. He would beg the adult child to send him money for gas and electric or other bills then drink it up. Often he complained about how unfair it had been that he had to raise the remainder of his children after his wife's death. To let him tell it, his kids owed him. After sucking the marrow from his children, the displaced children wanted nothing more to do with him. They left the old man to simmer in his own discontent; the only child who had remained at home was Popeye. Instead of being decent to his son, he despised Popeye because of the man's youth and virility. He was old now, and he hated it. He hated everything about being old. If he could take his son's youth as his own, big, popped eyes and all, he would. Even though he disliked his son, he secretly hoped Popeye would never leave home.

Popeye was hired at Timberland Steel when he was nineteen years old. He dropped out of the eleventh grade and went to the mill to put in an application. The plant's employment manager did not want to hire him. However, when the general manager spotted his name on the job application, he came from his office. He asked, "Are you Trevor Richardson's brother?" When Popeye admitted he was, the man asked, "Where is Trevor these days? He was one of our most dependable workers. Man, he worked for me when I was a foreman. Hell of a good worker." He looked at the application, "Earl, right? Earl Richardson?" He extended his hand and Earl shook it. The man said, "Look, we don't normally take high-school dropouts but I knew your brother and he was a great worker. Now I tell you what, I am willing to give you a chance, but you've got to take the correspondence course to obtain your high school-equivalency diploma. You do that, and I'll personally see to it you get a job with Timberland Steel." Popeye took the course and got his diploma. That was how he obtained employment at the steel mill; and not one time did he disappoint the general manager.

When Popeye's great-aunt developed dementia, his drunken father took the aged woman in. He made her assign him as power of attorney over her matters. Earl's father had tried to take possession of her car but he was too late. A week before the aunt gave Popeye's father power of attorney; the old woman had already signed the car title over to her favorite nephew, Popeye. This angered the old man. He had planned on getting possession of the automobile, selling it and spending the money on himself.

That evening at the dinner table Popeye told his pa he was letting a young, white lady use the car. The old man went off his rocker. He asked him, "What the hell is you gonna let some white bitch borrow that car for? Is you fuckin' her?"

Disgusted by his father's nasty language, Popeye shook his head and defended his action. "Pop, nobody's using the car. It ain't gonna hurt for her to drive it 'til she get herself situated. You don't have to be so foul about it?"

"Don't you go tellin' me how I should be. Ain't nobody ever gave us a gottdamn thing, and here my big-shot son, here he is givin' some white woman a car. You just as stupid as a fuckin' rock, boy. So now you is gonna start chasin' afta them Caucasian gals like yo' stupid-ass brother over in Las Vegas, huh? He followed that white cow to the otha side of the world. Don't even send a dime this way either. Guess she's gettin' it all." The old man shot a revolting look at his son, then added, "Keep on fuckin' 'round, and you liable to get taken by the bitch."

Popeye looked wildly at his dad and said, "This ain't right. You can't always be angry. It ain't healthy. What is so bad about me lettin' the lady use a car that neither one of us is usin'? You got the Chrysler, and I got my old Impala out there. Like I told you, I'm only gonna to let her use it 'til she get up on her feet!"

Popeye was trying to finish his supper but the old man would not let it rest. He blurted, "Gottdamn it boy, she's white; she was born up on her feet. Do you think she would be givin' yo' black ass a car if it was you that needed one? Do you?" Ken Richardson was fuming. He hated the thought of giving the car to anyone to use. He was very mad when he found out the old aunt signed the title over to Popeye. He was trying to pick the right moment to con the car away from his son, but he'd waited a moment too long.

Frustrated by his father's greediness, Popeye dropped the fork into the fried potatoes and onions and said, "Look old man, I told you I ain't givin' her a car. I'm lettin' her borrow it for cryin' out loud. Just get up off my back." He knew his father would not agree on his decision, but that was too bad. The car belonged to him, and he wanted Olivia to get some use out of it.

The angry man shoveled more food into his mouth as he stared his son down. He shook his head, conveying Popeye had turned out to be a pitiful specimen of a man. Aggravated, he angrily said, "You's a dumb-ass fool. I didn't know yo' ass was so gottdamn stupid."

The following day, Earl double checked the car to make sure it had all of its fluids and enough gasoline to get Olivia around for a few days. The old man looked at his fool son and cursed violently beneath his breath. He stood at the screen door watching as a black woman wheeled into their driveway. Ken saw the blonde sitting on the passenger side; it angered him to see the white girl on his property. He felt as though the pretty face had made an ass out of his son and he held back his crudeness by not approaching her. If he had, he was sure he would have told her to get the hell off his property. Ken Richardson thought if Popeye was that stuck on the lady, it served him right if she took advantage of him. He jealously mumbled to himself, *"I hope she takes him for all she can git. It would serve his punk-ass right!"* He stood staring at the lady, hoping Olivia would look his way so he could stare the blonde down; but she never did.

Olivia was excited. She and her friend, Veronica, raved over the car. They were outside of the car, then both of them were sitting inside, with Olivia behind the wheel. The ladies got out of the car and Olivia went over towards Popeye and took the key from his open hand. She gave him a gentle kiss on his cheek, and Ken Richardson could feel his blood pressure rise. He had hated white people for as long as he could remember. He thought his son would never have a girlfriend; had even been suspicious of Popeye's sexual preference for many years. It was a different story now; because now the old man feared his son would have a girlfriend, a white girlfriend. Ken saw the girl talking hard and long to his son as she turned the car engine over. Veronica had already pulled off; she had to make it back to work. Olivia had taken the remainder of the shift off so she was in no hurry. Popeye's father wondered how long Popeye would lean his narrow behind into the window of the car pointing out different gadgets and gages to the cute blonde. After Popeye explained the panel of instruments and reminded her to add air to the tires, he stood up. Olivia's head popped out of the car's window and she said something hilarious. The sound of their laughter penetrated the air waves, pounding unsolicited happiness into the old man's ears. When Olivia drove off, Ken watched Popeye as he bounced towards the house with a big smile on his face. At that very moment Ken Richardson despised the boy. He was so upset with his youngest son he thought about throwing all of Popeye's clothes onto the porch and kicking him out of the house. Then he remembered, Popeye was the only child still living in Timberland. If he chased him away, who would he have to argue with? More to the point, who would he have to curse out?

CHAPTER 21

FOURTH OF JULY

The sun blazed the small town of Timberland. The heat waves oozed into the atmosphere then singed into the inhabitants' skin. The trees were in an abundance of green, leafy foliage. They haloed the town in an amazing brilliance of emerald. Frivolously, they stood atop the mountains reaching towards the heavens to offer their praise to the Almighty. In a sensual, sassy interlude they swayed in flirtation, enticing the hot, sultry winds to kiss their amorous leaves. The floral beds knew how to enlighten the townsfolk to appreciate the summerfest, too. The petunias poised onto the summer's stage, prim, pleasurable and poetic. The daisies danced like delightful darlings, as damsels do on dazzling days. And roses would readily rise to meet sun-ripened rays, as the zinnias zestfully zipped into summertime with zeal.

Everyone anxiously stirred around the town preparing themselves for the best holiday of summer, the Fourth of July. It was not just any Fourth of July, this was the country's Bi-Centennial, Fourth of July 1976, and all of the United States was excited, even small town Timberland.

The sun was excruciating hot and the town happily welcomed it. It had been a long winter and the heat of the summer had been too long coming, so the Timberlanders refused to complain. The days were so hot the ice in lemonade lasted for only a few minutes at best.

It was rumored that a pan of Jiffy-Pop Popcorn could be popped on the sidewalk; and ice cream held no steady spot upon its softened cone. The old ladies walking about the town were sure to have their parasols over their heads to shade themselves from the searing sun. The children played and enjoyed the endless days of summer. They loved life and life loved their youthfulness. Summertime was a fun time in Timberland. Outings at Constitutional Park and picnics at Rocky Bluff were top on everyone's agenda. Everybody was carefree and happy.

The roses planted in front of the inn had a most exquisite aroma. They added a touch of elegance to the beauty of The Inn at Walnut Valley. Zorita noticed the American Beauties and looking at the roses inspired her to decorate the gazebo in the Fourth of July colors. She asked Betty to assist in fixing up the area with the steamers and flags. And when they were done they decorated the lounge and bar area as well. Inside the inn they taped white stars onto the mirrors and windows. The two of them hung red, white and blue streamers all around the bar and the stage where Junior Walker and the All-Stars would be performing later in the evening. When they were done, Nick ran streamers across the ceiling and looped the crepe paper onto the chandelier in the center of the room. When the decorating was completed the place looked very patriotic and Zorita was pleased. This year, the Fourth of July fell on a Sunday. After the people went to their places of worship there would be plenty of barbequing at Rocky Bluff and lots of children swimming at Constitutional Park. Zorita knew after the families celebrated the Bi-Centennial during the day, once the evening fell, the grown folks would be at her place to party the night away.

The Inn at Walnut Valley was filled with excitement the night of the Bi-Centennial celebration. Some of the patrons sat on the decorated gazebo watching the fireworks; some were mesmerized by the display as they stood on the porch of the inn. And some just milled around in the front yard of the inn gazing at the array of sparkling colors as they streamed their brightness along the skyline. When the Timberland fireworks were completed, the patrons went back inside to party to the tunes of Junior Walker and the All-Stars.

The band had the joint rocking with their tune, *I'm a Roadrunner*. Nick had somehow made contact with the sax player and the musician obliged the inn with a gig. Zorita could never figure out how Nick could pull off such feats; he teased her by telling her it was his little secret.

Olivia was late getting to the inn. She figured she would have to look all over the lounge area for Popeye. The man had been very nice to her, and she didn't want him to think she was taking advantage of him. When she'd attempted to give Popeye twenty dollars for the week of using the car, he would not take it. She wanted to give him more, but after all of her expenses, she was doing good to have even that much left to pay him.

It was the second week of driving the car when Olivia tried again to pay Popeye. She found him in the crowded inn.

Popeye was sitting with his friend, who came to Timberland for a quick visit. His friend's name was Two Thumbs. That's right, Two Thumbs. This fellow actually had two thumbs on his left hand; a regular thumb and a large appendage which formed on the side of his main thumb during birth. When his father spotted the abnormality upon the child's delivery, he insisted his wife name the infant Two Thumbs. She told him to forget it; nobody in their right mind would put such a name on their baby. She even asked the doctor to surgically remove the extra thumb, but the father vetoed it. He said it was God's way of letting him know his boy would have a thumb up on everything that would go on in his life. He even argued, if Indian fathers could name their sons Sitting Bull and Crazy Horse, he didn't see why his son couldn't be named Two Thumbs. His wife lost the argument, so Two Thumbs Thomas went on the baby's birth certificate.

Two Thumbs not only had two thumbs on his left hand, but a gift to fast talk as well. He talked extremely quick, double the speed a person would normally converse. Two Thumbs had been in and out of catastrophes. It seemed no matter what jam he got himself into, he would motor-mouth his way out of the trouble so quickly anyone witnessing it would not believe it. Once he talked the cop out of giving him a speeding ticket; he claimed his speedometer was broken so the cop let him off with a warning. He was so good at fast-talking that one of his friends said, "Man I know your name is Two Thumbs, but it should be Fast Talk. 'Cause you sure is a fast-talkin' motor-scooter."

Popeye was heavy in conversation with Two Thumbs when he noticed the man's eyes stray away. Two Thumb's eyes followed Olivia the moment she came into his eyesight. "Damn, where the hell did she come from? She sho' is a fine mamma-jamma," he said to Popeye as the lady came closer to their table. Popeye gave a weak smile and said nothing.

Olivia stood right in front of Popeye, she said, "Earl, can I see you for a moment? We got some business to finish."

She stood defiantly waiting for him to acknowledge her. Two Thumbs looked at the lady then gave Popeye a startle look. "Earl? Earl? Who the hell is Earl?" He gave Olivia a hard look, but the lady did not take her eyes off of Popeye. As Two Thumbs stared at the lady, she continued to stand haughtily waiting for Popeye to acknowledge her.

"S'cuse me, my man. I'll be right back," Popeye said. He could feel Two Thumbs eyes on him and Olivia as they walked over to the jukebox. Popeye fished into his pocket for some coins, "What do you wanna hear?" he asked as he inserted the quarters. He stood looking at the magnificence of her as he awaited her answer. He was over his paranoia of letting her see his big eyes. That pleased him because he loved looking at her and he especially liked it when she looked right back at him.

"Play whatever you want to play. I came to give you this." She took two twenty-dollar bills out of her purse and showed them to him. Through the red and yellow lights of the jukebox he could see the bills. "Don't even think about giving this money back. I've been trying to pay you what I owed, but you act like you don't even care about the agreement we had?" She grabbed his hand and forced the bills into his palm.

He accepted the money reluctantly. "That was your agreement, not mine. I see you're one persistent lady." Even though he didn't want to, he stuffed the bills in his pants pocket. He asked, "Can I buy you a drink, Olivia?"

She smiled. He loved it when she smiled at him. "Sure, I'll take a drink." She walked over to the marbled bar with him and he ordered a Tom Collins for her and a Smirnoff Vodka for himself. He noticed Two Thumbs had left the table so he escorted Olivia to it. She wanted to tell him how much of a blessing the car had been; she wanted to let him know how much she appreciated him trusting her with it. Before she could say a word, Popeye said, "Look Olivia, I didn't let you use the car for you to pay rent on it. It's not a rental car. I gave it to you to use 'til you can buy one of your own."

She touched his hand and said, "I don't want you thinking I don't appreciate the use of it. I don't mind renting the car, honest I don't. I know it will take me a while to buy a decent used one. That's why I wanted to rent your car each week. Because by paying such low rent for the usage I can save enough money to pay cash for a reliable used car."

"Tell you what," Earl said, "Why don't you add another hundred dollars to what you've given me and you can buy the car."

It was a ridiculous offer and Olivia knew it. She sipped from the Tom Collins drink. "I can't. The car's worth more than that."

Not to be undaunted, Popeye said, "Okay, make it two-hundred and sixty dollars more and the car is yours."

She laughed. "How can I pass up such a bargain?" She knew there was no sense in debating the price of the automobile with him. From the start, he really wanted to give the car to her. He had no intention of having her think the car came with an underlying motive. He realized the lady was only showing a good dose of precaution. Popeye figured that was probably why she insisted on paying for the use of the vehicle. Though he knew three-hundred dollars was an extremely low price for the car, he was bent on helping Olivia through her plight. It made him feel good to do so, whether or not he ever saw her again.

Two Thumbs roamed around the lounge area talking loud and hardy to the people he hadn't seen in a long time. He grew up in Timberland, but after high school he left the town. He'd returned numerous times for visits boasting on his various successes. He had several get-rich-quick hustles which he tried to entice his friends to take advantage of while his money-making projects were on the ground floor. There was his credit card hustle, real estate hustle, money loaning hustle, pyramid hustle, and insurance hustle. You name it and he knew a way you could get rich from it. He told everyone who listened, he was making big bucks. If his friends hung in there with him, they would end up being as wealthy as he. Twelve years later he was still up to his same old schemes. He boasted of his travels, Miami, Chicago, Las Vegas, New York City, and Los Angeles. He even said he had worked in the forty-ninth state, on the Alaskan pipeline, and was a tour-bus driver in Hawaii. He claimed he'd visited foreign countries as well, France, Brazil, Amsterdam, and Greece. Right now, he was back at home, in the state of Pennsylvania. It was rumored the man had gone no farther than Oaktown, Pennsylvania and was simply a mailman, nothing more. One Timberlander joked, *"He might have delivered mail from all of those fancy places, but that big liar ain't stepped his flat-ass feet on any of them places."*

Zorita was at her usual spot behind the bar serving her high and dry customers. She was dressed in a red, white and blue dress which she bought from K-Mart last week. Two Thumbs was roaming the lounge. He was trying to win some unsuspecting fool's admiration on his fabricated successes. If he could manage that, he knew he would be able to hit them up for a small loan. He was leaning across the bar trying to get Zorita's attention. She came down to his end to ask what his pleasure was. She was surprised when he leaned in closer and said in his fast-paced, but low voice, "Hey Zorita! Is everything copasetic? Girl you sho' lookin' mighty patriotic in that red, white and blue outfit. I was just wondering, can you do me a favor and cash this here check for me?" He discreetly showed her the personal check. "It's a good check; just that I didn't get a chance to make it to the bank Friday before it closed up. I sho' would appreciate it."

After being close enough to hear what he was putting down, she jerked back like a jackrabbit escaping the deadly jaws of a rattler. She asked in a loud, gruff voice, "Do I look like a bank to you?"

Even though the big woman said no in her unmistakable manner, he knew he still had a chance of extracting at least a portion of cash from Zorita. He continued on in his whispered, fast pace, "Then can you let me hold a twenty 'til tomorrow mornin'? Tomorrow's Monday, right? Yeah, that's right; tomorrow is Monday. Man, it sho' mess things up with the Fourth falling on a Sunday this year. That's what threw me off with gettin' this damn check cashed," he explained. Anyways, I'll pay it back tomorrow."

Zorita stared angrily at the man, "Negro please! I don't know you that well. You blow into town every now and then. I don't know anybody that know you well enough to let you hold twenty cents, let alone twenty dollars. Except maybe Popeye; get him to let you hold twenty bucks." It annoyed her that Two Thumbs would actually approach her and try to run a game on her. Zorita didn't take too kindly to the man trying to play her for a fool. She hated that. With a don't-give-me-no-mess attitude, she yelled at Two Thumbs, "If you don't want a drink, clear the bar and make room for a paying customer."

Zorita's loudness angered him, so he spoke not only fast, but just as loud as Zorita. "Damn Zorita, why you gotta loud-talk me? You don't have to be puttin' my business all over the place. Besides, I asked you to let me hold twenty, I'll pay it back. You ain't gotta be yellin' at me and shit, like I'm some damn kid."

She stuffed her hand in her pocket and felt the cold piece. She always carried it during working hours. She knew people felt she had money, and she did have money. She aimed to keep it too. And though she prayed to high heavens she would never have to use the gun, she knew she would not hesitate to bust a cap in some fool's ass if forced to do so. Zorita said, "Look man, I said no. If I let you borrow twenty bucks I might catch hell getting you to pay it back. Then it'd be just like giving you the money. Like I said, I don't know you that well." Two Thumbs gave her a warning look to let her know she didn't know who she was messing with; and she shot the same stare right back at him.

He returned to his table, but when he got there he found Popeye and Olivia occupying it. They looked quite cozy, but he didn't care.

He motioned to Popeye to pull himself away from the lady because he had something important to say. Popeye excused himself from Olivia and went to see what was so urgent. Two Thumbs, talking in his usual fast-paced style said, "Man, do you know that big-ass heifer wouldn't cash my hundred-dollar check for me. Shit, what kinda establishment is this anyways?" Before Popeye could give his opinion, Two Thumbs quickly asked, "Man, you got a twenty I can borrow 'til tomorrow when I can get to the bank. Here, you can even hold this here check; I'll sign it over to you. If I don't catch up with you tomorrow, you can cash it yo'self."

Popeye had witnessed Two Thumbs run his illusions on other unsuspecting Timberlanders who had fallen for them. He was smart enough to sidestep the man's tricky traps. He didn't know if this was a check-scheme con or if the man was really telling the truth about the check being good tender. He reluctantly said, "Man, I don't know. I ain't too cool about cashin' somebody else's check." He took the document out of Two Thumbs' hand and strained his eyes in the low lighting of the club to examine it. Two Thumbs' name was written was on the check and it seemed real, but even so, Popeye gave the slip of paper back to him. "Look man, I'll loan you the money. I can't be messin' around with this check. Look, I want my twenty dollars back tomorrow when I get off from work. Will you still be in town?"

"Yeah man, hell yeah," he quickly answered.

"Alright, Two Thumbs. Man, don't let me have to come searchin' for your ass to hunt down my money."

Two Thumbs had a wide grin on his face. He said, "Man you is out of sight! Thanks man, thanks." He vigorously shook Popeye's hands. "Popeye, man I promise I'll pay you back. Shit Popeye, it's me! Yo' main man, Two Thumbs! Have I ever stiffed you?" He thrust both arms to the side of him and gave a friendly laugh.

Popeye had a smirked of a smile on his face as he dug into his pocket and pulled out one of the twenty dollar bills to give his friend. He hadn't bothered to answer the man's question. He hoped to get repaid, but he didn't care; he just wanted to get back to Olivia.

"Right-On Brotha! Right-On! Man, I really 'preciate you givin' me this twenty."

"Give? You mean *loan* don't you?" Popeye corrected.

"Yeah, hell yeah! Loan, that's right. Loan!" Two Thumbs snatched the money from Popeye's hand then made his way through the crowd.

A week later on a Monday morning, Olivia went to the steel mill and had Earl paged. Popeye walked briskly out of the plant to the guardhouse. He could see Olivia through the window of the guard shack, sitting there laughing at something Tom, the guard was telling her. She spotted Popeye and came out of the shack to meet him. Softly she said, "Here's your money," she discretely placed the two-hundred and sixty dollars in his hand, giving the illusion to the curious eyes that she was shaking the man's hand. They walked away from the guard house. In an excited voice she told Popeye, "All I need is the title. How about dinner at Fast Eddies, my treat? You can sign over the title to me when we get there."

"What time?" Popeye asked her.

"Seven okay?" she replied.

"Yeah, that's good."

"Great, I'll pick you up at your house in *my* new car," she proudly announced.

An image of Popeye's angry father flashed before his eyes. He knew his father would embarrass him with his filthy mouth and nasty attitude. He remembered how his pa performed like a crazed man when Popeye told him he was letting Olivia borrow the car. It would set him off the deep end knowing Popeye actually sold the car to the lady for a paltry three-hundred dollars, when it was easily worth fifteen-hundred. He knew he could not have her pick him up at his home. Immediately he said, "Look, why don't I meet you there. No need for you to burn gas coming to get me."

Olivia looked at him. He noticed there was a disheartening look in her eyes. His statement triggered a memory of Bernard Elliot having her meeting him in secret places or taking her to certain establishments. She remembered Bernard taking her out, mostly at night, so no one would see the two of them together. Olivia did not like being hidden away like she was something to be ashamed of.

She said, "Look Earl, there's nothing wrong with me picking you up and treating you to dinner. You've been nicer to me than anyone I know. To me, it don't matter what people think. It only matters what I think of me and the people I let into my life. You being black, and me being white don't mean a thing to me. Go ahead; have it your way. I'll meet you at Fast Eddies at seven." She did not look happy and it pained Popeye. She turned her back on him and left. He noticed Tom staring at the two of them but he ignored the man. He did not want Olivia to be upset with him for anything, and he knew he'd have to straighten it out when he met with her later in the evening.

Popeye could not believe his luck. He was pleased to know he'd be having dinner with Olivia. He drove home like a maniac to get himself ready for the evening. Feeling like a teenage boy preparing to go on his first date he whistled as he showered, shaved and splashed on cologne. He pulled out his best shirt and slacks. As he passed the mirror he noticed his bulging eyes. Olivia never mentioned them, nor seemed sicken by them like other people had. He really wished he could do something about them. He went closer to his reflection and examined his face. He discovered if he smiled, a person would hardly notice his eyes. He changed the expression on his face in an attempt to look less popeyed. Serious look, surprised expression, happy look, concerned appearance, closed-mouth smile, wide-tooth smile. He liked the happy and smiling expressions the best. His dad stood off at a distance noticing his mugging reflections. Disgusted with Popeye checking his image out, he eased into his son's room and stood quietly by. Unable to stand it anymore, he nastily said, "Popeye, what the fuck is you doin'?" Embarrassed, Popeye quickly grabbed an afro comb and raked wildly through his hair. Ken waited for Popeye to put up an argument, but Popeye said nothing. Seething with anger that his son chose to ignore him, Ken Richardson spitefully eyed him. To farther antagonized his son, he nastily said, "Yo' crossed-eyed ass look like a fuckin' fool, chessie-catin' in that mirror. I don't know who you is tryin' to impress, but if it's a woman, yo' punk-ass can forget it."

PART FIVE

CHAPTER 22

RAMONA

Buying the inn had been a plus for Zorita. The first month of owning the inn a tax man told her she needed cancelled checks to verify her tax write-offs. This opened her eyes to farther safe-guard her hidden loot. All about the town, she had heard the rumors of how well-off she was. *Yeah man, you know she paid cash for that place. Goodness, can you imagine, cash money. Why she's so young! I'm telling you, she must be rich. Yeah, you right, that chick is loaded.* Zorita had heard all of the innuendos. She never told anyone about her finances and that simply fueled their imagination.

She found herself worrying about patrons and tenants with free access to the inn. It was different when she was in her home and the money was hidden in the basement. No one, but her mother and Miss Ada, knew how much money she possessed. She did not think they would try to steal it from her; they were the reason she had the money. When she paid Jack cash money for the inn, everyone seemed to have heard the news. She knew if they heard about the cash payment, they must have figured she had even more money. Zorita found herself at odds regarding the large sum of cash she had hidden in her room at the inn. Often she wondered if it would ever be discovered by a patron while she was tending bar. She knew there was a possibility that someone could pose as a utility worker to search in depth for the money.

So when the accountant advised her to open a checking account she knew it would be a good idea to get a safe deposit box for her loose cash as well. She used five-thousand dollars to open a checking account for her business. Even though she purchased the inn for twelve-thousand dollars, she had over twenty-five thousand dollars left over. It was an accumulation of funds from the demise of her husbands, her savings from Queen City Taxi, and the sale of her home. For fear of the bank going under, she paid a fee for the largest safe deposit box to store her tens of thousands of dollars. With all of the business her inn was generating, she knew it was best to put her loot into the bank's safe deposit box. In fact, Zorita found herself managing the inn even more successfully without the added worry for the safety of her cash.

~ ~ ~

Timberland, Pennsylvania is a rail town. It is the chief mode of transportation for exporting coils of steel, dry goods and agriculture. It is definitely the best commercial mode for travelers, departing or arriving. The nearest airport is fifty miles from Timberland. Timberlanders would tell their expected company it was best to drive or take a train to get to the town of Timberland. If they took a Greyhound, they had to get off in Oaktown then take a cab ride to Timberland. Lord help them if they wanted to fly into Timberland, because Timberland, Pennsylvania was not on the route of any major hub. If people were determined to fly, the best they could do would be to take a flight to Pittsburgh, then take a Greyhound to Oaktown, then a ten-mile cab ride from Oaktown into Timberland. This was way too much of a hassle, so folks mainly drove or took a train to get directly to Timberland.

Ramona Flores never knew anything about the inconvenience of flying into Timberland. She only knew she had to get herself to Timberland so she chose to take a train. Besides, Ramona had a terrible phobia of flying. That is why she took the long, two-day train journey from her hometown, Little Rock, Arkansas.

Ramona was medium height, very brown and extremely beautiful. She had long, black, wavy hair that had never seen a hot comb, nor perm solution. The teens, and even some adults of Little Rock, sometimes stared at her because of her attractive features. She knew she was pretty, and she was aware everyone else saw her in that light. Still, it had no great effect on her, because she was far from being conceited. She and her mother lived with her grandparents until she was five. Then her mother met a nice man and married him. Ramona and her mother moved out of her grandparent's home and went to live with her new stepdad in Arkansas. As soon as Ramona graduated from high school she took a job as an assistant photographer in a photo gallery. On September 24, 1978 she had enough money saved to leave Little Rock for good. She packed a suitcase, threw some toiletries into a cosmetic case, and took the Amtrak out of the southern town, never to look back.

Zorita took pride as the owner of The Inn at Walnut Valley. She wanted the inn to be a place for her customers to have a great time and a place where she could earn a good living. By her thoughts, she was still that fat teenager in Lincoln High. She wanted to prove to all the cruel guys and spiteful girls who disliked her that she could be successful in spite of their meanness. She felt a sense of pride and accomplishment with the many people who patronized her place. When the beautiful, dark-skinned girl arrived at Zorita's inn, the innkeeper was happy the young lady had chosen her place to stay.

"So you say you want to rent a room for a month?" Zorita said to the attractive, black girl as she motioned for William to take the young lady's suitcase. He picked up the luggage and cosmetic case and headed for the stairway. "She's gonna be up there on the second floor, in room number four." Zorita said to the teenage boy.

He stopped, turned and looked at Zorita, then put the large suitcase down. "Zorita, when you gonna get that elevator fixed? It ain't no fun draggin' this luggage up the stairs."

Ramona looked at William, and the young man suddenly felt stupid for complaining in front of the new renter. Zorita bellowed, "William, now don't tell me a big ol' strapping, young man, such as yourself, would have this girl carry the suitcase up those stairs. What's the matter with you, boy?" He quietly sighed, snatched up the over-packed suitcase, and walked up the stairs. Zorita looked at Ramona, then jerked her head towards Jack's old gambling room, which she'd made into an office. The newcomer followed her. "Have a seat," she pointed at the wooden chair. Zorita sat down behind her metal desk and pulled out a ledger. "I've had this place for going on two-and-a-half years now. I've seen a lot of people driving through Timberland needing a place to stay overnight; even out-of-towners visiting family that needed a room for a week or so. I gotta say you're my first out-of-town guest that's ever wanted to rent a room for a month. What's your name, child?"

"Ramona Flores," she replied. "I need to rest for a while and this town seem to be the perfect place to take a breather, don't you think? I figure within a month I will be ready to either move on or settle here. If I do decide to stay I'll get myself a job and an apartment."

The innkeeper wrote the girl's name in her ledger, the date and room number four. Zorita was never one to beat around the bush. She asked, "Why would you have to get an apartment? Don't you have family you can stay with until you figure out what it is you want to do?"

Ramona admitted, "No ma'am, Miss Zorita. I don't."

Zorita's brain seemed to explode whenever she heard someone address her as Miss. She remembered how Miss Ada got a thrill out of making everybody call her Miss Ada. She refused to power-trip the way she'd seen the old, fat woman do. She sharply replied, "Miss Zorita! Child, don't ever call me Miss Zorita. My name is Zorita Thurman. You don't even have to worry about my last name 'cause I've had so many I don't know what the hell my last name is anymore. And nobody ever calls me Miss, not ever. Please, just call me Zorita."

Ramona's southern manners had been programmed to always address grownups properly. Being careful not to offend the innkeeper again, she concentrated before speaking. She replied, "No Zorita. I don't know a soul in this town."

"You don't know anyone in Timberland? Why that sure is strange." Zorita shook her head. She could not understand how anyone could come to a town where they didn't know a soul. Why, even Miss Ada had at least known Slick Rick.

"How old are you child? You look awfully young."

"I'm eighteen. Believe me, I get that a lot. My mama says I'm blessed with good genes," the girl said with a nervous giggle.

"Eighteen, you look like fifteen which is too young to be traveling by yourself. There's a lot of weirdoes in this world. I hope nobody bothered you."

"Nobody bothered me, except this one man who wanted me to go with him. Said he had a pretty coat that would look real good on me."

"Lord! Girl, I hope you told him to stick that coat where the sun don't shine," Zorita said with great concern.

Nervousness came over Ramona, and an evasive manner emerged. She gently explained, "No, I didn't say anything to him. I had to hurry and get onboard the train."

"Good thing," the innkeeper said with a sigh of relief.

The young girl's eyes lowered. Unconvincingly, she said, "Yeah, good thing."

Zorita, sensing the story was not the truth tried to probe the young girl farther, but Ramona clammed up. The innkeeper had the wisdom to back off when she observed she was making the young lady uncomfortable. Changing the subject she asked, "So if you don't know anyone here, what are you doing in Timberland, Pennsylvania?"

"I had to move somewhere, so after I got enough money together I took my social studies map of the United States, closed my eyes, turned it every which way, then jabbed a hat pin on the map. Guess where I stuck it?"

"Timberland?" Zorita asked with a scrunched nose.

"No, actually I stuck it on one of the islands of Hawaii. Oahu."

"Oh, I see," Zorita exclaimed. "So why didn't you end up in Hawaii? How come you came to good ol' Timberland?" Zorita frown as she tried to make sense out of the girl's story."

"Because I didn't have enough funds to go to Hawaii on a week's vacation. No way can I afford to live there for a month. Believe me, I would love to live in Hawaii, maybe even open up a photo gallery there. I've seen pictures of the state and it's a beautiful place. It's so far away; it would cost more money than I could ever afford. Besides, I can't fly anywhere. I'm scared to death of flying. Anyway, I tried a second time; that time I stuck the pin right smack on Timberland. That's why I'm here." Ramona smiled and Zorita couldn't help but noticed how beautiful the girl was. The inn owner shook her head. Because of the brainwashing of Miss Ada, Zorita remembered shunning the darker-skinned people of her race. Zorita thanked God she had long ago liberated herself from Miss Ada's way of thinking.

The innkeeper said, "Make yourself at home during your stay. The kitchen's opened for breakfast from eight to ten. Dinner is from four to six. You're on your own for lunch, that's Nick's only break. If you miss the dining hours, than you'll have to either do without, or go to the Chicken Shack or Fast Eddie's down the street. If it's a good submarine sandwich you want, there's Dolly's Sub and Soup around the corner." The woman dug into the top drawer of her desk and search around for the key labeled number four. "Any problems with your stay here, and I do mean any problems, let me know. Ain't nothing I can't handle. Here's the key to your room. When you check out at the end of your stay, don't forget to return it to me. There's no spare one so don't go losing it?" She gave all her tenants the same warning because she hated making trips to the hardware store to replace lost keys. She watched the girl walk out of her office and towards the stairwell.

William Lewis had been working at Zorita's inn for almost three months, since graduating John Q. Adams High. He worked part-time as the groundskeeper. He was responsible for mowing, planting, pulling weeds from the flower beds, and picking up fallen walnuts. Sometimes he helped Zorita inside of the inn. She paid him twenty-five dollars a week, plus all he could eat. The eighteen-year old was entering the army soon.

William placed Ramona's luggage outside the door of room number four. He stood five feet, ten inches tall, was of medium build and had an extremely fair-complexion. Often people mistook him for white, but he proudly informed them he was black and had been black all of his life. He was a good-looking teen with a gentle spirit; yet there was a ruggedness about him that showed he had no fear.

Widow Paulette spotted William at door number four. The one question she asked, "Whose bags are those?" lead to a ten minute conversation with him. When William finally got free, he rushed down the stairs. He spotted Ramona on the landing and stopped to welcome her. He introduced himself. She smiled and told him her name. When he asked her if there was anything else she needed, she told him no. She thanked him for taking her luggage up, and continued up the stairs to room number four.

When he reached the lounge area he went over to Zorita, and said, "Where'd that one come from? God, what a knockout!"

Zorita wagged her finger in William's face. "Don't you be trying to make a move on her. She seems to be a good southern girl like myself." She chuckled at the raging-hormonal eighteen-year old as he left to finish the yard work.

She thought about checking with Nick to see how the dinner was coming. She always had the guest come and fix their plates and eat in the dining room off the kitchen. She warned all of her tenants, when they checked in, how much she hated roaches and rats so the only place they could eat was in the dining room or in the bar lounge. She also let them know they had to clean up after themselves. With the exception of Fred, no one was allowed to eat in their room. But she knew sometimes they slipped and did it anyway.

Zorita thought about her newest tenant. She hoped Ramona was not a party person. She could only imagine how the men of Timberland would flock all over the young girl once they saw her. She was sure their ol' ladies would want to jump on her in retaliation if they lost their men to her. Zorita did not want the fools tearing up her lounge over the attractive, new face.

Nick was busy fixing dinner when Zorita entered. He spotted her from the corner of his eye. "Afternoon Zorita; lovely fall day ain't it?" he asked, barely taking his eye off of the pot of chili he was stirring.

"Yeah, but it look like a perfect little storm has blown in," she announced.

Nick looked out of the small kitchen window which was nearby. He saw nothing but beams of sunlight ebbing through the openings of the walnut trees. "Zorita, you okay?" he asked. "Ain't no storm a'brewin' out there."

"I didn't say a storm was out there. I said a perfect little storm has blown in. It has blown right here in this inn." Nick turned from the stove and gave Zorita a crazy look. He had no idea what his boss was talking about. She laughed at the puzzled expression on his face, then said, "Forget it Nick! Forget it! Just fix me a cup of coffee."

CHAPTER 23

VACATION

It had been Popeye's suggestion to take the trip during the week of October 1, 1978. The ride to Washington, D.C. was fun for Olivia because she felt like a free spirit riding in Popeye's new, dark blue Mustang. For the sake of Olivia, this chapter is being told referring to Popeye by the name which she prefers, Earl. So to continue on with the story, Earl asked Olivia to take her vacation the same time as he, so they could enjoy the nice leisure trip and spend a romantic week together.

They had been dating for two years and everyone patronizing The Inn at Walnut Valley knew of their love for one another. The crowd would think it odd if Earl came into the lounge without Olivia. And Olivia would never dream of entering The Inn at Walnut Valley without Earl. The town always thought of Earl as a quiet individual, and he was. He didn't want any close friendships, because friends visited each other; and he was ashamed to admit he was thirty-two and still living with his dad. His aunt passed away a month earlier and his father was a basket full of complaints as to why didn't the old woman have at least enough money to be buried. As it was, Earl had to take money from his account to put his great-aunt in the ground. Even though his father had the power of attorney over the elderly woman's social security checks and insurances, the senior Richardson claimed he didn't have a dime to go towards the funeral.

Often Earl listened to his dad go on and on as to why he should be thankful the old man was giving him a place to stay. The senior also rambled on about how ungrateful all of his other children had been towards him. Whenever Earl would try to change the subject and inject something he and Olivia were doing, Ken Richardson would make negative comments about "that peckerwood lady," or "the honky bitch." And though this bothered Earl, he was afraid to stand up for his girlfriend, so he continued to withstand the barrage of verbal insults directed towards his lady.

After the death of his great aunt, Earl realized he was tired. He could no longer go on living life the way his dad wanted him to. Ken Richardson complained whenever Earl went out with Olivia, whenever Olivia called their house, whenever Olivia invited Earl to her place. It was too much for Earl to take; he felt an urgency to get away. Often when he talked to Olivia, she would share her high hopes of visiting different cities. After listening to his lady, her dreams became his dreams. He had never been outside of Timberland. Olivia had left the small town once. It was when her eleventh grade history class went on a field trip to Philadelphia to see the Liberty Bell. She often talked of how she wanted to go to Washington, D.C. to see the monuments. She opened up a brand new way of thinking for Earl, and he liked it.

Since Earl met Olivia, he began taking more pride in himself. People even noticed he didn't resemble the old Earl they once knew. With Olivia by his side, all of the people who knew him seemed to have great respect for the man. One by one he'd hear some of his friends call him Earl. One evening, when Betty delivered an order of chicken wings to the couple, she said, "That'll be three bucks, Earl." Earl looked at the older woman real strange. Betty glanced over at his lady and said, "Your woman seem to like callin' you by your given name, so that's what I'm gonna call you from now on. Besides, you look like an Earl."

He loved being with Olivia. Some evenings he would visit her at work when she was on her breaks. It made Olivia feel special. When one of her white co-workers was bold enough to ask her what she ever saw in the black man with the buggie-looking eyes; she told the worker she saw someone who loved her and to please refrain from talking harsh of him. There had been many whispers about the mixed couple, but Earl and Olivia shrugged it off. When Olivia's mother and stepfather discovered she was exclusively dating Earl, they let it be known they disapproved. Her mother sent word to her daughter that as far as she was concerned Olivia was dead. The young girl wiped her hands of trying to reconcile with her mom. She finally realized her mother loved only herself, and she and her brother had only been in the woman's way.

On the trip to Washington, D.C. Olivia noticed the stares of the other drivers, but she did not care. They spent the first day in Washington, D.C. sightseeing and enjoying one another. Earl found a quaint, little café where they enjoyed a romantic dinner. Later, when they checked into their hotel room, they made love and lay peacefully in one another's arms.

It was four o'clock in the morning when Earl was awaken by a muffled noise. Olivia was sobbing into her pillow. He reached for the lamp and turned it on. Earl leaned over and kissed her on her hair. He pulled her into his arms and moved her wet locks away from her face.

"What's the matter, Olivia? What is it doll?" he asked her.

"It's just that I'm so happy, and I've never been this way before," she confessed. "You just don't know what my life's been like before you came into it." She sniffled and cried softly, and Earl gently rubbed the falling tears from her eyes with his thumb.

Earl had been enamored by the young lady from the time he first saw her at the inn. There had been many times he wanted to tell her how much he cared for her. He kissed her. She kissed him back; gradually she pulled away from him. He said, "Honey, nothin' can be that bad. What is it?"

She asked, "Do you love me Earl, I mean really love me?"

He could hear the sincerity in her voice. He never told her he loved her, only because he was still thinking the relationship was too good to be true. No one had ever shown the man real love the way she had. Sure, before dating Olivia, he had experienced sex with many women. He was no fool. He knew they only wanted him to fulfill their needs; and he certainly had his own needs that had to be met. He lifted her chin with his finger and looked lovingly into her eyes. "I love you with all my soul, lady. Don't you know that?"

"Earl, you treat me like you love me. You treat me well; but you've never told me that you love me; and we've been together for two years now."

His head drooped and he said, "Olivia, look at me. What do you see?" His head was still hung low.

"I see a beautiful man," she replied.

He continued to hold his head in the downward position, "And how is my posture?"

"Why Earl, this is silly. What do you mean how is your posture? Your head is hung low and you look downright sorrowful; really pitiful."

"Exactly!" he replied. He raised his head and looked at her. There was a look of love in his eyes as he gazed into her baby blues. "How do I look?" She could see the love in the expression of his face. She gave in to the temptation and leaned over to kiss him. He stopped her.

"Aatt, aatt!" he said, as he gently turned his head away from her lips. "Answer the question." He looked at her again with more love, and a smile conveying his admiration for her. Again he asked, "How do I look?"

"Why you look wonderfully happy." To lighten the mood she tickled him and added, "And very, very sexy. That's how you look."

After a short laughter, Earl seriously asked, "Do I look pitiful or sorrowful?"

"No Earl, you don't. Why do you ask?"

"Because your second description is how I've been feeling since you've been in my life. The first description was definitely me before

I knew you. I don't walk around with my head hanging to the ground anymore. I am much happier and you gave that to me. In answer to your question, Yes, I love you. How could I not love you, when you have done nothing but brightened up my whole world?"

A solemn look came about her face, and he lifted her chin again with his finger. "What is it this time, doll?" he asked.

"I'm not a good person; there is so much about me you don't know. I feel like I'm deceiving you and it's paining my heart," she admitted.

Earl looked deeply into her eyes. He kissed her tenderly on her lips. With love in his heart he responded, "Nothin' you've done, nothin' you've been through, nothin' you can ever do will rip my love away. I would do anything for you; that's just how much I love you, lady. Even if you said, 'Earl, I'm in love with another man,' I love you enough to let you go. Because of this peace and happiness you have placed in my life, I will love you until the day I die."

"Would you love me if you knew terrible things about me?"

"I'd love you in spite of anything you have ever done, seen, said or been. If you've *done it*, than you must have had your own reason for doin' it. If you've *seen it*, then God must have had a reason for you to witness it; if you *said it*, God must have given you the words to say; and if you *been in situations*, good or bad, I can only hope God was walking right by your side, guiding you into my life. It ain't up to me to be judgin' you, or for you to be judgin' me."

"Earl, I'm not a saint. My life as a kid was horrible. Why, my own mother never wanted me. Fact is, to this day, she don't even speak to me."

Olivia wanted to tell him all about her awful childhood. She knew part of her life seemed more like a nightmare than real life. It was something she'd experienced but could not quite understand why she had to go through it. She wanted to share the remnants of her life with her lover, but she was afraid he would judge her the way Bernard Elliot had done. Often she felt very close to Earl, close enough to reveal the pain of her past. Just when she found herself wanting to divulge her life's turmoil, she'd see her stepfather, Jim Burns, threatening to kill her. Images of him flashed before her eyes and she could hear his voice threatening not only would he kill her, but her mother as well. Still, she knew she would tell Earl about her life. Earl had always been there by Olivia's side to give her the love she desperately needed. She knew he would remain by her side to shield away her pain as well. She wiped the last of the tears from her face and laid the story of her life upon the man's strong, loving shoulders.

CHAPTER 24

OLIVIA'S STORY

Olivia told her life's story from the moment she remembered best. She was seven and loved her brother, Steve, who was four years older than she. They were inseparable and they always brought fun and laughter to one another. He would take her to the Regal Theater; take her bowling, and sometimes fishing at his favorite fishing hole. They were close, in spite of their difference in age and appearances. Steve looked like his Italian mother and father, with his thick, dark hair and complexion of a well-tanned boy. Olivia was different. Her skin was extremely fair and her hair so blonde it looked like corn silk. Everybody in the Territino family noticed the variances immediately, but said nothing. All of their neighbors witnessed how nasty Sharon treated the little girl. Though they felt sorry for Olivia, few of them did anything to intervene. In Sharon's eyes, her son, Steve, could do no wrong. It was quite apparent to everyone that he was her favorite child. By the time Olivia turned eleven she figured nothing she did would win over the love of her mother.

Late one evening, when their parents came home from a night out, they tore into the house with such anger and rage it awoke Olivia. It was about midnight when they returned from the neighborhood tavern. Olivia could hear them arguing about something. They always argued after a night of drinking, but this argument was different. It was loud and violent, and she could hear scuffling and breakage of glass. When their arguing escalated into a shouting match, she clearly heard her dad say, "You're the one that had the affair. You went and messed with George Peterson and got yourself pregnant. You're telling me now you hate Olivia and want nothing more to do with her. Well too bad Sharon, because I've raised her same as I've raised our son; like she's my own flesh and blood. She don't have no idea she ain't my kid and that's the way I'm gonna keep it. Since she's looking more and more like that damn George, you can't stand the sight of her. It's not her fault you got pregnant by your boyfriend, so get the hell over it."

"You bastard! I ain't got to do nothing I don't want to. If she gets under my skin there ain't a thing I can do about it. Don't you get it, I hate that little bitch, she has done nothing but ruined our family."

"Don't be so sure that it's Olivia who's ruined the family," she heard her father say. He added, "Why don't you try looking in the mirror." Olivia heard more breakage of glass, then a few more choice words from her mother's mouth. Her mother told him to get the hell out, and never come back. It was about one in the morning when Sharon kicked Louie Territino out of the house.

All of the fighting had awakened Steve out of his deep sleep. He knocked on his sister's door, and entered without waiting for a response. Steve prayed his little sister was asleep. She was not. He was disappointed to find her sitting on the edge of the bed crying. "I'm not your real sister, am I?" she asked.

"You'll always be my sister and I'm not letting anything happen to you. She's not splitting us up; not ever," he assured Olivia.

The following day, when the Territino kids came from their rooms for breakfast, their mother informed them they were going to Kline's Diner to eat. Sharon sat across from them and smoked her cigarettes and drank her coffee as she complained about their father. It was over Olivia's pancakes and Steve's eggs and bacon their mother informed them she was divorcing their father.

A week later Sharon's boyfriend, Jim Burns, came to visit. Olivia became suspicious over her parents' argument on the night of the split-up. Had the argument been a rouse, created by her mother, to get rid of their easy-going father? She now looked at her mother's boyfriend with contempt and both she and her brother would say nothing to the man. When he start bringing gifts and giving money to the both of them, they figured maybe he was okay. The gifts eased their mind for a while, but it still did not ease the pain in their heart for their missing father. Whenever Sharon took the kids to visit their dad, she'd remind Louie how he was the cause of the family's unit being torn apart.

Jim Burns was friendly to Steve and Olivia, but Olivia noticed he was friendlier to her. When she felt his hand on her shoulder flopped down onto her developing breast, she said nothing. Maybe it was just the way his large hand overhung her shoulder. The next day when his hand drooped over her shoulder, he pinched the nipple of her budding breast. That was no accident and the eleven year old knew it. She went straight to her mother and said, "Mom, Jim pinched my chest." What distressed her was the fact that Olivia would have the audacity to accuse her boyfriend of doing something so sick. She flew into a rage and slapped the girl hard across her face. "Don't you ever repeat a lie like that again to anybody, you little bitch. You've been nothing but a pain in my ass. It's because of you your father left me for another woman. Are you trying to make Jim leave too?"

Whenever her mother's boyfriend would come around, Olivia made a point to stay clear of him. When he tried the money and gift trick again, she refused to accept them. Undeterred, he purchased a pair of tight, fashionable jeans for her; she tossed them in the outside garbage bin. Olivia never noticed her mother's eyes on her. Sharon made her daughter retrieve them and wear them the very next time Jim came to visit.

The man's hands were always on little Olivia whenever he caught her alone. One Saturday evening while her mother ran errands and Steve was shooting hoops at the school outside basketball court, Jim tried to put his hand down her blouse. She screamed and threatened to tell her mother. He said, "Your mom won't believe anything you say, so don't waste your breath. Besides, we're getting married as soon as she gets her divorce. You'll be my little girl. I'm going to adopt you and change your name to Burns like mine." A sinister grin came over his face and it frightened her. She ran out of her house and down the street to Jennifer's house. She begged Mr. Nesbaum to drive her to her father's place over on Bracker Road. There was an urgent plea; the neighbor knew something was wrong. When Mr. Nesbaum turned onto the short street, he saw police cars and an ambulance. At her father's house there were two officers in a conversation at the storm door. Olivia's heart was beating very fast. Mr. Nesbaum quickly parked the car. He warned her to stay put as he went into the house. When Olivia noticed no one at the door, she got out of the car and slipped into the house. She followed the trail of people. There were three men at the entrance leading to the basement. She crouched low behind them to see what they were looking at. Through the narrow, gapping spaces of their legs she could see her father hanging from a rafter. "Let me through, let me through," she screamed. She tried desperately to push her way pass the men.

Someone shouted, "Where did you come from? Hey, will somebody get this kid outta here; who the hell let her in anyway?"

Mr. Nesbaum grabbed Olivia by her shoulders. "Come on Olivia, there's nothing we can do." He took her back to his home where he quietly explained the grisly scene to his wife and daughter.

He called Olivia's mother. She yelled through the phone, "Bring my damn kid home. Louie Territino was a weak man, too bad if he hung himself." Mr. Nesbaum was a God-fearing man and knew of the cruelties the woman had inflicted on little Olivia many times before. He adamantly told Olivia's mother, under no circumstance would he bring the child to her at that moment. Sharon Territino slammed the phone in his ear.

Olivia's mother married the abusing man anyway, and gave him permission to adopt her children. One day Olivia's brother was sent home from school for illness. Olivia had been home with a bout of the flu, herself. Steve walked in on his stepfather raping her. He ran into the kitchen and grabbed a knife from the butcher block.

It was not hard for the man to get the upper hand on the teenage boy. He wrestled the knife from Steve and stabbed him once in the heart. When the law arrived, Jim Burns explained to the authorities he thought the boy was on LSD or some other mind-altering drug. He claimed Steve attacked him for no reason. He had to protect himself; in doing so, the kid fell onto the knife and was accidentally stabbed through the heart. Through the deception, the death was ruled accidental. With Steve out of the way Jim Burns forced himself on Olivia whenever the opportunity presented itself. The first time after Steve's death, when she tried to fight him off, he warned, "Remember, you're mom can accidentally die too, then there'd be just me and you. And you will be my little Lolita."

The exploitation of Olivia changed her perception of how her life was meant to be. When she became attracted to her teachers, it seemed perfectly normal because she had been taken so many times by the sleaze of a man. She chose the men with whom she wanted to have sex with. The more she was with the older men, the more she hated each time Jim raped her. She could not control his forcing himself on her, but she could choose other men which she wanted to have sex with. To her, it was a direct betrayal to her abuser. By letting other men have her, she discovered she enjoyed the power she had over them. They wanted her as much as they could have her, but she called the shots of when and if she would let them have her. That was one way she could squeeze the pain from her soul. She also took a portion of her life back by keeping her surname, Territino, instead of using her adoptive last name, Burns.

Olivia wanted to tell Earl the whole story, but she stopped short of a certain episode. She told him some of the life she had led before she had the good fortune of meeting him. She told Earl of Jim Burns and how he sexually abused her when she was a child. She told of the trauma when she witnessed her brother getting stabbed to death by Jim Burns. She told him of her affair with the school teachers; and revealed how Bernard Elliot had taken nude pictures of her. Tearfully, she informed him of how Mr. Nesbaum was shot and her participation in the cover-up. She divulged almost everything to Earl, but she could not bring herself to tell of her father's suicide. She always felt her dad died trying to protect her from her adulterous mother. And when Louie Territino knew he could no longer protect her, in sadness, he took his own life. That one thing, she kept to herself.

The shameful details she shared with Earl relieved some of the pressure she had endured from the distasteful life she'd once lived. He put his face close to Olivia's and glanced lovingly into her eyes. She was lost in love with the man. When he rubbed her hair, she leaned her head closer towards his stroking hand. He lifted her face, kissed her long and tenderly, then said, "Your days of mistreatment are over. Leave it in the past, sweetheart and look towards the future. That's what you must do." He continued, "What happened to you was not your fault. Blame the sick bastards that took advantage of an innocent child." He kissed Olivia on her forehead so she would not see the tears welling in his eyes. "That's who you blame, not yourself. Believe me! They will pay for their evil deeds in hell." The tears dropped onto his cheeks as he kissed his lover on top of her hair. "Trust me on that."

CHAPTER 25

ATTRACTION

Many, many years ago, when Nick Hutchinson was in the Navy, he served aboard ship. He was known as Hutch to his shipmates. He dealt with the white sailors and officers only when necessary. It pained him whenever he saw the colored storekeepers, machinist mates, and especially the hospital corpsmen go crazy over the various nationalities of women in the foreign ports. Whenever his friends invited him to go out and troll the beach for the exotic white ladies, he'd flatly refused. Hutch turned his nose up at his friends who engaged in the practice of collecting ladies' worn panties. It was their way of keeping score of the different races of women they made love to. German, Italian, Japanese, Swedish, or French, it didn't matter; those sailors would go after them all. The ship was docked off the coast of Sigonella, Italy when Hutch's friend, Mobile, asked him to join their shipmates for an evening out. "Man, why don't you come out on the beach with us and get some of that Italian pussy?" Hutch mentally cringed when he heard the sailors talked so bluntly. His shipmates rarely noticed Hutch's lack of using the crude language because he kept them laughing with his funny stories.

Petty Officer Hutchinson replied, "Naw man, I don't see me messin' with any of them women; you don't know what you gittin' into. Now a pretty little brown-skinned lady on the beach, I'll go fo' that."

"Shit Hutch, you missin' out, man. We gonna visit a town 'bout thirty minutes up the road, lit'le place called Catania. Man, the people are nice and the ladies are sweet. Hey man, you need to take advantage of all this different white pussy while you're abroad. You know, them colored gals back home ain't gonna stand for you dumpin' they asses for no white woman once you get back in the states. Shit, they liable to throw hot grits on yo' black ass."

The more Nick tried to be civil with his shipmate, the more Mobile insisted. Finally, Nick shook his head and said, "Man, you guys go 'head, knock yo'selves out. Messin' with them white ladies jist ain't my bag."

Mobile laughed loud and hardy at his friend. Yeoman Wilson added, "Yeah Hutch, them girls will let you do everything them colored girls won't. Man, it's a regular smorgasbord over here. They go for that freaky shit. You name it. Regular sex, booty sex, lickity dick, *and* lickity split. Hutch man, you better come on so you can lickity they split. You know what I'm sayin'?" All of the sailors in the lounge area were laughing at Nick Hutchinson and humorously continued to poke fun at him.

Nick knew what the yeoman was talking about, and he was having no parts of it. Before he could catch himself, he blurted out, "Man, is you talkin' 'bout eatin' pussy?"

Mobile poked his tongue out and quivered it quickly up and down a few times, then licked his lips long and slow. Proudly, he said, "Shit yeah." Then he added, "Hey man, don't tell me you ain't never ate no pussy?"

Hutch said, with a distain look on his face, "Hell naw, I ain't." He shook his head at his shipmate and added, "Man, that jist sound so nasty. Ain't no way I'm gonna be tryin' that. No way at all. That's jist sick. Jist plain sick, man."

The shipmates all whooped and roared with laughter. Petty Officer Davidson was slapping his knee and nearly busting a gut at Nick's lack of experience. Then somebody from the crowd yelled,

"Can you believe that shit? Ol' Hutch here is still a lickity-split virgin; probably a lickity-dick virgin, too!"

Nick laughed with his shipmates. They had him on that one; he joked with the sailors and told them, "Hell, y'all can laugh all you want. There still ain't no way I'm gonna be pokin' my head 'tween no lady's legs or stickin' my thang in they mouth. It jist ain't gonna happen." He shook his head and continued, "Sick, sick, sick; jist plain sick."

Mobile, still laughing, slapped his buddy on the back and said, "Man, I use to say the same thing. And then I ate some. Gotttdammnn!! Hey, all I got to say Hutch, man, is don't knock it 'til you try it!"

Petty Officer Nicholas Hutchinson never tried it; he stayed true-blue to his belief. The man had sex with only the Negro and brown-skinned ladies throughout his military and civilian life. And he never, ever experienced a lickity anything; which suited him just fine.

~ ~ ~

Nick had been opposed to the young, white crowd coming into the lounge. When Jack of Diamond owned the place, there had only been two or three white customers at the most. Even then, Nick had not been cool with the idea of them coming to the bar. After Zorita took ownership, a whole lot of young whites began patronizing The Inn at Walnut Valley. It was hard for the cook to wrap his mind around their patronage. On occasion he would voice his displeasures to Zorita, telling her it was unnatural having the white clientele in a black-owned establishment. But Zorita was a business woman. The whites coming to her inn meant her place of business was becoming a more successful neighborhood establishment. Nick noticed a lot of young, white men and women venturing into The Inn at Walnut Valley after the graduation party in 1976. Much to his dismay, the two schools utilized the inn for their graduation parties again in 1977 and 1978 as well. They were just white patrons as far as he was concern. The cook had noticed the attractive Olivia when she first patronized the place back in 1976, but he never showed an interested in the young lady. She was just like any other white face in the bar that he felt shouldn't be there. He figured they were kids who should be taking their business to Hillbilly Haven in the white section of town. But over the years when some of the whites moved to a larger cities to pursue their career, and some headed off to college to figure out what to pursue, and some pursued one another in matrimony, he noticed the thin blonde still came around.

Nick never had an interest in white women; but the more he saw the blonde snuggling next to Popeye, the more he wanted Olivia. How could someone like Popeye have a woman like her? It also bothered him she had never once looked his way. Some of the other white girls had flirted with him; he always ignored them. Olivia, however, seemed as though she didn't even know he was alive.

After two years of Nick noticing Olivia's devotion to the unattractive man, he had become inquisitive about her. He did everything in his power to get her to notice him. She never so much as gave him a second glance. He spotted the girl sitting with Popeye one Friday night, both of their heads romantically close. Popeye held the woman lovingly as they sat listening to a local singer belt out one of Al Green's songs, *Love and Happiness*. They ordered two hot met sandwiches from Nick's kitchen. When Betty grabbed their order for delivery, Nick told her he'd deliver the food himself.

"Here you two lovebirds go," he said. Olivia gently pulled away from Popeye's arm and took the sandwiches from the tray. When Popeye handed the three bucks to Nick, the cook said, "Hey man, they's on the house." Popeye's right eyebrow rose as he gave a questionable look to Nick, then he looked over at his woman. She was busy eating the hot met sandwich oblivious to the fact a wage for her affection had been set into motion. Popeye bit into the hot met with his eye still on the cook. The juice from the spicy sausage squirted onto his hand. Nick, sensing Popeye's suspicion said, "Can I get y'all anythang else?"

"An order of french fries," Olivia said. She batted her eyelashes at Popeye as he sucked the juice off his fingers. He cut his bulging eyes at Nick. "You heard the lady, an order of french fries. And tell Betty we need some hot sauce for these mets."

"Hot sauce? Okay, my man!" Nick said, as he stole a quick, last glance at Olivia.

There was something about seeing Olivia all hemmed up under Popeye's arm that had Nick curious as to what he may have missed out on. Maybe he had been wrong by limiting himself to dating only within his color. On a couple occasions he had spied on Popeye and Olivia as they sexily, slow grinded to the melodies of the musicians and the jukebox. Though he would never admit it, secretly, he was jealous of Popeye. Often he had wondered what the beautiful, young, white girl had seen in one of the town's ugliest, black men. Nick found himself attracted to her, not because she was white, not even because she was beautiful, but because she had totally ignored him, and she was completely in awe with Popeye.

Nick had three beautiful women he successfully juggled around. He was quite fond of them, too. But Olivia had awakened an exotic passion in him. Passion he had denied himself all of his life. After he delivered the hot met sandwiches to the couple, and got a good look at Olivia, he returned to the kitchen smiling all over himself. Betty had noticed the grin about his face as he threw two handfuls of frozen french fries into the hot grease. The sizzling, crackle of the cold fries hitting the rolling, hot liquid sent some of the burning oil popping onto his flesh. Nick wiped the grease off as it stung his arm. He still had that stupid happiness on his face when he looked up from his scorched skin and spotted Betty staring at him. She shook her head as if something had sickened her. "What?" he asked perplexed.

She shook her head a couple more times, then threw the dish towel over her shoulder. As she walked away, she said, "You is one disgustin' old man."

CHAPTER 26

PHONE CALL

The payphone, on the second floor of the inn, rang at seven o'clock in the morning. Nick grabbed it and said, "This is Nick the Chef."

It was Olivia's voice he heard at the other end of the receiver, "Good morning, Nicholas. This is Olivia. I got the message you slipped to me beneath the plate of french fries. What is so urgent that you would have me call you first thing in the morning?" She asked him in the most glowing tone.

The melody of her voice was sweet in his ear, and he was even more intrigued with the young lady. He needed to have the twenty-year-old, no matter what. Nick did not want to come across as a country-bumpkin so he was careful to properly enunciate his diction. "Yes Olivia, I want to know if there's any chance I could see you? Outside of the inn, that is."

There was a long hesitation and he wondered what she was thinking. When she did finally speak, Nick was surprised to hear a change of tone in her voice. Abruptly, she asked, "Why?"

The lady's unexpected switch of demeanor momentarily rattled him. He could tell she wasn't interested in him by the way her voice had turned from comforting warm to icy cold. Trying to maintain his composure, he continued, "I would like to know you. You seem like a wonderful lady, and I was hoping you would let me take you out to dinner."

"Do you know Earl is my boyfriend?" she asked with an air of sophisticated arrogance. Even so, it didn't intimidate Nick. He was use to classy women, especially when they were sure of themselves. The three ladies in his life were the height of elegance, so Olivia's brashness did not deter his interest. Nick had hoped she would not mention anything about Popeye. It led him to believe the lady was truly devoted to him. He knew he was doing Popeye wrong, but didn't care. It wasn't as though he and the man with the big, popped eyes really knew one another. He gently replied, "I know you and Popeye like each other, but what does it have to do with you and I being friends?"

"It has a lot to do with it. I don't just like Earl, I love Earl! How would it look, me having dinner with you, when Earl is my man?" she sharply questioned the cook.

He could not understand why he felt the urge to tell her that she could do better than Popeye. He decided to keep his concerns to himself. Instead, he said, "I can respect that. I wanted to let you know how much of beautiful person I think you are. Hey, it don't hurt to have more friends. Look Olivia, I think you're a real classy lady and I'd like to get to know you; that's all."

"And by getting to know me, are you referring to screwing me?"

Her bluntness caught him off guard. "Wow! That hurt. You should know I'm not like most of the guys who trip all over themselves trying to run games on pretty ladies. I'm only interested in a friendship with you, that's all I've got in mind," he tried to convince her.

With a staunch attitude, Olivia sternly said, "Sure it is. Let's be honest, shall we? I noticed you when I first start coming to the inn two years ago. You, who seemed to be so full of yourself; I know you got a few women who throw themselves at you. Well, I'm not like that. I won't be one of your weekday whores."

The lady had shocked him. Most of the patrons of The Inn at Walnut Valley knew he liked the ladies, but no one ever mentioned his affairs, because he never bragged about the women he laid with. He was right in telling Olivia he was not like most of the other men. He kept his mouth shut when it came to discussing the women he had conquered. His buddies, he noticed, couldn't wait to share the whole sordid detail of their interludes. He regrouped from her comment and said, "Nor did I ask you to be my weekday anything. I just thought it would be nice to know you as a friend. Sorry I offended you."

He was ready to say goodbye when he heard her say, "Wait! Wait a minute. Don't get upset because the truth hurts. I figured you to be an unfriendly guy, that's all. I guess you're okay. Besides, it ain't like we plan on doing it. Maybe we can have breakfast. But I don't think it's a good idea to have breakfast at the inn. Like you said, we can meet somewhere outside of the place." She laughed, "Besides, it wouldn't be right having you cook for us." Can you meet me at the Oaktown Village Restaurant, about ten miles from here?"

"No problem," he said mundanely, expressing no excitement.

"Okay, I'll meet you there within a half an hour."

Nick had already fixed the inn's breakfast because he hoped something would jump off with the blonde this morning. He was brimming with anticipation on what the possibilities of a breakfast with Olivia could bring. He explained to Zorita the food was prepared and asked her to oversee things because he had to make a run. He drove his old Chevy in pure excitement to the Oaktown café. A wide smile came upon his face when he saw Olivia sitting at a booth waiting for him. He sat across from her and admired her as she took a sip of coffee.

"Didn't think you'd mind if I started without you," she said, as she raised her mug towards him.

"No, not at all," Nick replied with a seriousness about him.

The waitress came over; she stood chewing gum and clacking it very loud. Any other time it would have perturbed Olivia. She considered it a discourteous gesture when a person snapped their gum within carshot of other people. This morning she had other things on her mind. The waitress asked Nick if he wanted coffee. When he said he did, she poured him a mug of steaming hot brew, topped off Olivia's mug and placed two laminated menus on the table. She clacked her gum, blew a big, pink bubble and let it pop as she left to refill some of the other customer's mugs.

"So why is it you want to get to know me?" Olivia asked, as she took a taste of her refreshed java. She locked her eyes onto his, curtly raising her eyebrow.

"I beg your pardon?" Nick said, still trying to maintain his perfected, English façade.

"Why the interest in me? Was that your way of making a pass at me, by slipping me the note to call you?" she asked.

He flashed a wide smile. To remove the seriousness from her rigid disposition, in his regular diction, he said, "Lawd, have mercy, 'Livia gurl if you was a plate of honey I'd sop my biscuits in you." She laughed, then Nick added, "And when I finished sopping my biscuits and enjoyin' them vittles, I'd lift up the plate and lick the damn thang clean." Olivia, burst into laughter and used her napkin to wipe the dripping coffee from her mouth. He took a sip of his coffee and said, "Course, I was makin' a pass at you. Gurl, you is one stylish lady. Why any man in they right mind would want to be with you. Hell, you~is~fine, jist~fine~as~wine," he sang in a poetic rhythm. "Whooew wee! That's if you don't mind me sayin' so."

She looked pleased. She stated, "I can see how those lady friends of yours can be so attracted to you, Mr. Hutchinson. You are quite a handsome man, and I find you humorous as well."

Though he didn't show it, Nick was shocked the young girl knew so much about him. Determined to find out how she had come to know his business, he came right out and asked, "How the hell do you know so much about me, 'Livia? It jist don't seem fair you is knowin' thangs on me and I ain't hardly knowing anythang about you."

"What does it matter? I just do." Then she casually asked, "I only want to know one thing. Why are you coming on to me when everyone knows Earl and I are in love?" He hated hearing Popeye's name come out of the pretty lady's mouth. It was like seeing a beautiful rose with a cockroach crawling out of it. But that didn't too much matter to him now. After all, it was he, not Popeye, sitting directly across from the fine-looking Olivia. At this point, anything could happen; and that possibility created an arousal in him. "Nick, I know you know Earl and I are a couple, so how come you insist on getting to know me?" she questioned.

Nick looked at her and smiled broadly. He winked at her and said, "Hey, you's a real fox, gurl. Can you dig it?" It flattered him that she had taken the time to learn so much about him. She knew his last name and she knew about his girlfriends. Though he appreciated the fact she had such an interest in him, he wondered if he should be concerned. He'd never had a crazy woman in his life. Many times he'd heard his buddies talk about such nutty ladies; he was hoping Olivia wouldn't turn out to be psychotic. Wanting to know more about the young girl, with a puzzled look on his face, he questioned, "Hey 'Livia! Gurl, what you is?"

Olivia smiled at his improper use of grammar. She asked, "What do you mean?"

Once again, in a more serious tone, Nick asked, "What you is? I'm talkin' 'bout yo' horoscopic sign."

Olivia stifled the laughter that wanted to escape. To clarify his inquiry, she asked, "You want to know what's my zodiac sign?"

He had a big smile on his face, "Yeah gurl, what you is? I'm a Taurus, myself. You know; the bull. Yeah 'Livia, I'm like that bull. Strong~ real~strong. Can~last~real~long."

The lady smirked at his attempt at poetry. She answered, "Nick, I'm a Scorpio. Why?"

A sly grin came across his face. He took a sip of his coffee, eyed her sexually, then said, "Yeah, I'll bet you is. Gurl, you is lookin' like you got a lot of sting in you!"

Olivia laughed at his joke, then reached over her coffee mug and pinched him on his cheek. He was thirty-four but he looked as though he was in his late twenties. Many women were interested in him. They only had to look into his dreamy eyes to realize he could lead them straight to his bed. Nick knew a lot of women meant a lot of problems. That was why he limited himself to only three girlfriends. He had discovered if he had three, and made sure each knew about the other, he would have no women problem. And he was right. A long time ago Olivia would have been involved with him if he had shown an interest in her. But even so, she knew she would have to be his exclusive lover. If she had to share him, she would not have wanted him. She refused to be Miss Thursday, friendly with Miss Monday, Miss Tuesday and Miss Wednesday.

Right there at the breakfast table, over grits, bacon, eggs and pancakes, she proposition Nick. She would let him enjoy the company of her for one, and only one time. After that he was to forget about her and leave her alone. When he asked Olivia why she would consent to let him make love to her, she admitted she had wanted him the first time she laid eyes on him. But back then, he seemed uninterested so she steered clear of him.

After they both finished breakfast, Olivia followed Nick's car to a motel a block away. Nick had seen the motel on the way into Oaktown. Little did he know, Olivia had been at that very motel many times with Bernard Elliot. He went into the office and rented a room. They spent the whole morning and into the afternoon entangled in passion. It was some of the best sex Nick had ever experienced, even down to the lickity split, which he happily explored with Olivia, as she ventured, equally uninhibitedly into his erotic zone. And when he thought he could give no more, she allowed him to cool down to rebuild his stamina; then they made love all over again. He knew the promise which he made to Olivia would be hard for him to keep, but he would try his best to honor it. Olivia found herself fascinated with Nick, but she would not allow herself to experience a deep, emotional tie towards the man. He was more handsome than she had first thought and she hoped she hadn't made a mistake bedding the good-looking cook. It was curiosity which lead her to want to experience Nick inside of her, but it had to be on her own terms, not his. Now that she had enjoyed having sex with him, she wasn't so sure whose terms it had been on.

CHAPTER 27

PHOTOGRAPHER

The town of Timberland had taken a while for Ramona to adjust to. For one thing, the scenery was absolutely hypnotic to her. She had arrived in the early fall to the tiny city, and it amazed her to be surrounded by such beauty. Ramona was outside snapping pictures of the natural brilliancy of the leaves on the walnut trees, which had changed into its colorful, short-term apparel. She was mesmerized by the bordering mountains. When she spotted a lone house high up on the mountainside, she could only imagine the magnificent view the homeowner could see of the village.

Ramona had taken some nice shots of the walnut trees. Squirrels were scampering about, chasing one another up and down the rough bark of the tree trunks and racing across outstretched branches as she snapped away. She was busy focusing on a tree and was not paying attention to anything else when she was startled by Zorita's voice. "Why I've never seen anyone take a picture of a tree. Why on earth would you want to photograph a tree?"

"Good morning Zorita," Ramona shrugged her shoulders. "I can't help myself. They make such splendid subjects. Why look at them, they're beautiful! Simply beautiful."

"Beautiful?" Zorita asked, in a questionable tone. "I have never heard anyone describe a tree as beautiful. You're beautiful, but those trees, why they're just plain ol' trees."

Ramona's nervous giggle escaped, and when she noticed Zorita was awaiting a reply from her, she became flustered. An air of self-consciousness engulfed her and she found herself wanting to get pass the big woman without hurting her feelings. She said, "Oh my, look at the view with you standing there by that red bush. Is that a burning bush? Zorita, stay right where you are. Okay, now how about a big smile?" Zorita was flattered. No one had ever been pleased with her looks enough to take a snapshot of her. Since she was enjoying the attention so much, Ramona took the remaining six shots of Zorita. She told the innkeeper to move to the row of trees, then around to the front by the gazebo next to the large bouquet of hardy mums to finish off the roll.

"Oh, I can't wait to see how those pictures come out," Zorita said, with excitement. "Make sure you show them to me." The young girl said she would, and headed for the porch of the inn. When Ramona entered the building she noticed a white girl sitting at the end of the bar with her head hung low. It was only eight-thirty in the morning, and Ramona wondered what the girl was doing there so early in the day. The usual crowd for Nick's breakfast specials was there, but rarely did Zorita have to tend the bar first thing in the morning for a breakfast customer. Ramona tried to slip pass the blonde. Just as she put her foot on the first step of the mahogany staircase, Olivia looked up and asked, "Have you seen Zorita?"

"She's outside. She'll be in shortly, I'm sure," Ramona replied.

"Okay," Olivia replied; then the blonde quickly added, "You must be Ramona."

Ramona could not conceal her amazement and it showed in her face, "Yes, why yes, I am. How did you know my name?"

Olivia tossed her long hair to the side, "I heard someone mention something about a quiet, pretty girl, named Ramona, renting a room from Zorita for a month who was thinking about moving here, and you are going up the staircase. It's got to be you they were talking about." Olivia added, "You been here about two weeks now, right?"

Ramona adjusted the weight of her camera bag on her shoulder. "That's right," she answered.

"Got a job yet?"

"No, I don't; I've just been relaxing. You know, not really taking the time to look around town just yet for a job. This place is like a dreamland and I've really been enjoying each moment I've been here."

"You think it's a dreamland, huh? Where did you say you came from?" Olivia laughed sarcastically, she added, "Everybody I know has been trying to move the hell out of this one-horse town, and here you are thinking how great of a place it is." For some reason Ramona's naivety reminded her of herself, how she had once been an innocent child, how desperate she had been to take control of her life. Olivia could not understand what would make Ramona move to Timberland, Pennsylvania when there were other energizing cities in which to live. Those cities, she was sure, had many single men from which to choose. But the blonde had no way of knowing Ramona did not move to Timberland to get herself involved in a romantic relationship. She was much smarter than that. Olivia offered, "They got an opening at Kroger Supermarket. Are you interested?"

It had not been the type of job Ramona had longed for, being a cashier and bagging groceries. Graciously, she said, "I got another two weeks before I explore Timberland's job market, but thanks for the tip." She smiled curtly and continued ascending the flight of stairs before the blonde could add another word to the conversation.

Zorita came into the bar with a handful of hardy mums that had grown in abundance around the gazebo. She placed them in a vase of water in her office then she went over to the solemn blonde. "What in the world are you doing here at this time of the day, Olivia? You're normally here with the evening crowd. You mean to tell me you want a Tom Collins this early?"

"Yeah, I sure can use one," she quietly admitted.

Zorita took the key from around her neck and unlocked the half-door entrance to the bar. She whipped up a Tom Collins, added a cherry and straw then placed it on a napkin in front of the lady.

"What you lookin' so doggone sad for?" she asked. "Girl, look like somebody's snatched all of your joy away."

Olivia toyed with the stem of the cherry. She twirled the cherry around several times, then bobbed it up and down in the Tom Collins drink. She held the cherry suspended over the tall glass then let it plop down into the mixture a few times. Olivia grabbed her wallet and paid Zorita. As Zorita put the money in her cash register, Olivia mumbled into her drink, loud enough for the innkeeper to hear, "Earl asked me to marry him."

"Huh, what'd you say?" She had heard Olivia, but couldn't believe her ears.

"I said, Earl asked me to marry him."

"What?! You mean you and Popeye are getting hitched? Child, when is the wedding?" Zorita asked with eagerness.

"I haven't said yes, yet." The twenty-year old took a sip of the potent beverage, then grabbed the cherry and popped it into her mouth. She crunched down hard on it then tossed aside the stem. Zorita waited for Olivia to say something else about the event, but the blonde said nothing more.

Sensing the young lady was deep in thought, Zorita said, "Oh, I see." She started polishing the marbled bar top as Olivia sat there staring into her half-finished Tom Collins. Zorita knew when it was better to keep the conversation going with her customers and when it was best to keep her trap shut. As she polished the counter, she said not another word.

CHAPTER 28

RENT

When Zorita took over the place, she promised Jack of Diamond she would let Nick stay with free room and board for as long as Nick cooked for the inn. The man was a great cook and she loved his specialty dishes. Even so, the innkeeper had thought long and hard about approaching her cook. In a tactful way she wanted to tell him it was now required for him to pay a weekly-room rate. She was all about business, and though she enjoyed his cooking, and his wild sense of humor, she knew it was time to let him know of this change. It wasn't even that she needed the money. She still had her dead husbands' insurance money, and the funds from the sale of her house, put aside. If she could get him to pay rent it would help her out on the gas and electric; eliminating the need to go into her tucked-away stash.

It was a slow day in the lounge area when she chose to approach Nick concerning the matter. The scarcity of customers would emphasize her need to implement the room rate. She figured she would give him a discount of fifty-percent. Besides, she had noticed Nick's free room had a revolving door when it came to entertaining not one, but three fine, black women of Timberland. But what Zorita didn't know was how cool-natured all three of his women were with one another. Nick had told each about the other, and still they wanted to have a piece of his love. They did not mind sharing the good-looking man with the amazing personality. No sooner than one would dance out, another would waltz in. Sometimes they would bump into one another and cordially speak, smile and be on their way. If Marlena came to visit his room, you could bet it was Monday night. On Tuesday nights, Patsy sometimes sashayed into his room, wearing a black trench coat and shiny, sexy boots, with not a stitch on beneath the coat. And Wednesday nights, Yolanda rocked his world. She often pestered him to move in with her and her husband. But Nick wasn't taking any chance the lady's husband swung both ways. Besides he had almost killed a man in the navy for wanting to do unnatural things to him.

Zorita was standing in the doorway of the kitchen looking at Nick busting suds in the sink. Somehow, he felt her presence. With his hands still in the soapy water, he turned his head around, "Zorita, gurl how long you been starrin' at the back of my head?"

"Not long," she said, trying to ease into the real reason she was there. He was waiting for Zorita to say something else, but she didn't. He had been around his boss long enough to know when she needed to talk to him.

Nick dried his hands, grabbed the carafe and walked towards Zorita. "Coffee?" he asked.

"Thanks," she grabbed two mugs, and sat at the small corner table; the same table Nick had been hired by Jack of Diamond back in 1970. Nick poured her cup, then his. She said, "Nick, you know business is business and I appreciate everything you've done around here for the inn."

Nick had taken a taste of the hot coffee and place the mug down when Zorita's words registered in his brain. He spurted out, "Aww shit, here it comes, here it comes! You gonna fire my black ass ain't you?"

Zorita laugh, "Naw man. Why would you ask something like that?" She took a drink from her coffee mug.

Nick answered, "Well, only 'cause you come talkin' 'bout 'business is business'. It sound like you gonna let my ass go."

She took another sip of the coffee then proceeded carefully. "Nick, I need a cook. Not just any cook, but a damn good cook.

You! I'm sorry to say, business has been slow, unfortunately I have to start charging you for your room. I can't let you stay rent-free any more. I need for you to pay fifteen dollars a week; now that's half of what I normally charge. Don't worry though, I won't be charging you the usual five dollars a day for your meals. Your meals will remain free."

She looked at Nick over her raised coffee mug. She noticed his mild manner changing. The longer her eyes rested upon his face, the more she noticed a scowl gradually appear. When his features had reached a full-blown look of an angry man, he furiously said, "I rememba when I first started workin' here, Jack was chargin' his tenants only ten dollas a week. Then, about five years later, he charged twelve dollas a week. Only raised the rent once in the all the years I been workin' fo' him, and even then, it was only by two dollas. When you bought this inn from Jack, you upped the room rates to twennie dollas a week, right off the bat. Then last year you raised it another ten. Now you want me to start payin' fifteen dollas a week to live here? And where is I suppose to git the money from. You gonna start payin' me to cook?" Nick shook his head in disbelief. He leaned across the small table and glared into Zorita's eyes; "Jacka Diamond said I could stay here free as long as I cooked fo' this place. That deal you done made with Jack 'bout me livin' here rent-free was sealed. So, is you sure that's what you want? Fo' me to pay a weekly-room rate of fifteen dollars?"

Undeterred by Nick's rationality, Zorita said, "Yeah Nick, that's what I'm saying. Look around, you notice up there on the second and third floor we ain't got but five people living here. You, me, Paulette, Fred and Ramona. I got three empty rooms that ain't generating revenue; and if I count you and me, that makes five rooms with no rent coming in. Besides, I'm paying a lot of money to keep the lights on in this place. Now if that's a problem, then I'm sorry. But that's how it is."

Nick abruptly stood up, snatched his chef's apron off and hurled it to the floor. "That's jist fine! You is somethin' else Lady Zorita. Guess you ain't never heard the word integrity, 'cause yo' promise didn't mean shit." He rattled on, "You accepted Jacka Diamond's deal, now you is sayin' the deal's off." Nick kicked the rumpled apron across the floor. "That's oooookay! One of these days, lady, you is gonna figure out there's thangs mo' impo'tant than money. A deal's a deal. It ain't somethin' you suppose to be breakin', gurl. You can find yo'self another chef 'cause I ain't payin' no rent. I quit!" Before Zorita could negotiate with him, he stormed out of the kitchen. She could hear his voice trailing from the lounge area, "I'll have my shit outta yo' place in ten minutes." She heard his footsteps dissipate up the stairs.

That wasn't the way she had perceived her little talk about the rent to have gone. She sat there pissed at herself for not taking into account what she would do if Nick refused to pay a room rate. She thought he would pay it without a fuss, it was only fifteen dollars. But she was wrong. "Gottdamn it," she mumbled to herself. "What am I gonna do for a cook?" She got up from the table and dumped the mug of coffee into the hot, sudsy water. She walked from the kitchen and caught a glimpse of Nick's back as he stormed towards the double doors. He carried two overstuffed shopping bags, one in each hand. She had no idea what she would do without Nick in the kitchen. He had been a big money-maker, filling all of the inn's take-out orders, cooking for the tenants and fixing short orders for the drinking customers of the bar and lounge. It was Nick who made use of the walnuts from the property's walnut trees. He had used those nuts to make and sell walnut pound cakes and all of his other walnut delicacies, including banana-nut bread and walnut ice cream. His delicious, sweet recipes had put a lot of cash into Zorita's pocketbook. He was gone now, and he had taken his secret walnut recipes with him. She went behind the bar and poured a double shot of Crown Royal and downed it. She spoke to the reflection in the bar mirror, "I need to kick my own ass."

PART SIX

CHAPTER 29

ANNIE

Annie Elliot and her twin boys had just got out of Linda's car. The two women had taken their children to Constitutional Park to collect fall leaves for a school assignment. She was inside her house and about to close the door when she spotted two white men in business suits coming up her walkway. Immediately, she told her boys to go to their room. She instructed them to put their school projects away and get their books out to read. When the children were out of her sight she stepped onto the porch to greet the men. "Can I help you gentlemen?" she asked.

The taller man, Detective Pilcher, had a small scar over his right eye and his hair was disheveled. He said, "Ma'am, I'm Detective Pilcher. This is my partner, Detective Martin. We're looking for a Mr. Bernard Elliot." They flashed their badges, almost simultaneously.

"He's my husband. Can I ask what this is in reference to?" Annie asked, in a pronounced voice of control.

"Ma'am, we're investigating a child pornography case. We have reason to believe your husband might be involved."

The statement sent her heart racing, but in a cool voice, she said, "Child pornography, you say?" She stood defiantly, "And what make you think my husband would be affiliated with anything remotely associated with the sexual exploitation of innocent children?"

Already, there were two neighbors curiously looking in the direction of her home. One was raking the leaves, and the second neighbor was picking up debris from her walkway. When the neighbors lingered a moment more than Annie figured necessary, she swung the storm door completely opened and invited them into her home. She contained them in the small foyer area. "Like I was saying, why would Bernard be involved in such deviate behavior? He's a school teacher, a decent family man, with a wife and children. He loves us too much to even think about anything so immoral."

The two men made a quick mental note of the immaculate living room. Detective Martin said, "Ma'am, we don't doubt that." He discreetly glanced around again; he had a little smile on his face. He added, "You have a lovely home ma'am and we don't mean to do anything to disrupt it. Unfortunately, there's been a complaint and we have to follow up on it. Believe me, we wouldn't be here if we didn't have to be."

She knew what they wanted. It was obvious they were digging for whatever they could come up with. There was no way she would let them search her home nor interrogate her unless they had a warrant. She asked, "Why are you here?"

"Beg your pardon, ma'am?" Detective Martin asked. "What do you mean? We told you we're here to investigate a child pornography case."

"I asked you, why are you here? You're detectives right?" she interrogated.

"Yes ma'am we are," Detective Pilcher spoke up, wondering how she had turned the table to question them.

"Then if you . . ."

"Mama! Mama! Dewitt took my red leaves and won't give them back. He pretended like he was going to trade me three yellows for three of my red ones. Now he won't give me the yellow leaves like he promised."

"Donald, mama's busy right now. Tell Dewitt I said to give the leaves to you?" She yelled, "Dewitt, don't make me come in there!" She stooped and quickly swatted Donald's little bottom. "Go back to the room, honey. I'll be done shortly." While she had busied herself with the child, both detectives looked feverishly around the living room. Once the child was situated, she resumed. "As I was saying, if you have questions regarding this matter, then you should be questioning my husband, not me. So if you'll excuse me, I have very active twins I must tend to." She opened the storm door for them. As they walked out, she added, "If you think my husband is involved with something so sordid, you're incorrect. You gentlemen are looking in the wrong direction."

Once they were back in their car they both agreed what a smart cookie the woman seemed to be. It was quite apparent she would not give her permission for them to look around her home without a search warrant. "Yeah, she's pretty smart," Detective Pilcher said to his partner. "Frank, did you get a look at that house? Whew! How can those black people afford such a fabulous house in this nice community? And on a teacher's salary?"

"Jerry, it beats the hell out of me. It pisses me the hell off knowing they actually live better than I do; better than you too, gottdamn it!"

The beginning of school put Bernard in his glory. He had missed being in the presence of the pretty school girls during summer recess. When he arrived home from his day of teaching, he noticed his wife's character was irregular. Unable to ignore the woman's strange behavior he asked, "Something bothering you, Annie?"

She rolled her eyes at him, bit her bottom lip, then said, "Two detectives were here earlier today. They said you've been involved in child pornography. Is that true Bernard?"

Bernard wondered why his children weren't around. He wondered why there was no smell of fried pork chops or baked cornbread. He jerked the noose out of his tie and walked towards his wife who had planted herself in the corner of the sectional sofa. He stood a few feet from her and said, "Sweetheart, of course it isn't true. How could you even fix your mouth to ask me such a terrible thing? I would never become involved in such filth?" He approached and leaned over to kiss her on the cheek, but she turned away. Annie grabbed a envelope from the wedge of the sofa. It was an envelope Bernard had hidden away in the blind attic. Bernard backed up; he asked, "What is that?"

"You know damn well what it is," she snapped.

"How would I know Annie? I've never seen it before."

"Don't treat me like I'm one of your students. You know exactly what this is, you filthy pervert. And here I thought you were a halfway good husband. I suspected you had women, but never did I even think you were a child molester." She flung the packet of photos of naked teenage girls at him. The Polaroids scattered out of the business-sized envelope right in front of Bernard's feet. She ran as he bent to pick up his collection. When he retrieved them all, he placed them on the stand then headed towards the bedroom where she'd locked herself in.

"Annie, open this door right now," he demanded. He leaned his ear against it, listened and pounded again. "Open up." Annie said nothing. All he could hear was drawers being opened and closed and wire hangers sliding across the aluminum pole. He beat on the door some more. "Open this damn door Annie before I bust this son-of-a-bitch down." There was nothing, not a word, only faint sniffles. The twins were not there; where were they? She had no car. Bernard purposely kept her from driving by not purchasing a second car. It was his way of knowing she was stuck at home while he was out having his affairs. Everywhere Annie went, her husband had to take her, or she'd take Queen City Taxi. As a last resort, she'd catch a ride with her friend, Linda. Though she was a highly-educated woman, she had fallen right into his trap and did not take on a career of her own. She stayed at home to raise their sons, as he suggested. He had supplemented their income by selling the nude photos. The envelope Annie flung at him would have bought him three-hundred dollars.

Annie now knew about his illegal activity; and according to her, the law was actively investigating him. He knew he was losing his family and in desperation he start pleading for Annie to let him explain. She was disgusted with him. She realized she was married to a man who stole the innocence of children. Through the door he begged her to forgive him; even said he didn't know what he had been thinking. He never thought he would be caught so he became bolder each year with the young girls. The more he took advantage of the teenage girls, the more he thought he could get away with it. He had even begun thinking about experimenting with little boys. He was a predator and he only thought of one thing, his next innocent victim to fulfill his sick, sexual appetite. He pleaded and begged for his wife to stand by him, but it did no good. He leaned helplessly against the wall, his body slowly slid down. He sat against the wall with his legs crumpled within the hallway. When his wife came out of the room with a large suitcase, he cried up towards her, "Annie, Annie, listen to me baby. I didn't mean to . . ." Annie cut her eyes at him, stepped over his legs without saying a word, and marched out the front door into Linda's awaiting car.

CHAPTER 30

OLIVIA WORRIED

When word got out about the teacher's involvement with black and white school girls, the citizens of Timberland were livid. Every parent whose daughter had been a student of Mr. Elliot's extensively questioned their girls. If the parents felt they were not getting the truth out of their teens, they'd question their daughters' friends.

Olivia had just got out of the shower when the two detectives knocked on her apartment door. She had on a pink, terry-cloth robe and her hair was wrapped in a matching towel. Excited, Olivia rushed to the door. She thought it was one of her friends who was helping her with the small wedding she and Earl were having at Holy Baptist Church of Christ. Surly disappointed when she saw the two men standing on her porch, she hastily asked, "Can I help you?" Her smugness shifted to underlying fear when the detectives showed their badges.

Detective Martin cleared his throat, "Are you Olivia Burns?"

Annoyed, upon hearing the surname, Burns, the young lady answered, "I'm Olivia. What is it?"

"Ma'am, I'm Detective Martin and this is Detective Pilcher. We're here to ask you a few questions about Bernard Elliot."

Olivia tried to conceal her distress. In a normal tone of voice, she said, "Mr. Elliot was my English teacher. What could you possibly have to ask me about him?" She stood rigid and said nothing more.

Detective Pilcher sensed they would get nowhere with them standing on the outside; he asked, "Could I trouble you for a glass of water?" He added, "Ma'am, do you mind if we come in? This wind is really whipping up." Olivia felt uncomfortable letting the men into her home; she had nothing on beneath her robe.

"Umm, wait right here, I need a minute." She closed the door and rushed to her bedroom. Olivia threw on a pair of jeans and a long sleeve white cotton blouse. She removed the pink towel from her wet hair, rewrapping it with a clean, white towel. Olivia ran back to let them in. As they made themselves comfortable on her black, leather sofa she went to the refrigerator to pour each man a glass of water. She speculated; were they there because of Bernard Elliot's involvement with underage girls, or because of the death of Mr. Nesbaum. Either way she knew she would have a hard time pretending she didn't know anything. It was only a few days ago she had heard gossip about the investigation of the teacher. This concerned her because in four days she and Earl were to get married. It looked as though she would have to face the fact her ugly past might be rearing up to ruin her beautiful future. She sat Indian style in the black, leather chair. Olivia pulled the ashtray on the end table towards her. She had picked up the disgusting habit the same day she heard the gossip about Bernard. Someone told her cigarettes would ease her nerves, and her nerves were shot. "Cigarette?" She tilted the pack of Winstons toward the men. They both declined. "Okay, so what is it, guys? What brings you to my place?"

"Miss Burns, what can you tell us about Bernard Elliot?" Detective Pilcher asked.

She tried to conceal her anxiety when the detective called her by her adoptive last name. Olivia took a puff from the cigarette, "Please detective, I go by my real last name, Territino. I don't use that adoptive name because of personal reasons. My name is Olivia Ann Territino." She sucked on the cigarette and then quickly blew the smoke from her mouth. "What do you mean, what do I know about him? He was my teacher," she said, convincingly.

Detective Pilcher's face was as solemn as a granite stone. He said, "We've heard from a pretty good source you were involved with him."

She knew the detectives could have received that tidbit from any one of the citizens of Timberland. It seemed as though the whole town kept up with her business far better than she could keep track herself. In her coolest manner, she confessed, "Okay, so Bernard and I had a fling. Big deal. Anyway, we've been broken up for over two years. We're two grown people who had a relationship. No law against that, is there?"

Detective Pilcher said, "Come on, Miss Burns, umm Territino. We all know you and Elliot were having an affair while he was teaching you at Lincoln High. Maybe in your young mind you didn't think anything was wrong with a thirty-something year old man having sex with a sixteen or seventeen year old, but murder is a different story.

She almost gag, quickly she cleared her throat. She said, "Murder? Who died?" She flicked the ashes off her cigarette then took another quick puff.

"Have you ever heard of a David Nesbaum?" Detective Martin grilled her.

"Yes." At this point she was not divulging any more than she had to.

"Miss Territino, how do you know of him?" Detective Pilcher asked.

"He was my ex-roommate's father," she said, devoid of emotion.

"Did he ever come into your house the night he was found murdered?" the taller detective asked.

With an angelic face, she replied, "Why would you ask me that? The man was found outside of our apartment, dead in his car."

"Miss Territino, that's not answering our question. Did Nesbaum ever come into your apartment on the night of his death?" Detective Pilcher angrily repeated.

"No!" she lied with a straight face. She knew if she admitted Mr. Nesbaum had been in her place it would open up a flood of questions she was unwilling to answer. It could possibly make people think she had something to do with his death. She would deny the fact that David Nesbaum was inside the apartment until the moon turned into Swiss cheese. Mr. Nesbaum's death had been a complete travesty to her. She had suffered greatly knowing she had been the indirect cause of the man's demise. Both detectives stared at her but she simply stared back. When the tension was a bit strained, she asked, "Is there anything else?"

"Umm, no ma'am. We think that will be all for now." Detective Martin took a drink of the chilled water; they left the lady's home.

They knew the lady had been intimately involved with not only Bernard Elliot, but David Nesbaum as well. She had been discreet with Mr. Nesbaum and told not a soul about the relationship except for her fiancé, Earl. Olivia never suspected that Mrs. Nesbaum pretended to be asleep while she and her husband quietly made love in the bathroom. It was Mrs. Nesbaum who had given that information to the investigators the moment she heard her husband had been murdered. Even though the authorities had that fact, they could not pinpoint Olivia as the person responsible for the homicide; therefore the case was never solved. After a year and a half of no active investigation on the case, Mrs. Nesbaum went to the Timberland Police Department. The widow inquired when they plan on finding her husband's killer. The detectives were given orders to take another look at the case.

The morning they interrogated the young lady in her home, they knew she was lying. Mrs. Nesbaum indicated she suspected her husband of having continued the affair even after Olivia moved out of their home. The evening her daughter went out of town, Mrs. Nesbaum knew her husband had gone to visit Olivia.

The detectives were sure the only way they would be able to get the truth out of Olivia, was to pull the young lady out of her comfort zone. They would have her come to the precinct. Olivia had been working the day shift to help out a co-worker who needed to switch hours. The detectives showed up at her job and asked her to come to the precinct for more questioning after work. There was no way she could get out of it so she decided to prepare herself and maintain the sturdiest mental armor she could muster up. When she was done for the day she went straight to the Timberland Police Department. If she thought she would saunter in, bat her eyelashes, and breeze out, she was very mistaken. No matter how coy and cute she tried to be, it had no affect on the men. They played good detective, bad detective with her. They questioned her long and hard, pounding their fist upon the metal table. When she told them she felt she needed a lawyer, Detective Pilcher shouted, "Looks like she had something to do with the Nesbaum murder. She's asking for a lawyer now." She was nervous and she would have taken the detective's offer to smoke her cigarettes, but they didn't seem to work for her. Her nerves were still shattered, and she couldn't take any more of the belligerent interrogation. That was the moment the moon turned into Swiss cheese. It must have been something she had seen on television, or something she read somewhere; either way, she blurted out, "If I tell you everything I know, what's in it for me? I did not kill Mr. Nesbaum; and I don't want to be implicated in his murder."

When the detectives told the young lady they would grant her immunity if she handed over the person responsible for Nesbaum's death, she told them everything. Olivia even admitted she was an accessory after the fact. She felt relieved as she revealed the secret. They already knew about her affair with Bernard Elliot. She readily admitted to seducing David Nesbaum while living with the Nesbaum family. She concluded by saying she was almost sure the man had let himself into the apartment specifically to see her on the evening of his death. According to Olivia, it was simply bad timing. Bernard Elliot was there making love to her, and when Nesbaum saw she and Bernard doing it on the couch he angrily ran towards them in a fit of rage. That's when the teacher shot him in self defense. She admitted, she was sure David Nesbaum would have harmed them if he had reached the both of them. The recording had been transcribed and when she signed the typed statement they released her. As she drove home, she remembered how Bernard warned her not to tell a soul about the murder. Deep down inside she was glad the truth was finally out. It had weighed heavily on her ever since the death of her friend's father. Today she felt free.

When Olivia arrived home, she sat on her sofa and cried. The pain of Mr. Nesbaum's death had been trapped deep in her psyche. Like the steam escaping a teakettle, it had finally been released. The liberation of the secret was flowing out of her in the form of tears. She tried to smoke to pacify her nerves, but the cigarette did not work. Frustrated, she put it out in the nearest ashtray. She needed to do something to relax, so she took a shower to drench away the pain. She stood beneath the falling water and cried until she could cry no more. And when she was done feeling sad and sorry, she perfumed her body and dressed herself up. For the very first time since dating Earl she headed for The Inn at Walnut Valley without her sweetheart.

CHAPTER 31

FOLLOWED

The world is filled with people who look at their life and sing their sad, *If Only* song . . . *If only* they had been born to good parents, *if only* they had lived in a better part of town, *if only* they hadn't been abused, *if only* they had a great paying job, *if only* they had gone to college, *if only* they had a better looking body, *if only* they were more attractive, *if only* they were another color, *if only* they were healthier, *if only* they were rich, *if only* they were famous, *if only* they were younger . . . *if only* . . . *if only* . . . *if only;* and the song goes on. But the truth of the matter is, no one has any reason for singing the *If Only* song. Because it is up to each person to take care of their own situation no matter what the reality of their life may be. Sometimes a little wisdom really does go a long way. And if only they'd used an ounce of common sense and dust themselves off, it could save a pound of unwanted consequences.

But Olivia could never quite figure out what was common sense, and what was just her senses acting common. Since the neglect and raping of Olivia Ann Territino, she did what she wanted, whenever she wanted, however she wanted to do it. She had tried to straighten out her life, but somehow she could never quite figure how to dust herself off and cautiously start all over again. Many times she blamed her failures on the inadequate parenting of her mother. It was her mother who had put her in harm's way by letting the pedophile,

Jim Burns, into their lives. Her past had caused her bouts of anxiety; still, she always wanted people to think she was in control. But she wasn't. Her life had veered way off track and she didn't know how to put it on course again. Her choices were always based on how she felt. Sometimes when she thought she was making a good choice, because at the moment the choice felt good, it would end up being a bad choice that would have an adverse effect on her life.

After she had taken the long shower, perfumed and put her makeup on, she found her mood had changed for the better. As she was driving to The Inn at Walnut Valley to start an early evening of partying, she spotted Nick walking on Chase Street. She had not spoken privately with the man since their tryst in the Oaktown motel. Seeing him boosted her spirits even more. She quickly swerved her car to the curb and shouted, "Hey Nick, where are you going?"

He leaned into the young lady's car and said, "Hey 'Livia gurl! What's happenin'?! I sho' am glad to see you. You know my car done broke down and I got to get over to pick up a package from Western Union. I was jist gonna git me a cab, but if you can give me a lift I sho' would 'preciate it."

"Sure Nick. Hop in," she told him in a happy voice. Knowing she would be in the company of Nick made her heart leap. She had been cursing the fact her beloved Earl was still out of the city. He had to take his father to a visit a friend in Bald Eagle, Pennsylvania. The old man had rammed his car into a tree the night before and had no transportation. She was a bit concerned about Earl's absence. Even though he was due back tomorrow, the wedding was so close in time. It annoyed her; she needed Earl at that very moment, and he was hours away.

Since Earl was off with his father, Olivia was more than happy to see Nick. He got into her car and flashed his beautiful smile. She was so ecstatic to see him that she leaned over and gave him a hard kiss on the lips. Happy to know the young lady was as thrilled as he was to be in one another's company, he took a chance and slid his tongue between her lips. He was pleasantly surprise when Olivia's tongue entwined his. He could taste the butterscotch candy which she had been sucking on before he entered her car. When they finished kissing, Nick reared back and looked at her. He said, "Gurl, look at you. Why you is lookin' like a million bucks, lady. Why is you all dressed up? Is it your birf-day?" He looked as though he had thought of another reason for her fancy attire. He said, "Aww, shit naw! I bet you done hit the jackpot. That's it, right? You done hit the jackpot, ain't you?"

Olivia laughed at her friend's comment as she steered the car away from the curb. Nick was funny and he seemed to know how to bring out the sparkle in her. She knew she could easily love him, but the man had so many women. Though she loved Earl, she found herself wishing her fiancé had a sense of humor as witty as Nick's. Her Earl was always serious and he took life so stringent. There was no other way he knew, but to be sincere; because he loved her with his whole soul. Olivia adored that trait in him. At times, she wished she could take Earl's sensibility and Nick's sense of humor and mesh them together. If she could, she would have the perfect man, because sex with both was great. She knew she could not make the two men into one; so for now, Nick was her salvation. The moment he climbed into her car all of her troubles from the interrogation vanished from her memory.

Olivia parked the car right in front of the building. When he jumped out of the car and ran into Western Union, she looked into the rear view mirror to check her makeup. She patted her hair in place and refreshed her lipstick.

Nick got the three-hundred dollars his friend Gilmore had wired him. Poor Nick. He bought his hard luck on himself because of a principle. It was a principle he had believed in all his life, a person's word was meant to hold substance. He could not understand why anyone would throw their promise to the wind. Consequently, when Zorita went back on her agreement of his free room, he found himself no longer able to trust her. He wondered what would be next. Months later would she make him pay for his meals too? He had held up his end of the deal; he felt she should have held up her end as well. For now, he had no real job and no decent earnings to supplement his loss of the free room and board which he had once worked so hard to earn. He now worked handy-man jobs to hold him over; and he hated handy-man work. He lived a meager existence, paying twenty dollars a week for a room at Fort Timberland Hotel and eating whenever he could grab a seat at the homeless shelter. On some occasions he'd help the hotel manager by keeping the place clean. But cleaning toilets and dumping trash was not for him. His forte was preparing hardy cuisines for hungry crowds. It was the talent God had given him. He longed for another great job as a chef in a well-equipped kitchen. When night rolled around he was generally by himself. His three girlfriends had found other fun-time men to hang with. Sure, at the beginning the women gave him money when times were hard for him. But before long, they had tired of his neediness and left him to fend for himself. It was out of desperation he telephoned his buddy, Gilmore, and begged the man to wire him some money. Sympathetic to Nick's troubles, the friend wired him three-hundred dollars.

Now Nick had three-hundred bucks in his hand, and the privilege of being chauffeured around by a beautiful lady. "Hey 'Livia," he hollered. She looked in his direction as he walked towards her car. He waved the money in the air, "Babycakes, we's rich gurl, we's rich." A driver, who had just pulled into a parking spot two cars behind Olivia's automobile, had witnessed Nick's windfall. As soon as he got into the car, Olivia quickly pulled away from the curb.

That was one thing about Nick, if he had money, whoever was with him had money. He was a freehearted soul, a trait his ex-girlfriends loved about him. Excitedly, he asked Olivia, "What do you want to do, since it's your birf-day and I done hit the jackpot." She laughed at his comment and asked him to get her a cigarette from her pack. He did, slipped it between her lips, then lit it for her. "Gurl, what the hell you smokin' that mess fo'. Don't you know they call them thangs cancer-sticks fo' a reason. Look at you, why you ain't even inhalin' it." She took another short puff. Nick shook his head, "Look gurl, take me over on Elmwood Street. I can get some good shit from over there." Olivia smashed out the cigarette and did as Nick instructed. She forgot not only her troubles with the detectives but she also forgot about making it to The Inn at Walnut Valley as well.

"Right there, that blue house," he said. She parked the car and waited. He made a quick in, quick out of the shabby house. When Nick got back into the car, he discreetly showed her the bag of weed.

Olivia had never smoked grass before. She found herself getting happy with the anticipation of trying the marijuana with Nick. The adrenalin filled her with excitement as she drove. She knew she was in for some fun with Nick. "Where to Nick?" At this point, she was gamed for anything her friend suggested.

Nick said, "Hey, let's go back to my place; I got a room at Fort Timberland Hotel. That's if you don't have to go and be with *yo' precious Earl*."

She snickered, and excitedly said, "Nick, *my precious Earl* is out of town. This is your lucky day!"

A wide grin came across his face. "Hot damn," he hooted. "I told you, Livia! I told you, gurl. I done hit the jackpot, didn't I gurl. I told you!" They both laugh.

Olivia was feeling very comfortable with Nick riding in her car. She reached her right hand over and rubbed high on his thigh, trying to reach his groin area. With a big smile on her face she said, "Look like we both hit the jackpot, Nick."

Every turn she made, a car few automobiles back took the same turns. As she whipped into the hotel's parking lot, the car that had been tailing her was caught by a red light. Olivia parked the car and she and Nick took the elevator up to the seventh floor. The room was nothing fancy. The owner of the hotel used the last floor for indigents and downtrodden men and women who could afford to pay the weekly twenty-dollar rooming fee. Nick's place was full of clutter and soiled clothing. The bed was unmade. It looked as though he had never picked a thing up the whole time he'd lived there. He threw the marijuana onto the rumpled bed as Olivia stood looking at the unkempt room. For a moment she wanted to turn and run from the chaos, but then Nick's sense of humor kicked in. "I see my maid, Hilda, done ran off with my butler, Charles. Shit! I knew I shouldn't have paid them in advance." He laughed, "I'm gonna fire they asses soon as they get back from that cruise I know they done took." Olivia laughed heartily, and the filth of the place was tossed aside. She watched him as he rolled the joints. "Here gurl, smoke this." He showed her how to smoke the weed to maximize her high then lit one for himself. After they both smoked some joints, the two of them laughed themselves silly. They ate all of the Fig Newtons and split the big Hershey that was in Nick's nightstand. The couple laid in bed and experienced one another's passion; and when they were done, they smoked a little more. They found themselves laughing at absolutely nothing, then hitting the sack for more sex. As Olivia was going for her third organism there was a loud thrust at the door and then another, on the third thrust the wooden door came flying open. Olivia thought the grass was playing tricks on her and hid beneath the sheet. But Nick knew it was no hallucination. As Olivia hid, Nick angrily confronted the intruder. "Who you is? And why you is bustin' in my door?" he asked, unashamed to be standing naked in front of the man. When he saw the gun in the intruder's hand, Nick threw his hands up in the air and shouted, "What I did? What I did? Is it the money? Man, you can have it. Jist let me git it fo' you." Olivia was still beneath the sheet. She was so stoned from the grass she actually believed the intruder would not know she was there. She heard Nick shout, "Man, no. Please, no. I'll give you anythang you want, jist don't shoot me." Olivia thought she was warped from the dope. She thought, *Please just let this be some bad marijuana, please.* When she heard the popping sound, her heart beat faster. This time she knew it was not the weed doing a number on her.

The man had spotted Nick earlier when the ex-cook first hopped into Olivia's car. He followed them to the Western Union place. He would have done his horrific deed right there, but too many people were moving about and he did not want witnesses to view the murder. When Nick stopped at the drug-dealer's house, it was the same situation. Some little girls had drawn a hopscotch diagram on the sidewalk and three of them were busy testing their skills. A house away, some girls jumping double-dutch, and some little boys wheeling themselves around on their Big Wheels were in full view. It wasn't the scene he wanted a child to witness. A murder. He followed the couple as they headed for the Fort Timberland Hotel. He was caught behind a car at the stop light. When the light changed he pulled into the hotel's parking lot and spotted the empty vehicle. By then the couple were out of the car and headed for Nick's room. The man waited and waited for them to return to the car. When he had tired of waiting, he entered the hotel in search of his intended victim. He had killed Nick. Beneath the sheet Olivia heard another shot but could not tell what the shot hit. A woman screamed and Olivia heard the man belligerently order her to shut up. The man drugged the woman over to Olivia's covered body. He knew she was beneath the sheet, in spite of her delusional attempt to hide. With the barrel of the gun, gently he removed the sheeting off of Olivia, exposing her naked body. When she looked passed the gun her eyes focused upon the weapon-wielding, crazed man. He held a small, brown woman tightly by her arm. To Olivia he said, "I told you I'd kill you if anything happened to me and my family. Since I've lost my wife and my boys, you lose your life." Her ex-lover shot her once in the head.

CHAPTER 32

GUNMAN

Ten minutes before Bernard's attack he had grabbed a housekeeper and threatened to kill her if she did not help him locate Olivia and Nick. When she took him to the seventh floor and pointed out Nick's room, it angered him the woman didn't have a pass key to let him in. He kicked the door in. At the very end of the hall was Winehead Rubin.

Winehead Rubin called the front desk earlier when he first heard the whimpering of the housekeeper through his door. Now the noise was more intense. When he peeked out his door and heard Nick pleading for his life he knew there was imminent danger so he called again to tell the desk clerk some crazy man was holding the housekeeper hostage and had burst into Nick's room. When the first shot was fired in room 707, Winehead Rubin panicked. When the wino made the third call, the desk clerk informed him Gus, the security guard, was on his way up. Shortly after the guard arrived Rubin heard a second shot. Again he peeped out of his door. What he saw sent him scrabbling back into his room, locking the door behind him. He punched in the number for the front desk again and told the clerk, "Man, this crazy fool has just shot Gus. I think he's dead; he's lying in the hallway. This cat is a crazy-ass fool; you gotta get us some help up here." The clerk ran over and shut off the power to the elevator. By then, Olivia had been executed.

Four police cars and a Tactical Unit Squad were dispatched to Fort Timberland Hotel. When the patrolmen arrived, the Tactical Unit Squad climbed the stairwell with their guns drawn because they did not know what the situation was. Bernard forced the maid to help him push the large dresser against the damaged door to barricade the room.

Two of the cops stood in the hallway and called to the gunman. He did not answer. The negotiator asked him to tell him his name. Bernard refused to tell them. He yelled out, "I've got this lady in here. I swear I'll kill this bitch if you come through that door. For hours they bantered back and forth. When he finally broke down and told the cops his name, he requested to see his wife and twins. No one could find his family. Linda heard about Bernard's desperation over the live-news report. She would not give away her friend's safe-house location. All through the hours Bernard ranted about how he was being framed for the Nesbaum murder. He adamantly proclaimed his innocence. When he realized he may be spending the rest of his life in prison, he thought about killing the small woman. He even considered going out in a hail of gunfire. If he shot it out with the law enforcement, it would force them to end his life. He had a full clip in his pants pocket and knew he could get at least four, maybe five of them if he was lucky. He heard the hostage negotiator trying to talk sense into him through the megaphone. Even that man's voice had long ago irritated him.

Bernard began talking to his hostage, "What's your name?"

"Marie Sanchez," the woman answered.

"You got children?"

Marie had not a child on this earth, but at that particular moment she said, "Yes mister, I have two sets of twins."

He broke down and began to cry. He missed his twin boys and his wife, but his love of teenage girls and easy money had somehow seemed more important. In his lifetime, he had ruined countless of teenaged girls' lives. Counting today's kill, Bernard had murdered four people. The man had been paranoid from the moment Olivia tossed him to the wind. When he realized the police were on to him and his wife and kids had left him, it sent him over the edge.

He thought about what harden convicts did to child molesters once they were sent to prison. It terrified him to know that once he was locked up with murderers and serial killers he may very well get his just due. He lifted the gun and pointed it to the housekeeper's head; she began to cry. He forced her down on her knees. "Close your eyes," he shouted. She did as he told her. She thought of her husband, her mom, dad and her teenaged brother and sister. She would never see them again. "Say your prayers 'cause I'm going to put an end to your gottdamn misery." She shut her eyes, tears trickled down her face. She began saying The Lord's Prayer. When she heard the loud gunshot, then a thud to the floor, she screamed. Though she had heard gun fire, she felt no pain. Marie knew she was dead but it didn't make sense because she still heard herself screaming. When she opened her eyes, there before her was a very dead Bernard Elliot.

She jumped to her feet and ran towards the barricaded door and pounded furiously upon it. She screamed for help and when the marksman from the tactical unit asked her where the gunman was, she screamed he was dead. "Get far away from the door," he warned. She did. The Tactical Unit Squad rammed opened the door with the battering ram. They stormed the room with guns drawn and snatched her out of the room.

"Thank you Jesus, Thank you Jesus," she praised as she gave the sign of the holy cross upon her body.

Bernard Elliot, the child molester, was sure this would be the day he would murder Olivia. He had hoped to kill her and no one else. It was only pure misfortune that Nick asked the pretty blonde to give him a lift. Bernard knew this would be the day he'd send Olivia to hell. He just hadn't planned on joining her the very same day.

PART SEVEN

CHAPTER 33

CELEBRATION

Gus, the brave security guard, was laid to rest at Provinski and Sons Funeral Home. During the funeral ceremony, the white citizens were infuriated that Sharon Burn's daughter may have been the very cause of the guard's demise. Whispers got back to Sharon about the craziness of her daughter. The woman told anyone who questioned her regarding Olivia's involvement with black men, she had written the girl off long ago. There were innuendos surfacing about her husband, Jim Burns, raping Olivia when she was a little girl. People stated it was the reason the girl had become a wild-child. Sharon steadfastly denounced the rumors. She stated Olivia had lied on her stepfather to get her father to return to their home.

The people openly cursed Bernard Elliot's soul. When the reverend gave the teacher's eulogy, he stated Bernard was a child of God in spite of the man's faults. Few people attended his funeral. Most all of the black community gathered at Holy Baptist Church of Christ and mourned Nick and Olivia's murder. The morning after the security guard was laid to rest Olivia's funeral was held. It was packed. That afternoon Nick's funeral had standing room only. It was a sight to behold as the mourners grieved the loss of two of their favorite citizens. Popeye's grief was painful. He and Olivia were to be married at the church and now he was there attending her funeral. The town looked upon him as Olivia's mate, and expressively gave their condolences to him. It had been a hard time for Popeye. Through his grieving he found it unbearable to be around anyone. A week after Olivia's funeral he moved out of his dad's house and into his own place. Zorita closed down the bar and lounge area for two days; and though she knew it made no lucrative business sense, she did not care. It pained her to lose the cook and one of her favorite customers. The only satisfaction she had was knowing Miss Ada didn't have her hands involved in the deaths of Nick and Olivia.

The inn was in full swing a week after the deaths of Nick and Olivia. Zorita's put together a memorial celebration in memory of her two friends. She hired a local group comprised of both black and white musicians who could imitate the latest singing groups and even did Motown renditions from the sixties. Betty offered to prepare and serve the food. She told Zorita she, her husband, and her married daughter would be more than happy to help. Zorita declined. She wanted Betty and her family to enjoy the celebration. That is why she hired Sissy's Catering Service to do all of the cooking in the kitchen of her inn. The drinks were half-price for the evening.

Zorita had experienced losing four people she cared about, through violent deaths, Randy, Percy, Nick and Olivia. In spite of knowing very little about Olivia, she was already missing the young lady's beautiful, smiling face. As the crowd partied to the music of the band, Zorita found herself thinking of Ramona. Her mind was constantly on the girl and she couldn't figure out why. Maybe because Olivia and Ramona were both young and beautiful, maybe it was the way both ladies smiled, maybe it was the way they were both carefree, each in their own special way, or maybe it was their innocence and inexperience of life. Zorita had hoped Ramona would come down and celebrate with them, but she did not. The innkeeper knew Ramona was not a bar person, but even so, she thought the lady would join the celebration as a kind gesture. Zorita felt a great need to see Ramona; she called on Betty to take over the bar for ten minutes. Zorita went up the stairs and knocked on Ramona's door.

"Yes? Who is it?" she heard the young girl's voice.

"Ramona, it's me. It's Zorita." Zorita could hear the door unlock and when it opened she saw the girl standing there in green pajamas. This threw Zorita off a bit because it was only eight-thirty and she was already dressed for bed. Zorita said, "Are you alright Ramona? I was hoping you would come down tonight and celebrate the memory of our friends, Nick and Olivia."

The young lady's eyes were red and Zorita could tell she had been crying. When Ramona saw Zorita standing at her door she began crying again and the droplets flowed down her cheeks. Concerned, the innkeeper asked, "What's wrong, Ramona, is it because you miss Nick and Olivia?"

The girl wiped away the wetness with the back of her hand. "I miss my mama," she said. "I really miss her a lot." The eighteen-year old walked back into her room and sat down on the bed's edge. She reached for the double-frame photo that sat on the small desk, looked at it and clutched it to her bosom. Another tear rolled down her face.

Zorita felt helpless standing in the door entrance watching the girl sob, so she walked into the room and pat the distraught girl's back. The innkeeper said, "Why don't you call your mama, honey? You don't even have to call her collect on the pay phone. Go in my room and use my phone. I'll pay for the call myself."

The young lady said nothing; she held her head next to Zorita's big belly and silently cried as the innkeeper gently pat the girl on her shoulder. Zorita waited for Ramona to say something, but the girl only sniffled. Zorita moved her belly slightly away from the girl's head and looked down at her. The young girl's long, black locks covered her face; she used her fingers to comb the hair back. Zorita felt bad, she hated seeing the child upset. Ramona pulled the double frame away from her bosom and lovingly kissed both photos. She looked up at Zorita, "I appreciate you letting me call my mama. But truth is I can't call her. We had a big argument when I graduated from school. We both said some real nasty things. For a while we lived in the same house and never even spoke because of the anger. My dad told me it was wrong of me to be upset with her. Said everything my mama ever did had been all for me."

"That's even more reason for you to call her, Ramona. You got to patch this thing up. You can't go being mad at your mama and not speaking to her. That ain't nice. I'm sure she will be happy to hear from you." Zorita grabbed the chair from the desk and sat down in front of Ramona. As soon as she did, the girl clutched the picture ever tighter and then boo-hoed all over again. "Ramona, honey you got to go call her. I see this thing is tearing you apart."

"You don't understand, I can't call her Zorita, she died three weeks before I came here," she wailed even harder.

Shocked to hear the words come from Ramona's mouth, Zorita did not know what to say. She had not expected the girl to have such a weight on her shoulders. Sympathetically, Zorita asked, "She died?" Zorita began to feel even sadder knowing she had insisted the girl call her mother only to find out the woman was dead. She sorrowfully asked the girl, "What happened to your mama, Ramona?"

"Cancer. I wasted time being mad at her. Mama never even hinted to me she was dying. Even when I saw her sick, I didn't have brains enough to figure out something awful was wrong with her."

Tactfully as she could, Zorita asked, "Why were you so upset with your mother to the point of not speaking to her?"

Ramona looked at Zorita and said, "She waited until I graduated from high school to tell me she wasn't my real mother. Said she had to let me know. But even though I wasn't her daughter she loved me as if I were her very own. I didn't know she only had weeks to live and that's why she really told me. She wanted to clear her conscience before she passed away. Anyway, I was angry because I felt she should have told me a long time ago." The young girl wiped a tear from her face, "When I asked her who my real mother was, she said it would do no good to tell me because she was not even sure if my real mother was alive. According to her, when I was a newborn baby she saw a woman drowning me in a pond near her home in Macon, Georgia. She saved my life and raised me as her own."

Zorita felt chills flow through her bloodstream. She quickly grabbed the double-framed photo from the girl's hand and looked at it. In one photo she saw her cousin, Sally Mae, holding the hand of a very young Ramona and standing by her side was Kashif. In the second photo she saw a very frail-looking Sally Mae, then Ramona dressed in a graduation cap and gown, and a much older Kashif.

CHAPTER 34

MIDST OF DEATH

After realizing she was face to face with her very own daughter, Zorita had no voice. She could not find the words to ask the girl anything about her life. She wanted to know how she had end up in Little Rock, Arkansas with Kashif, who was really Ramona's real father, and Sally Mae, who had taken on the role as the child's mama, but was actually Ramona's second cousin.

Zorita left the young lady's room. When she heard all of the celebration filtering up through the open stairwell, she wanted no parts of it. She suddenly felt sick. She could not bring herself to go down and mingle with the crowd. The innkeeper knew if she returned to the lounge, she would only make her patrons uncomfortable with her somber state. She sat confused in her room. It had been a strange encounter, because in the midst of the deaths of her friends, she had discovered the life of her daughter.

As she sat at the desk in her room, she thought about calling Miss Ada and her mother to find out what happened the night she gave birth. She remember all of the months being locked in the basement and feeling the baby move around inside her big stomach. She had grown to love the child; even though Pearl constantly told her Miss Ada was going to make her put the baby up for adoption. It bothered the pregnant teenaged Zorita that Miss Ada was going to force her to give up her infant. She remembered how relieved she was to find out

God had taken the baby to heaven. When her mama told Zorita that Miss Ada said her baby was born dead, she believed the woman. So after moving to Timberland, Pennsylvania, Zorita concentrated on giving it her all in making her life work as best she could. She had tried to have children with her two husbands and Albert to make up for the one she'd lost. With each man, she was greatly disappointed. She believed her childlessness was God's way of punishing her.

Betty, who was in great shape to be a grandmother, flew up the first flight of steps with great speed. By the time she got up to the landing she was winded so she walked up the next set of stairs. When she got on the second floor she spotted the door of Zorita's room slightly opened. She peeked in and she saw her boss-lady sitting at the desk, "Zorita, did you forget you only needed me for ten minutes? What happened?"

Zorita was very strong. Even though she never cried when her husbands were murdered and Albert ran off, she was crying now. Betty could see the tears in her eyes. She knew how proud the woman was. She did not dare ask her boss, who was more of a friend to her, what was wrong. She simply said, "You know what, Zorita, I can handle the bar for the rest of the night if you want me to."

"That would be nice," Zorita said to Betty. "That would be real nice. I ain't feeling too much like going back to the lounge. Look, could you close up the place when the last customer leave? If not, come and let me know and I'll be down to take over."

"Don't worry. I'll take care of everything for you. Me and Rick will lock up at one o'clock when it's time to close shop."

"I sure do appreciate it." And with her boss's response, Betty closed Zorita's door and ran down both sets of stairs. Zorita sat at her desk trying to figure out what had happened while she was delivering her baby. She pulled the bottle of Crown Royal out and drank a little. She thought some more, then drank some more. She continued to think and drink, and drink and think until she felt numb. She got up from the desk and got into her bed. She was out like a light as soon as her head hit the pillow. In her dream she was back at the side by side, porch house in Macon, Georgia giving birth to her daughter. Her body hovered over the birthing bed and looked down to see Miss Ada taking the baby out of her. Her floating body followed Miss Ada and her mother to the park's pond where she witnessed the women taking turns drowning the newborn. She saw someone retrieve the baby's body but she could not see the person's face. Zorita awoke sweaty and anxious. She wanted to go across the hall and take her brown-skinned, eighteen-year old baby into her arms and cradle her. She had missed so much happiness because of the wickedness of the two outlandish women.

As much as she wanted to have a mother-daughter relationship with the girl, she knew she could not tell Ramona she was the girl's real mama and expect Ramona to accept her with open arms. How could she tell the girl, *You were drowned to keep you out of Miss Ada's unconventional family, but Sally Mae pulled you from the pond and saved you.*

After the bizarre dream, Zorita could not get back to sleep. It was about four o'clock in the morning and she was wide awake. She went downstairs and found no one in the lounge area. Betty and her husband had tidied the place up and locked up as promised. Zorita poured herself a stiff shot of Crown Royal, swallowed it then downed two more.

She felt the cold steel piece in her dress pocket. Touching it gave her the urge to go over and put both, Miss Ada and Pearl, out of their miseries. She sat behind her bar and thought about her teenage pregnancy. What she figured sickened her. The thought of her baby in a cold, watery grave upset her to tears. Zorita knew she had to face the two women.

It made sense; Sally Mae telling the girl she pulled her out of the park's pond. When she was locked in the basement she had often heard Sally Mae arguing with Pearl about her whereabouts. But Pearl always stuck to the same story. Her cousin had been her only true ally. Even though they had parted on bitter terms, Sally Mae never stopped trying to figure out what had happened to her cousin. Zorita surmised Sally Mae had watched vigil over the house when her baby was born. When she saw either Miss Ada or Pearl, or both carrying the infant to the nearby pond, she followed and saved the infant from drowning. It must have been later that she tracked down Kashif to let him know he was the baby's father.

CHAPTER 35

CONFRONTATION

Zorita slid her old spare key into the lock of the house which she had once shared with Pearl and Miss Ada. She was not surprised to discover they had never changed the lock in the many years she had been away. She drew her gun and stealthy walked into the darkened living room. She had not seen the women since the death of her second husband. Zorita quietly followed the night-lights to Miss Ada and Pearl's room. Once she made it to the room she felt around for the light switch then turned it on. Despite Miss Ada big size she jumped out of the bed as quick as a jaguar. The woman reached beneath the bed and came up with a baseball bat.

"What's goin' on; what is it?" Pearl said, as she arose from her sleep. She sat up in the bed, and when Zorita and the gun came into focus, she said, "Zorita what is you doin' pointin' that thing at us?" Miss Ada didn't say a word but she was thinking, *This yellow bitch might end up in the hospital before it's all over.* As Zorita stood aiming the gun at the both of them, Pearl, in an attempt to put a scare into her daughter, said, "Zorita, is you done lost your mind? You best get the hell outta here before Miss Ada kill your ass with that baseball bat."

"What? Like she killed Randy? Like she killed my Percy? Like the fat cow tried to kill my baby?" Zorita said in a cool, even tone.

When Pearl heard the baby part of Zorita's accusation, she had to think hard as to what her daughter was talking about. When she could not come up with anything that made sense within ten seconds of pondering her brain, she angrily said, "What the hell is you talkin' 'bout Zorita, killed what baby? Your ass ain't had no baby for Miss Ada to kill. And I know you ain't talkin' 'bout that baby that was born dead in Macon."

Zorita had long ago dismissed addressing Pearl as Mama. The angry innkeeper wields the gun into the direction of her mother. She blurted, "Look Pearl, don't you go acting like you didn't help Miss Ada try to kill my baby when she delivered her. Well y'all might have tried to kill her but . . ."

"Is it true Miss Ada? Was Zorita's baby born alive, or was it born dead like you done said?" Miss Ada did not answer Pearl. She stood with the baseball bat in a swinging stance. She had been prone to hot flashes and this night her naked body was drenched with perspiration. The intensity of her body heat, maximized by her fat, blubbery, folds of flesh, lead her to sleeping in the buff. She stood with no clothes or wig on, with the bat in swinging motion. The old woman was ready to take out Zorita if she had to. Miss Ada knew she had long ago lost hold on their daughter. It had been for the sake of Pearl and even Slick Rick, that she hadn't harmed a hair on Zorita's head. But this very morning the woman knew she might have to bludgeon the girl to death. Pearl, upset by Miss Ada's silence, asked again, "Well is it true Miss Ada, did you kill Zorita's little baby?"

Zorita injected, "No, she didn't kill my baby. My baby is very much alive. No thanks to that big heifer. I want to let you know . . ." she waved the gun back and forth between the two women, "You two bitches best stay away from me and my daughter or I will kill both of your asses."

As she turned to leave the room, Miss Ada flung the bat at Zorita. Though the bat didn't hit her, Zorita quickly turned and stared at the big, black woman. She wanted to shoot a bullet through her skull. Instead, her eyes narrowed. She shook her head in a show of pity for the old woman. Then, just as she turned her back and was headed out of the door, Miss Ada snarled, "Ever wondered why you couldn't get yourself in the fam'ly way with your husbands?" Zorita stopped dead in her tracks, turned and looked defiantly at Miss Ada. The old woman wanted to send a deep pain through the core of Zorita's soul. She said, "I done fixed you girl. Whilst I had your legs pried open afta deliverin' your ugly, black baby I yanked your plumbin' out. You can't ever have no chill'rens. So if you is tellin' me that black thing survived, then whoop-dee-do. If she's as black and ugly now as she was when she was born, she's in for a fucked-up life."

Zorita held the gun down by her thigh. She said to Miss Ada, "My heart bleeds for you Miss Ada. You're one crazy bitch and I am so glad you're out of my life." She looked at her mama, "And this is the type of existence you want?" She shook her head in empathy and said, "You two deserve one another." She walked out of the house and drove back to her establishment. She talked to the car's dashboard, "They ain't worth me killing and going to prison. God has seen fit to let me have my baby back.

CHAPTER 36

SEARCHING

Miss Ada had never set foot in The Inn at Walnut Valley. Pearl had been in the club only once when Jack of Diamond owned the place; a man enticed her to meet him there. When Slick Rick reported this to Miss Ada, the big woman warned Pearl if she ever went near the inn again, or deceived her in any way, she would kill her. Since that day, Pearl never mentioned anything about The Inn at Walnut Valley, not even when she heard her daughter had purchased the place.

Miss Ada was silently angered by the way Zorita turned out. She thought back how beautiful Zorita had been as a child. She and Pearl were so proud of her. But when she grew into a teenager that seemed to be where they lost control of their pretty daughter. When Zorita moved out of their household Miss Ada began to detest the girl. She found her to be a very ungrateful, self-centered wench, considering all of the things she and Pearl had done for her.

Miss Ada dressed her fat body as Pearl rolled over to go back to sleep. Pearl said, "Can you believe our daughter? Wonder what she was talkin' 'bout, sayin' her baby's still alive?" Sleepily she added, "I sure hope she is alive 'cause that would make us grandmas."

Not if I can help it, Miss Ada thought. She went to the dresser and checked her wig to make sure she had it on straight. She wanted to tell Pearl she should not get too excited about being a grandma because she was sure the baby was dead. She knew she drowned the infant deep in the water, and there was no way it had survived. Pearl went back to sleep as Miss Ada walked four doors down towards Slick Rick's house.

It was five-thirty in the morning and already Slick Rick was up drinking a cup of black coffee. Miss Ada said to the woman, "Remind me to change that gottdamn lock today. That damn Zorita, done come into the house this morning with a muthafuckin' gun aimed at us. Coulda easily killed me and your Pearl whilst we lay sleepin' in bed.

"Son-of-a-bitch Miss Ada, why the hell did you let her get away with it? I know I said I wanted her for myself, but you ain't gotta take no shit like that from her."

"The girl is my creation. It was me who picked out Pearl and I found a nice-looking white man for Pearl to get pregnant by so Zorita's little ass could be born. I hate she don't want to be in our lives no more. Guess I got to accept it. She's got her own way of doin' things." She dug her fingernails deep into the wig to scratch an itch that had annoyed her. The old woman continued, "What do you make of this Slick? That yellow heifer told us her baby . . . rememba that black thing I told you I delivered when that cow got herself knocked up as a teenager?" Slick Rick nodded, yes she did remember, "Well anyways, she says that the bastard baby of hers is alive, not dead."

"What? Ain't no way. Thought you said you done killed it? Said you done drowned it. Didn't you tell me that?"

"I did Slick. I drowned it good. As far as I knows ain't nobody in Macon claimed to finding a baby, dead or alive. I even put bushing over the body." Then Miss Ada got to thinking out loud, "Maybe somebody did find it and revived it. Zorita said it was a girl. I figured if somebody did save it, then the girl would be eighteen years old by now."

Slick Rick's ears perked up. "A girl? Eighteen? Wonder where she might be? I'm wonderin' how she look. I certainly would like to see the young thing, wouldn't you Miss Ada? Why I bet she's liable to be a pretty girl, bein' she's Zorita's kid."

Miss Ada could feel sprouts of jealousy spiking through her sinful heart. She loved Slick Rick. She loved her deeply. In fact, at one time Slick Rick had been her main lover. But where Miss Ada loved having one woman as a companion, Slick Rick liked messing around with many women and it worried Miss Ada. That was why she moved back to her hometown of Macon, Georgia to get away from Slick Rick and all of the woman's different lovers. Whereas Slick Rick would get different ladies to let her do whatever she wanted to do with them, then go on to the next one, Miss Ada wanted only Pearl as her woman. When they were forced to leave Macon, Miss Ada took the Greyhound Bus back to her old lover. She laid up with the woman until the two of them could figure out what they would do to keep her little family together. Miss Ada had loved being the woman again. Slick Rick knew just how to make her feel with her strap-on dick. With that thing she could screw Miss Ada better than any man had ever done. And when it was time for Miss Ada to go back to Georgia to retrieve Pearl and Zorita, Slick Rick sat the big woman up with an old car and a hundred dollars so she could relocate her little family. When Miss Ada returned with the beautiful Pearl and her fat daughter, Slick Rick fell in love with the cute, petite Pearl. She made Miss Ada bring the little lady to her bedroom and together the two old women had their fun with Pearl.

It ran through Miss Ada's mind of how Slick Rick wanted Zorita when the girl turned eighteen and graduated from high school. And she would have tricked Zorita into coming over her way if the girl hadn't come back from Hershey married to that jailbird of hers.

Now Slick Rick has been informed Zorita's offspring might be alive instead of dead; and Slick Rick wanted her, as she had wanted Zorita. She didn't know where the girl was but she was determined to locate Pearl's granddaughter. Slick Rick planned on forcing her into submission with her and Miss Ada. Since they missed out on Zorita, she felt Zorita's daughter would be easier pickings.

Slick Rick went over and caressed Miss Ada. She said, "You know I want Zorita's kid. I don't know what she look like. I don't even know where she's at. All I know is I want her and I want her in the worst way. Even if we have to kill Zorita to get at her. I say we go snoop around and find out where that bitch is got the girl hidden. We'll take her for you and me; not Pearl. That dumb-ass would never go for it."

Even though it had been quite daunting for Miss Ada to listen to all of the things Slick Rick wanted to do to the girl, it sound so sensual she couldn't wait to share the bed with Slick Rick and the fresh meat. Slick Rick kissed Miss Ada and slid her slimy tongue between the big woman's thick, black lips. She groped Miss Ada's huge breast like a man hungry for love, then pulled one out and lapped all over it. The big woman suggested they go lie down, but Slick Rick told her now was not the time; they had to find the whereabouts of Zorita's daughter. The sprouts of jealousy had disintegrated from Miss Ada's heart. She said, "Just knowin' I'm gonna be sharin' that girl's pussy with you has gotten me all hot and bothered. I'm gonna go home and beat the shit outta that bitch of mine 'cause I think she musta said somethin' to Zorita 'bout me tryin' to kill off that baby; then I'm gonna screw her brains out." Miss Ada pulled her elastic-waist pants and drawers down and said, "Just touch it for a little while to hold me over." Slick Rick jabbed her fingers around inside of the woman, tongue-kissed her long and hard, then sent Miss Ada on her way.

Slick Rick had often gone to The Inn at Walnut Valley when Jack of Diamond owned it. By the time Zorita purchased the place, Slick Rick had discovered a bar at the other end of Timberland which discreetly catered to gays. Even though she got a lot of action from the bar, she was always looking for something new and exciting. She would scout various locations about the town, such as supermarkets, Laundromats, and bowling alleys, to obtain sexual gratification from the different women she'd enticed. After getting in bed with Slick Rick, some of the women were shocked to discover what they thought was a man, was really a woman. Most would secretly return for more of her style of sex. These women shall remain nameless due to husbands and boyfriends. The men didn't have a clue their women were also getting their needs met by the man-like woman. And the ladies who had played around in her bed wouldn't dare be caught socializing with the lesbian in public.

When Miss Ada told Slick Rick about Zorita's child, the woman was on a mission to find out as much as she could about the girl. She loved a challenge. She decided she would kidnap her if she had too. It would not be the first time she had taken a lady against her will. And unlike Miss Ada, Slick Rick was not stuck on color or size. White, tan, brown, jet-black, skinny, fat, short, tall, pretty or ugly was of no factor to the thin woman. She liked them all.

That evening Slick Rick parked in the back parking lot of the inn and waited patiently. When she spotted Betty coming out, she tooted the horn to get her attention. When the inn-worker recognized it was Slick Rick she reluctantly walked closer to the woman's vehicle. Many times Betty had heard things about Slick Rick and the rumors were enough to get her antennas to quivering wildly. Alert signals warning her to beware, engulfed her. She hesitantly stooped down and looked into the darken car. Slick Rick said in her masculine voice, "Hey Betty! Girl, I thought that was you. How you been?"

"Been fine Slick Rick, been fine."

"Me too. Hey, I hear Zorita's got a daughter. I was wonderin' if you knew anything about it?"

"Can't say I do. Why you askin'?"

"Just curious. That's all. Can't seem to picture Zorita with a kid. Can you?"

"Ain't up to me to picture her with or without a kid. Ain't none of my business." Betty's voice had all the splendor of dry, crumbling leaves.

For two days Slick Rick had been asking all around town if anybody knew anything about some kid Zorita claimed to have. Everyone she asked pretty much said the same thing. Even though Zorita had been married twice, and had shacked-up with Albert before he flew the coop, they had no clue of the woman having kids. Slick Rick was getting very disgusted and thought about busting into the tavern after closing hours to jack Zorita up for the information. She knew that would only make matters worse, so she sent Miss Ada on a mission to find out all she could. The following evening when the two of them put their notes together, they basically had the same story. No one knew a thing about some eighteen-year old daughter that was supposed to be Zorita's child. But then Miss Ada thought about a conversation she had. She said to Slick Rick, "Somebody did tell me 'bout a new girl that's been stayin' at that Walnut Inn place for the past three weeks. Said they heard she come from down south but couldn't be sure 'cause the girl talks all proper and shit." Slick Rick's ears wiggled with excitement.

"A new girl in town? How can that be? I ain't seen nobody new in town, is you?" Slick Rick asked her part-time lover.

"No, indeed I ain't," Miss Ada replied. "I heard Zorita's business was slow with rentin' rooms out, but I ain't seen a soul that's new walkin' 'round town. Let-me-see, who was it that done told me 'bout some strange gal? Let-me-see. Oh yeah, I think it was that old widow woman, Paulette. I'm pretty sure that's who it was. I seen her the other day at Rexall drugstore and she was tellin' me there was a lady livin' in the room right next door to her room at the inn." She nodded eagerly, pleased she had remembered. "That's right, I rememba her sayin' the lady's room was right above the stairs. Said it was room number four and the widow said her own room number was number three. Said somethin' about God putting the lady next door to her so she could protect her 'cause the lady's so innocent. She's a weird-ass, old woman. I tell you, she talked so much; I had a hard time gettin' away from her. In fact she was pickin' up some things for the lady at the drugstore." Miss Ada slapped her knee in jubilation. "Yeah, that's who it was, that widow woman. Anyways, I asked her how come the person couldn't come in the drugstore and get her own stuff. She said, 'Why Lord, she's shyer than a born-again Christian at a nudist colony.' Says hardly nobody knows about her 'cause she don't show her face anywheres in town. She mostly stays at that place of Zorita's."

Slick Rick's ugly, black face brightened with a wide smile; she broke into a long, wicked laugh. Her decayed, beige teeth looked like tiny dominoes scattered in her mouth. Miss Ada joined in with the laughter as though there must have been a joke she had missed somewhere within the conversation. When she realized she didn't have a clue what they were laughing about, in a perplexed pitch she asked, "What is we laughin' 'bout, Slick?"

Slick Rick broke into an even hardier, deep-bass laughter. "Don't you get it? That has got to be Zorita's daughter. All we got to do is figure out how to lure her out of that inn away from Zorita's fat ass."

CHAPTER 37

REPAIRMEN

Inspection for The Inn at Walnut Valley occurs every three years. It had been inspected on March 1, 1970 and passed with flying colors. However, later in the year, right before Nick Hutchinson was hired as a cook, the elevator conked out. On March 1 of 1973 and 1976, Jack of Diamond bribed the old building inspector both times to look the other way regarding the elevator. So, from 1970 to 1976 he had simply kept the gates chained and locked and placed an out-of-order sign on each gated door. The man had good intention of getting the elevator fixed, but his need to gamble took precedence over almost everything else. Of course he made sure the bar was well stocked, and there was plenty of food in the place to keep his tenants, lounge clientele and take-out-order customers happy. But repairing the elevator? Well, let's just say the elevator car stayed stuck in the basement once it broke down. When Zorita purchased the building in 1976, she left Jack's out-of-order signs and locked chains on the gates. She tucked away the keys to the locks in her office desk. Zorita had the money to get the elevator fixed, but since the customers were use to it being out of commission, she saw no reason to have it repaired.

The old inspector, who had been repeatedly paid off by Jack, retired September 1, 1978. A week later the new inspector arrived at The Inn at Walnut Valley to inspect the building. Zorita complained that Jack had informed her that the next inspection was due on March 1, 1979, another six months off. Inspector Beckerman stated the city sent out a notice informing her that the Certificate of Occupancy inspection was now being scheduled every two and a half years. The innkeeper reluctantly let the man inspect her place. Sure enough, everything passed except the elevator.

When the inspector informed Zorita she must get the elevator up to code, she contacted Tri-State Elevator Repair Company. The manager of Tri-State Elevator, Scott DeSoto, informed Zorita it would be about three weeks before the repairmen could get there. When three weeks came and went, Zorita placed another call to the headquarters' service department only to be told she had to wait her turn because of a backlog. The repair orders were mostly for conventional elevators; Zorita's elevator was the only gated-elevator on the list. On one occasion when Zorita called and complained of the delay, Scott told her the contraption was a relic and parts might be hard to find. "So because it's old, are you telling me that you can't repair it? Is that why you keep giving me reason after reason as to why nobody's been here?" The manager assured her it was not what he was trying to convey. He informed her that his company was responsible for the tri-state area and he only had three teams of men to handle the elevator repairs for the regions. Patiently, Zorita continued to wait as her name moved slowly up the list. All in all, it had taken the company a month and a half to get someone to the small town to check out the elevator at The Inn at Walnut Valley.

On Monday, October 16, 1978, Zorita received a call around six a.m. from Scott DeSoto giving her the heads up that the crew would be there in two hours. By eight a.m. Zorita sat at the bar anxiously awaiting the arrival of the men. The weather had changed from a slight drizzle to a steady rain. To make the morning even more discouraging for Zorita, by eight-thirty the repairmen still had not shown up. There was a cool air about the town. Through the lounge's large windows Zorita noticed a sheet of fog rolling into the valley. Not wanting to waste time waiting for the late repairmen, she polished the marbled counter, straightened the bottles of liquor and even wiped the tables down a second and third time. Eight-forty-five turned into nine-fifteen.

The men showed up at nine, twenty-two and Zorita wondered where they had been for almost an hour and a half. The weather had turned from a steady rain to a downpour by the time the men arrived at her inn. A crew of three men rushed into her place dripping wet and anxious to get themselves out of their outer garments. Zorita had placed large area rugs down for them to wipe their feet, then took their wet coats and hung them in the coat room of her lounge area. When they had all unraveled, the man with the reddish hair, beard and mustache, spoke for the group. He mentioned they were Team Two from Tri-State Elevator Repair Company. His name was Gregory and the other two workers were Vic and Elmer. By eleven-thirty they had the elevator all torn apart trying to figure out what had cause the car to become inoperable.

It was noon time when Gregory, the head of the work crew, knocked on the opened door of Zorita's office. "Ma'am," there was a slight hesitation in his voice. "Ma'am, I don't know how to tell you this, but we've torn apart the main mechanisms of the elevator and it look as though this is going to be a real expensive job." Zorita looked at the mechanic and said nothing. This made Gregory a bit edgy because he did not want to start ordering the needed parts for the old gated-elevator, then not receive payment for the job once it was done. To snap her out of the trance he thought she was in, he said, "Ma'am? Did you hear what I said? This job is gonna cost big bucks. Are you sure you want us to continue on with it?"

She had dealt with Scott for weeks upon weeks. Each time she had to use her business voice on the phone to assure she would receive high-quality service. She carried the same professionalism over to the repair men whenever she had to converse with them. She responded, "Hell yes, I want you to continue. It's been six weeks that I've waited to get this elevator fixed so this inn could pass inspection? Do you think I would be waiting this long, have you travel such a distance, let you tear the elevator apart, only to tell you not to fix it because I don't have the money to pay for it? Do you?"

"Well, ma'am, I guess not. I need to let you know before me and my crew go any farther on this job, you're looking at three-thousand dollars. We can get the elevator to go to the second floor, but it won't make it to the third floor. Then when it does get to the second floor, for some reason it slides itself back down. It stops on the first floor, or sometimes it will land in the basement. There's no rhyme, nor reason for what this thing does. Anyway, I've got to order some parts to fix it properly." Still Zorita said nothing. Nervously, the repairman continued, "Our policy, ma'am, is to charge for the initial service call, which is two-hundred dollars. Once we've determined what the problem is, and you agree you want the work done, we require one half down. So Ma'am, if you want us to continue then you must pay us the service-call fee, plus one half of the total cost of the repair."

"You're saying you want a check for seventeen-hundred dollars, correct?" Without waiting for an answer she pulled her check book out of the desk drawer. She scribbled on the document, tore it from the check book and presented it to the lean man.

The inn was shut down for the day due to the elevator repair. It was quite doubtful if it would open up for the evening's crowd. This didn't too much concern Zorita; even getting the elevator repaired to appease the town's ordinance hadn't worried her. There was only one thing she concentrated on these days, and that was Ramona. After she realized the girl in room number four was the child she thought had died at birth, Zorita lost interest in most anything concerning her place. The Inn at Walnut Valley had been the main love of her life after husbands had been murdered and her sweetheart, Albert, had been exposed as a coward in the war. It was the purchase of The Inn at Walnut Valley that replaced her sadness with a warm spot of joy in her soul. Now God had sent her daughter to her; and all she could think about was being around her newly-found child whenever she had the chance. She did not know how long the girl would stay at her inn. Already, Ramona had been there for three weeks. Zorita's biggest fear was maybe the young lady would leave and go to another city, one more populated than the small town of Timberland and she would never find her daughter again in the crowd. Ever since she found out the girl was indeed her child, she wanted to see her every chance she could. She only saw her a couple times a day when Ramona came down to have her meals. Even then, the lady rarely said anything; she simply ate her meal and returned to her room. With Nick no longer running the kitchen, and Betty working at the inn whenever she could, Zorita had less time to linger around trying to catch glimpses of her daughter.

The whole wet day had passed and Zorita found herself wishing the repairmen had never shown up. It had been twelve hours since the team of men had started on the task. Now it was nine-thirty in the evening and Zorita's patience had worn ragged. The repairmen had neatly cleaned up their mess and left the elevator car stuck in the basement. Long, lean Gregory swaggered over to Zorita's office and stood in the entranceway. "Well ma'am, we'll have to return eight o'clock tomorrow morning, right after breakfast." Disgusted, Zorita sighed and went back to writing her grocery list. Gregory walked to the elevator shaft and yelled up to Vic, then down to the basement to Elmer, "Okay you guys, let's wrap 'er up. Tomorrow's another day." When they left, they stormed out like gangbusters and headed for Main Street where their company manager had booked a room at the Holiday Inn for the crew.

Zorita went up to check on her guest. She knocked on Ramona's door first. She heard the unlocking of the door. When Ramona appeared she looked tired. Zorita said to Ramona, "Sorry about all of the racket with this elevator repair."

Ramona's shiny, black hair fell onto her face but the girl left it there. She said in a very low, sad voice, "Don't worry. It was of no great inconvenience to me. S'cuse me," then she closed the door. Zorita thought it was odd, but blamed it on the rainy, dismal day and the repair team ruining the normal routine of the inn.

Zorita went next door to Paulette's room and knocked on the door. When she apologized to Paulette the elderly woman said, "Child, them people didn't change any plan I had for the day. Why, I did the same thing I do almost every day, sit in my room watchin' my portable, colored television my son bought me." The woman stuck her head out the door and peeked down the hallway. She had once been the neighborhood's busy-body when she had a neighborhood to live in. The Inn at Walnut Valley was now her neighborhood and she kept tabs and noticed every tiny detail that went on in the place. When she looked down the passageway, with her sharp eyes, she immediately spotted the discrepancy of the elevator. She pointed towards it, and then asked, "How come the chain is lying on the floor. Zorita, they didn't put that chain and lock back on the gate like you had it."

The innkeeper looked towards the elevator. She was too tired to go trekking down the hall to chain and lock it. She wondered if Gregory had taken the keys to the locks with him. He certainly had not returned them to her. She did not want to chain and lock the gates without knowing the whereabouts of the missing keys. Frustrated, she warned, "Just don't go near the thing. Those idiots, I don't think they know what the hell they're doing. It's a damn shame. I waited all this time trying to get that elevator into working order, and those fools seemed to be sitting around playing tidily-winks."

"Don't worry. Me and Ramona are so use to walkin' down them mahogany stairs that it's almost a shame for you to be wastin' your hard-earned money gettin' the elevator fixed in the first place. Ain't nobody used it in years. She laughed as she pat her hips, "Besides, I need the exercise. Walkin' up and down them steps for breakfast and dinner then takin' Mr. Fred his meals up on the third floor is plenty of exercise. Yeah Zorita, you coulda saved yourself a lot of money by leavin' the darn gates chain and locked up."

"I have to get it up and running. That's what the inspector told me. Something to do with the Certificate of Occupancy. You have yourself a good evening Paulette."

"I sho' will. I'm watching *The Carol Burnett Show*. Gee, I'm tellin' you this rain was an all-day thing. Six o'clock news said it's gonna be a nice day tomorrow. Thank God."

"Goodnight Paulette," Zorita abruptly said to the woman. Paulette got the hint, she politely retreated. Zorita started for her bedroom. She stopped, then turned and faced Ramona's closed door. She wanted to knock on her door and tell the girl everything she could remember; she came to her senses, turned around and flipped the switch to dim the lighting, then went into her room.

CHAPTER 38

RAMONA'S STORY

The evening was long for Zorita. She was exhausted by the repairmen, drained by the downpour of the day's rain, and uneasy because she did not know how to approach Ramona to tell her that she was the girl's natural mother.

Zorita generally feared no situation, nor no one. Regardless of that fact, the woman suddenly felt a magnitude of panic. Her nerves were on edge so she pulled the Crown Royal out of her desk drawer. She took three shots of the liquor, put her nightgown on and crawled into her bed. No sooner than she got in bed she heard a hard knock at her slightly opened door. Aggravated the talk-aholic still had the need to yap some more, the innkeeper drug herself out of bed. She was astonished to see Ramona standing there. "Zorita, I can't sleep," she said in a solemn voice.

"Why Ramona, I was thinking about fixing myself a nice cup of hot chocolate. Would you like some for yourself?" Zorita had the alcohol in her system and really didn't want any hot chocolate; but she figure it would be a nice gesture to show the girl. It sound like a pleasant thing a mother would do for a daughter who could not sleep.

"Yes, I would love a cup of chocolate," she gingerly replied.

"Good, why don't you come on downstairs and join me. I sure could use the company." Zorita felt so much happier that Ramona decided to come to her room. Even so, she could not figure out why Ramona was there because she never talked to anyone unless forced into conversation. When the girl approached Zorita, the innkeeper could feel her palms sweating and her heart racing. As the young lady followed her down the dimly lit stairway Zorita wondered if she should reveal the fact that she was Ramona's real mother. She decided she'd say nothing and simply savor the moment of being in her child's company. When they approached the kitchen, Zorita pointed at the small table and chair. "Have a seat child. It won't take long for me to heat up the milk."

Before the girl sat down, she said, "Zorita, here's the photographs I took of you. They turned out real nice. Look how photogenic you are."

The innkeeper took the snapshots, "Lord, why look at me. I ain't ever looked this good in all my days. Thank you child, I sure do appreciate these pictures." Zorita looked at the scenic pictures of the fall foliage and was amazed at the brilliancy of the photography. "Ramona these are some nice shots of the walnut trees. Boy, oh boy! Is that what you were looking at as you were taking pictures of them? Why the changing colors are beautiful, like you said. You got a real talent."

Ramona commented, "That's what Mr. Rubenstein told me. I use to work in his studio. He said I had an eye for detail."

"Well you sure do." Zorita smiled, put the photos on the countertop and continued making the hot chocolate. Ramona sat at the table in a quiet state. She did not say a word after the initial conversation of photography. Zorita, unable to stand the silence said, "I am so glad those knuckleheads are out of here. They got this place in a darn mess. Tell you the truth girl, I can't wait 'til they get their butts back in here and finish up this job." Still the girl didn't say anything. Zorita came to the table with two mugs of chocolate, both topped with marshmallows. As she stood at the table with the cups of hot chocolate she noticed a small puddle of tears in front of Ramona. She put both cups down. "Why, what in the world could have you crying, Ramona. You're still missin' your mother, aren't you?"

"Yes, I do miss my mama. I was thinking how badly I messed things up right before she died. I figured my mother was making up the story about finding me in a pond. I was determined to figure out if it was true or not. I knew it would do no good asking my stepfather because he always told me I should pay attention to what my mother said because she loved me. I went back to Macon and was told what I needed to know." Zorita became uneasy. She could feel the unsteadiness of her legs. "My grandmama told me what really happened and I was happy to find out the truth. She said my mother did find me in some water. She even walked me over to the pond which mama pulled me out of. My grandmother is your Aunt Stephanie, married to my grandfather, your Uncle Ted Frazier. They are your aunt and uncle, right?"

"Yes, yes my child. They are my aunt and uncle." Zorita wanted to talk to the girl about her birth; she simply didn't know what was truth and what was pure speculation. She retrieved the apple pies from the counter then sat at the table with her daughter.

"So my mother was really your cousin, right?"

Zorita looked the girl in her eyes and said, "Yes." She drank her chocolate then nervously took a generous helping of the apple pie.

Ramona continued telling of her young past. "When I returned to Little Rock, I was very angry at my mama. I treated her cold because I'd found out she really wasn't my natural mother." Ramona touched Zorita's hand, and sadness engulfed the young girl's demeanor. "But I didn't know! She kept getting sicker and sicker; then finally she died. That's when my dad told me she had been dying of cancer. I didn't know. I just didn't know she was dying." She sniffled, and wiped her nose with a rumpled tissue. "Why couldn't he tell me she was dying while she was still alive? I wouldn't have given her the cold shoulder and snubbed her the way I did. I would have loved her and thanked her for saving and raising me. I was angry with my father when my mother died. Because all of those years my mama was alive he kept the lie going to make her happy. After mama died my dad told me she couldn't have children. Said she'd convinced herself God had given me to her, so she made him continue to make me believe he was my stepfather and she was my real mother. That's just how much he loved mama."

The innkeeper asked, "So that story about you sticking a pin in the map was just that? A story?"

"That's all it was, something I made up. I didn't have the heart to tell you all of this as soon as I met you; so I kept quiet. I guess with Olivia's dying and with me trying to get over my mother's death, it was all too much for me. I'm sorry I couldn't hold it in any longer." She took a drink of her hot chocolate and continued. "It was my grandmama who remembered hearing the old woman your mama took up with once lived in a small town called Timberland, Pennsylvania. That's how I found you. I called the long distance operator for Timberland and discovered you and your mother were living here. Once I arrived and I found out you owned this inn, I decided it was best to rent a room. I actually couldn't believe how easy it was to locate you. But then again, this is a small town and I guess it's true."

Zorita finished her hot chocolate and nervously gobbled down the marshmallow. She asked, "You guess what's true?"

Ramona continued, "You know, what they say about small towns. That everybody knows everybody. I certainly had no problem when I asked the cab driver if he knew where I could rent a room. He said, 'Sure, there's the Holiday Inn or Zorita's place, The Inn at Walnut Valley.'"

Zorita's nerves bunched together and she could feel herself getting sick. She excused herself and rushed to the bathroom near the lounge area. She flipped the light switch on and barged into the stall scarcely making it to the commode. She felt terrible. It was not the way she wanted her daughter to perceive her, as a woman who had no control, a weak woman. She figured it was the Crown Royal, hot chocolate and marshmallows, and the apple pie. Not to mention her jumbled nerves from the death of Nick and Olivia, the elevator repair men, and yes, even the information her newly-found daughter had given her.

Zorita took a few minutes and cleaned herself up. When she got back to the kitchen she discovered the girl was gone. She thought she'd heard footsteps on the mahogany stairs while she was cleaning herself up. She knew Ramona had left the kitchen and went back to her room. She wanted her daughter and she wanted to tell the girl what had really happened for her to be placed into the pond. She felt she owed her child at least that. She put the cups in the sink and then ran the dishwater to clean them. As her hands sat motionless in the water, warm tears trickle down her face. She pulled herself together, wiped away the tears and went upstairs to her room.

Zorita's head hit the pillow and hit it hard. She wanted to talk to Ramona so badly, she end up dreaming about the girl. In the dream she saw herself putting the baby in a small woven basket then placing the basket into the pond, sending it on its journey. She saw a woman at the other end of the pond retrieving the baby and when the dream showed her the woman's face, it was the round face of Miss Ada. She screamed to the top of her lungs but no one heard her as Miss Ada stole her child. She awoke in a cold sweat. The dream bothered her so much she rushed out of her bed and ran across the hall to Ramona's room. She could see in the softly-lit corridor that the door to her daughter's room was wide open; but she couldn't see into the darkened room. She knew something was out of line. The young girl locked up everything, even when she went to the bathroom down the hall. Widow Paulette, on the other hand, never locked her room. She had a fierce belief God would take care of her; a locked door would be a turn-off to the people God sent her way. Paulette popped her head out of her room, glanced down the darkened hall, then said, "Look Zorita, look at that man, why he's got Ramona with him." Zorita saw Slick Rick struggling to drag the girl towards the gated-elevator. She quickly flipped on the main light switch. Zorita leaped forward quick as lightning towards Slick Rick, who was struggling to pull Ramona towards the elevator. Her daughter's eyes were large and begging for help because Slick Rick had slapped duct tape over her mouth after Ramona's first and only scream. "Let go of my daughter. Let her go, you can't have her." She continued to yell and curse Slick Rick as she tussled to get her daughter free of the woman's grasp. She pulled with all her might as Slick Rick managed to get the gate opened to the elevator. Slick

Rick was in a fight of her life, but in her haste she failed to make sure there was an elevator to get into. She was so intent on getting Ramona out of Zorita's grasp, she never noticed someone on the opposite side of her. It was Fred, the hermit who lived upstairs. He had come out of his room to use the bathroom. When he heard the commotion, he took the obscured, rickety stairs near the elevator down to the second floor to check out the disturbance. Once he saw the intruder trying to abduct Ramona, he plowed his hard fist into the side of Slick Rick's face, forcing her to let go of Ramona's arm. The woman fell backwards and when she realized there was no elevator to sustain her fall she grasped at the darkened air, reeling backward into the black pit. She grasped and clawed at the nothingness up until the very last moment of crashing onto the top of the elevator at the bottom of the shaft. When Zorita pulled her daughter close to her bosom, she hugged and kissed the girl about the forehead and face. "Oh my sweet baby, I'm sorry. I'm so sorry," was all she could say. She gently peeled the duct tape off Ramona's mouth. Zorita looked in Fred's direction to tell him how much she appreciated him saving her daughter's life. The man was nowhere to be found.

She took her daughter back to her room and insisted Ramona get into her bed to calm herself from the incident. Zorita discretely removed the gun from the hidden compartment of her desk and slipped it into her pocket. Ramona sat on the edge of the bed and cried. The girl sniffled and wiped the tears off of her face. Her voice choked as she questioned, "Why did he break into my room? What in the world did he want with me?" The girl's look of confusion led Zorita to know she would have to tell her all about Slick Rick and her parents. After informing the girl of the three women, Ramona collapsed onto the pillow and cried herself to sleep.

Zorita thought about calling the police concerning the death of Slick Rick, but she decided she would wait until the morning. She wondered how Slick Rick found a way to get into the inn. When she was sure Ramona was asleep Zorita left her door opened and went across the hall to Paulette's room. Widow Paulette was sitting up in her bed praying over an opened bible. Zorita asked her to go into her room and watch over Ramona and the widow happily did so. The innkeeper went to the second floor entrance and saw it was locked up tight. Then she went up to the third floor and found the third floor's door was locked and intact. She wanted to tell Fred she appreciated him saving her daughter's life but when she looked into his smelly room he was snoring so hard she knew she should wait until the morning. When she got back downstairs on the second floor she checked her daughter's room, she could see where the door's lock had been picked. She knew that was how Slick Rick gained entrance into the girl's room. She went downstairs and discovered the back door slightly ajar. She closed the door but was unable to lock it because of the damage done to it.

It had been a trying day and the night proved to be beyond belief. Her daughter admitted to searching for her and once they found one another, in a flash they almost lost each other. When she returned to her room she was happy to see her daughter asleep and Paulette at the desk with her head resting upon the opened bible. She closed her door and went back downstairs. Zorita barricaded the damaged door best as she could with the small kitchen table and the two chairs. The angry innkeeper grabbed a dining room chair and sat in the kitchen with her gun close at hand. If anyone else tried to break into her place, she was sure she'd be forced to shoot them as a last resort. She never went back to sleep for the remainder of the night.

CHAPTER 39

COPS

Zorita felt very bad about the death of Slick Rick. She often wished the three lesbians would leave her alone; now one of them laid dead in her establishment. The following morning the innkeeper repositioned the small kitchen table and chairs. She telephoned the operator to report the break-in. Officer Merchetti walked into the lounge with his partner Officer Berkley. "We heard there's a problem here. What seems to be the matter?" Officer Merchetti asked.

Zorita paced herself as she told the story the way she figured it best to tell. "Well officer, I got up to put on some coffee for the elevator repairmen who are to suppose to be here in about an hour. I looked into the shaft to see how far along the repairmen had gotten on the job. Something didn't look right, so I grabbed the flashlight to check it out. That's when I saw him."

Officer Merchetti took his hat off and scratched his bald head. "Saw who?" he asked, looking around questionably.

Using the flashlight as a pointer, she aimed it towards the elevator. "Go back there and look into the elevator shaft and see for yourselves." She gave the turned-on flashlight to Officer Merchetti and said, "Follow me." The officer shined the light into the darkened shaft and saw the body of Slick Rick on the top of the elevator. The officers thought they were looking at a thin-built man, and Zorita went along with their perception.

"How the hell did he get down there?" Officer Berkley asked. He glanced over at Zorita expecting her to provide an answer. "How did he even get himself in here to fall into this shaft? Are you sure he isn't one of your customers from the night before?"

"Of course I'm sure. I wasn't opened last night for business. I've had this elevator safely secured ever since I've own my place. Had to call in Tri-State Elevator Repair to get it fixed. When they came yesterday, the repairman asked me for the keys to unlock the gates." She sadly shook her head. "You'd think they'd have enough sense to relock the damn gates when they left for the evening."

The officers looked at one another, then Officer Merchetti said to Zorita, "Ma'am, where is the rear entrance to this place?"

"There are rear entries for all three floors, but the doors are always locked."

"Where's the back door to the first floor?" asked Officer Berkley.

They both trailed her to the kitchen. When they got to the door Officer Berkley checked it out. Immediately he spotted marks made on the lock and pointed them out to his partner. "I believe this is our point of entry," the officer said to Zorita.

Zorita had a quick mental synopsis as to what she felt had happened. Ever since she discovered Ramona was her daughter, Zorita made it a habit of sleeping with her door slightly ajar. She knew when Slick Rick came up the staircase and spied her asleep in her room the wicked woman did not want to chance going back down the staircase with the struggling young lady. The commotion would have, more than likely awakened Zorita. Once Slick Rick grabbed the girl, in order to avoid taking the risk of waking Zorita, she decided to take the gated-elevator down. Zorita recognized the fact she had awaken in time to help save her daughter's life.

Officer Merchetti asked, "Do you recognize that car out back? Does it belong to any of your patrons?"

She tried to contain herself when she saw Slick Rick's car in her parking lot. Pretending she knew nothing about the vehicle, Zorita said, "I have no idea whose car that is. My regular tenants don't own vehicles." The officer got on his shoulder microphone and said, "Eileen, run this tag for me. BK8-976, Pennsylvania tags.

Moments later a squelch came over Officer's Berkley's radio, "Bob, that car belongs to a lady by the name of Rachael Jarvison. That name comes up with some aliases. It seems our Rachael Jarvison goes by Rick Jarvis, also has a street name of Slick Rick. Those are strange aliases for a female," the woman added.

"Okay, you got an address on this Rachael Jarvison, Rick Jarvis or whatever the hell you say she goes by." Eileen came back on the radio and gave the officer the woman's address.

"Okay, thank you; ten-four." He said to his partner, "You know we've dealt with that Rachael Jarvison person last year, it was alleged she attacked a woman in the Constitutional Park bathroom."

"The queer woman? Yeah, I do remember the jailhouse being in such an uproar because she was dressed like a man. Is that her in there on top of the elevator? Damn, I thought it was a man. Well she won't be accosting anybody else. You can bet your ass on that."

The second officer said to Zorita, "Ma'am if you got somebody coming to work on that elevator then you best get in touch with them and inform them there's a body in the shaft. We have to seal it off as a crime scene to investigate if this is accidental or a homicide."

It was almost eight o'clock, she figured Gregory and his crew would be late again. Zorita paced the porch as she waited for the three men to show up. The police officers had contacted the crime-scene investigators and soon there were four additional people milling about in her inn. An attractive, petite woman investigator was in charge. She wore her dirty-blonde hair in a cute flip, with a part on the side and looked no older than twenty-eight. She introduced herself to Zorita as Investigator Sandler.

The innkeeper knew it would be a matter of time before Slick Rick's death would be blasted all over the news. She was not looking forward to getting a visit from Miss Ada and Pearl. They were sure to put her through the wringer. The repair crew arrived twelve minutes after nine; they were over an hour late. The men hustled towards the building in a mad rush ready to start tinkering on the elevator. When they saw Zorita deliberately blockading the doorway, they stopped one behind the other. "What's going on here? Why the cop cars?" Gregory asked.

Zorita stood defiantly with her big arms crossed. She said in an authoritative voice, "Seems you guys rushed out of here so fast last night you never put the chains and locks back on the gates; and I have no idea what you did with the keys." At that point Gregory fished into his pocket and pulled out the keys to the locks. Without a word he dropped the chain holding the four keys into the innkeeper's hand. She put the keys in her dress pocket and continued on, "Thanks to your little error somebody broke into my inn and got themselves killed trying to take the elevator down. That's what's going on." They followed her into the inn. They spotted the yellow, taped-off elevator. Vic and Elmer peered down the darkened shaft; Gregory had no desire.

The team leader could see lawsuit written all over his resignation papers. Gregory knew he was in hot water on this one. Gated-elevators were not his thing so he never thought about securing the elevator perimeters once he closed the gated doors. The chain and lock was simply left neatly against the wall for each elevator.

Without thinking he said, "Well I guess there's no way we can work on the elevator today, is there?"

"You've got to be kidding me. Man, do you see all these officials around here? The police told me I can't even open up today, let alone have you guys work on the elevator. It's best for you to call your office and inform them. And once you get your boss on the phone, I want to speak to him. This accident should not have happened." she said in an opinionated voice.

"So you're saying it's okay for me to use your phone to make the long distance phone call to Scranton?" he asked with a sadden expression.

Zorita warned, "If you don't call, I will. Because I want to know if it is your company's policy to leave gated-elevators unsecured once you're done for the evening. A person is dead because of your negligence. Thanks to your company, I'm forced to lose even more money by being shut down for goodness knows how long."

Gregory's face reddens, and Vic and Elmer looked worried. They all ran last evening's work scenario through their minds, trying to determine why the gates were left unsafe for the inhabitants of the inn. When it came down to it, the team leader knew he would be blamed for the disaster. His co-workers made their way out of the inn as Gregory picked up the telephone receiver. Slowly, he punched in the telephone number. The nervous man could feel the sweat rolling down his chest as he awaited Scott's rugged voice. "Tri-State Elevator Repair Company," the man's voice snapped loud and quick.

"Hello. Scott, this is Greg."

"Yeah, what is it Greg?" Scott asked in a rushed manner. "Make it fast 'cause I got Smitty on the other extension. I got him checking on a possible job in Maryland. Somebody paid a quarter of a million dollars for a turn-of-a-century mansion. Town called Cumberland I believe. Yeah, that's right, Cumberland, Maryland," he explained as he quickly looked over his messy note pad. "In the town's historical area. They need some work done on the elevator there. It goes from the basement to the fourth floor tower. Seems the old scientist who owned the place had a laboratory up on the third floor. Heard he never let anybody go up there to see it." Scott abruptly sneezed. "S'cuse me," he roared. "Anyway, weirdest thing happened. For some reason when the old man died, the elevator got stuck between the second and third floors. Guess he got his wish, 'cause can't a damn soul get to the third floor or the fourth floor observation tower unless they hike a shit-load of stairs. I'm hoping Smitty can put in a winning bid for us to secure that job." Getting back to the team leader, he bellowed, "Greg! Man, what is it you want? I got bigger fish to get on my hook than to be dealing with that small job you got over there in Timberland, Pennsylvania."

"We got a problem here Scott. It's a big problem."

Scott shouted, "A big problem? Let me tell you what a big problem is. A big problem is if I don't get that damn contract over there in Cumberland, Maryland. That's easily a fifteen-thousand dollar job. That's a big problem! So, don't be tellin' me, 'It's a big problem.' Fact is, I don't even want to hear anything about a problem. It ain't we got a big problem, it's Team Two that's got a problem. It's Team Two who's gonna fix it. You're the team leader and what do team leaders do? They oversee everything and take care of anything that jumps off."

"I can't fix this problem, Scott. Somebody died," Gregory blurted into the phone.

"I know I didn't hear what I think I heard. And if I heard it, I must be having a fuckin' nightmare and somebody better wake my ass up. Did I hear you say somebody died?" Scott yelled in Gregory's ear.

"You heard right Scott. Somehow the gate was not re-chained and somebody fell down the elevator shaft."

"Are you fuckin' kiddin' me? How did that happen? Son-of-a-bitch!"

"It was an accident," the team leader defended.

"Accident my gottdamn ass. A fender-bender is an accident, dropping a hammer on your foot is a damn accident. Leaving the gate unsecured at the end of a day's job, now that's no accident, it a gottdamn disaster waiting to happen, and obviously it has. What did the owner say?"

Gregory didn't answer his boss. He pitifully shook his head and handed the receiver to Zorita. "Scott wants to know how you want to handle this." As he walked towards the door two police officers walked up to Gregory and began questioning him about the unchained gates.

Zorita cleared her throat then put the phone to her ear. She spoke in a tone of business. "Hello Scott, this is Zorita, the owner of The Inn at Walnut Valley; Zorita Thurman."

"Yeah, yeah, Zorita; we've talked quite a bit over the pass weeks. Zorita, what the hell is going on there? Gregory's told me there's been an accident." Out of customer courtesy he refrained from flavoring his speech with peppered verbiage.

In a cool and civil tongue Zorita explained, "That's right Scott. You know I've been more than patient with trying to get this elevator fixed so I can get my C of O renewed. When you finally send a team of men, I happen to get Curly, Larry and Moe to entertain me. Thanks to the neglect of your men I have a dead body lying on top of the elevator car in the basement. I am not, I repeat, I am not paying you a red cent for the repair of my elevator. I have police officers swarming about my place due to the pure negligence of your men. I can only pray my establishment's business don't slack off because of the stigma of this death."

"Zorita, you can't refuse to pay my company. I've sent you a reputable crew and I'm sure they've been very responsible in providing you with the best professional service," Scott tried to assure the innkeeper.

"The best professional service? Ha! Yesterday you called me very early and told me your men would be here at eight in the morning. They showed up at nine-thirty. Is that their best professional service? They had a two-hour lunch, is that their best professional service? Last evening they left at almost nine-thirty. They did not secure the gates with the chain and locks which they removed, is that their best professional service? And coming in here at nine-thirty this morning, when they told me they'd be here first thing at eight a.m., what is that? I'll tell you what it isn't. It isn't their best professional service. By you saying they provide the best professional service does not make it so."

After getting blasted by Zorita, Scott continued to keep his cool. He said, "I can understand your concern Zorita, but in all fairness they are good men. Maybe their punctuality leaves much to be desired but there had to be a reason the men were not there at the times specified."

With his explanation the innkeeper fumed. Zorita belligerently said, "I'll tell you this Scott, I expect to have my elevator put back together and in no way am I'm paying for this disaster. If I have to call the Better Business Bureau on your company and give a negative report, I will. If I have to call Cynthia Braxton of Channel Five News and have her alert the public about your company, I will. I'm sure she'll want to know who's going to pay for the funeral. Poor people in my community don't have a bunch of money so it's going to be rough for the family to come up with burial expenses. And while we're on the subject, who will pay for all of the revenue I have lost because of this. Should I get my lawyer involved with the negligence of your corporation? Do you understand what I'm puttin' down, Scott?"

She was still irate when she thrust the receiver back into the hand of Gregory, who had returned after the police officers' interrogation. Zorita stormed out onto the porch. She anxiously tapped her foot from the frustration of the conversation. Vic and Elmer were in deep conversation as they smoked near the walnut trees.

Back inside, Gregory was getting his butt chastised up and down by his supervisor. "What the fuck happened Greg. What happened man, this is not good," Scott's nasty language was once again singeing the phone wires.

Gregory tried to sugar-coat the whole situation. He tried to lead his boss to believe it really was an accident. Scott heard numerous complaints before from other clients concerning Team Two. He burned into Gregory's ear, "Don't tell me it was a gottdamn accident again. It was no accident, it was like the woman said, pure negligence. We got somebody that has died on account of your *accidentally* leaving the gottdamn gates unsecured. If this company gets sued I will make sure your ass is left penniless. I want you to do everything you can do to make that lady happy." Gregory wiped the sweat off of his forehead as his boss shouted. "Sounds like you made a gottdamn mess out of this one. Don't you dare charge her a damn cent. There ain't no way we can pull anything over on this broad; she's too gottdamn smart for that. This is one you ain't capable of sweeping under the rug so you better do your best to clean this shit up."

Gregory came out of the inn, his face crimsoned. He walked to his truck and then returned to Zorita. "Scott told me to return this to you," he handed her the check she had written the day before.

"What does this mean I don't get my elevator repaired? You're gonna leave it torn apart?"

His face colored some more, "No ma'am, that's not what it means. As soon as the policemen have finished all they have to do, we will continue the repair. Look lady, we're awfully sorry about what happened here. Scott has given us another three more days to get this job done and it won't cause you a dime. He says he sends his apologies to you and condolences to the decease's family for what has happened. We'll check back tomorrow morning, eight o'clock sharp. Maybe they'll be finish by then. UPS is gonna deliver some parts we need for the elevator sometime today, or maybe tomorrow." Gregory briskly scratched his red beard and he nervously used his fingers to comb his mustache. He added, "Scott said you'll be receiving a check by registered mail for five-thousand dollars. That's one-thousand to cover your loss of revenue, and four-thousand dollars for the expenses and grievance for the family of the dead man." He sadly shook his head in disbelief that the whole episode happened. He continued, "Do you want us to wait until the cops are gone before we chain and lock the gates?" When Zorita told him she'd take care of securing the gates, the man slowly descended the porch. She watched the men as they got into their truck and sped away. As they zoomed down the street she tore the check up into the smallest pieces and tossed it to the wind. Slick Rick's little accidental death saved her three-thousand, two-hundred dollars, plus added more money to her stash. Since she knew the woman had no family, she figured it best to cremate Slick Rick's body and put the remainder of the money into her safe deposit box. She recalled the image of the lifeless body sprawled on top of the elevator car. She mumbled to herself, "*Slick Rick, you ain't so slick anymore.*"

CHAPTER 40

FIGHT

Just as Zorita predicted, as soon as the death of Slick Rick hit the news, Miss Ada and Pearl drove to the inn. Miss Ada pushed the double-doors open with such force it startled Investigator Sandler who had returned to ask Zorita a few more questions. When the two women spotted the innkeeper talking to the investigator, Pearl lagged behind while Miss Ada stormed over towards Zorita. The old woman swung back and plummet her fist hard into Zorita's mouth. Investigator Sandler tried to grab Miss Ada but before she could get to her, Zorita start wailing on Miss Ada. The two fat women rolled around on the lounge floor trading punches and vulgar insults while Pearl stood looking on. The small investigator tried to break the women up but it was like a small, cute piglet trying to pry apart two angry hogs at war with one another. Investigator Sandler was new to her job and this was her first-solo crime scene to oversee. Nervous about the women's entanglement and with the women being way too big for her to break apart, she lost her senses and fired a shot into the air. The sound echoed throughout the lounge. The loud noise of the gunshot and the plaster particles which showered them caused the women to separate immediately. Zorita's jaw was swollen and her left eye blacken. The investigator quickly cuffed Miss Ada while the big woman was disoriented. On her portable police radio she called for a car to be dispatched to The

Inn at Walnut Valley. Pearl sat at a table boo-hooing about the fight. From the tussle, Miss Ada's dentures worked their way out of her mouth and her wig came off. No longer having teeth in her mouth she sound like Donald Duck as she spewed threats to Pearl, "You wucken witch. You coulda welped me. You wust stand dare doin' wucken nothin'. Gawddammit. I'm gonna kill your muthawuckin' ass when I get my hands on you, witch!"

Pearl sat and cried. As two policemen rushed into the building to escort Miss Ada to jail, Pearl looked sorrowfully at her daughter. She wanted Zorita to understand she was forced to be there. Pearl stared at her lover as the cop had her by the cuffs and bravely said, "Miss Ada, what you expect me to do? That's my daughter. I can't help you fight my daughter. I've done a lot of things for you. Things I didn't even want to do." Pearl looked at Zorita and said, "Zorita, I'm sorry. I sold myself to that ol' devil of a woman. That's all I did, just gave my whole life away." Angry at herself for the direction she had taken her life, Pearl snarled, "I pretended like I was into bein' gay and I ain't never even liked doin' it with no woman. Boy, did I mess myself up; but Miss Ada, I'm done with you. Comin' to this here inn to hurt my daughter is *just the straw that done broke this here camel's hump*."

The cop jerked on the handcuffed woman; and Miss Ada jerked and wrestled back to let them know nothing scared her. They held a tight rein on her and when she realized, that she could not get free to rip Pearl's guts out, she retaliated by saying, "Yo' witch-ass wasn't no damn good in wed anyways. I'm glad I'm rid of you. Watch your wack witch. I swear I'm gonna murder yo' ass like I killed that sorry-ass Randy." The cop snatched her away and Miss Ada spurted Donald Duck profanities to the big officer as he drug her outside to the awaiting patrol car. The shorter officer used Miss Ada's wig to scoop up her dentures and held the wig as if it was a dirty diaper.

Pearl got up and walked over to Zorita who was sitting at another table nursing her black eye. It looked like the swelling would take days to go down and it was the same story with her jaw. Zorita looked up towards her mama. Pearl wanted to touch her daughter, but years of manipulation and deceit ripped that privilege away. The small woman began to whimper. She loved her daughter, yet now she feared her. She was afraid to say anything to Zorita. Somehow she felt Zorita would blame the whole thing on her. Pearl could not accept the blame being dropped right smack on her shoulders. She knew she was the cause of a lot of heartaches in Zorita's life, but this was not one of them. She started to say something; a strange utter came out, then nothing more.

Zorita loved her mama, even with all of the turbulence that had gone on in the confused woman's life. She reached for her mama's hand and as she held Pearl's small hand, Zorita stood up in front her. Even though Zorita was so much bigger than her mother, at that moment the innkeeper felt like the woman's little child again. She let her mother embrace her. Finally, the words came from Pearl's mouth, "Zorita, I know I was not the best mama. I'm sorry. Baby, can you forgive me and try to forget how I let Miss Ada take advantage of us." Zorita broke the embrace.

She never thought she'd see the day her mama would find the strength to stand against Miss Ada. Zorita said, "I will never forget Miss Ada, nor will I ever forget you. Everything you and the woman did affected my life and made a direct impact on the woman I have turned out to be. Even so, I love you because you're my mama, through all the good and bad times."

"Oh Zorita, I'm so . . ."

"Pearl, it ain't necessary for you to say another word. You did the best you knew how to do. I'm a grown woman now; I got my own life to live. God gave us all a mind to do what we want to do, and live the way we want to live. I will live on my own terms." She grimaced in pain as she gently rubbed her swollen jaw. "I ask you to respect my choice, the way I respected your decision for you to live the way you wanted to live. What all you and Miss Ada did made me a better person. I might be a little tougher, because of how I was raised by you and your woman, but overall I'm okay."

Pearl was saddened. She had tried to niche out a life for herself without contributing anything at all to society. She admitted, "I can't believe what I did to myself." She then asked, "Did you know I was a prisoner?"

Zorita could not believe her ears. "A prisoner? What do you mean you were a prisoner, Pearl?"

"Just that! I couldn't come and go as I pleased. Okay, so Miss Ada would let me run errands; but whenever she thought I was coming up with a plan to leave her, she'd beat me. She'd beat me for every little thing and when I tried to stand up for myself she'd beat me even more. The woman's crazy." Then, as though a wayward thought came to her, she said, "I just want to know one thing, Zorita."

"What is it, Pearl?"

"Is your daughter really alive or was that a lot of crap you were layin' on me and Miss Ada?"

"Yes my daughter is alive, Pearl. Sally Mae saved her from drowning in the pond."

Pearl's eyes brightened. "Oh Lord, that means I'm a grandma don't it, Zorita? I'm a grandma!"

"Pearl, don't tell me you didn't know that's why Slick Rick broke in here last night? She was trying to kidnap my baby and take my girl for herself. You're telling me you knew nothing about it?"

Pearl looked square in her daughter's eyes, "I swear Zorita. I ain't knowed nothin' 'bout what Slick Rick or Miss Ada was doin'. Miss Ada always kept a tight noose about my neck. She was afraid I would tell you all of her and Slick Rick's secrets. They only used me for sex and bein' they flunky." Pearl threw her right hand upwards and gave thanks to the Almighty. "Lord, thank You, thank You." She added, "Look like God's done chopped off the head of the snake by takin' Slick Rick off of this here earth." She leaned in close and whispered in Zorita's ear, "Slick Rick was the head of the snake. Miss Ada is the body of that serpent. Now all I got to do is wait until that serpent's big, fat body stop wigglin' around and 'round."

CHAPTER 41

VIBRANT RAMONA

Moments after Pearl left the inn Zorita began thinking hard. Did Slick Rick have others like Miss Ada lurking in the corners of Timberland, ready to extract vengeance on her, or worst yet, her innocent daughter? Before something bad happened to Ramona, Zorita knew she must take steps to protect her child. She remembered Gregory mentioning his crew was staying at the Holiday Inn. Zorita knew it would be the first place a person would look. Years ago Percy had taken her to a hotel a ways from Timberland, in the town of LaVala. That was where she would hide her daughter. Zorita explained to Ramona and Paulette she felt it best for the two of them to leave the inn for their own safety. She called Slumber-Time Lodge and told the hotel clerk she had two customers in need of a room. She gave money to Paulette to pay for a room for her and her daughter to share. She would take the calculated risk she could trust the widow with Ramona. When the cabbie arrived the driver told her Max had given instructions not to charge Zorita for his service. Zorita thanked him and loaded Ramona, the widow, and their satchels into the cab.

The following day when Pearl came to the inn and asked to see her granddaughter, Zorita apologized and explained the girl was gone. There was no Ramona or Paulette at the inn, only Fred, the hermit-tenant, three overnight travelers and Zorita. Pearl was out of luck.

"But when can I see her?" Pearl's voice was thick with anticipation.

Zorita was leery. She knew there was always a possibility the woman could manipulate her young, naive daughter and she was not willing to take that chance. She replied, "Pearl, I can't answer that. My job is to protect my daughter, so forgive me if I ain't too excited about having The Frazier Family Reunion right at this very moment with you. I'm not going to trust you with my baby. I thought I'd lost her, but now I've got her back in my life and I'm holding onto her. Anyway, you act like you didn't know anything about my baby being drowned when she was born?"

With a dash of attitude, Pearl retorted, "I ain't knowed no such thing, Zorita. How would I know that? You heard me say the woman was a devil. The devil don't always tell you what he is up to, he just tell you what he need to tell you, so he can get what he need to get from you."

"Look Pearl, I'm not going to argue with you, I don't trust you when it comes to my child. You might buddy up with me and my daughter so you can turn her on to Miss Ada, or yourself. There's no way I'll let that happen." Her voice strained as she continued to explain. "I might have been subjected to the way you two women viewed life, but I'm not letting you or anybody else force it on Ramona."

"Ramona? Is that my granddaughter's name? I wish I could meet her. I bet she's a lovely girl. Honest Zorita, I'll just sit in the corner and look at her. I promise. I won't so much as say a word to the girl. She won't even have to know I'm any kin to her."

Zorita said, "I'll have to think about it before I make up my mind."

With no definite answer of when, where, or even if Pearl could ever see her granddaughter, Pearl left in defeat; she drove herself back to she and Miss Ada's home. For the first time she felt free of the rigid hold of the woman. She noticed the light blinking on the answer machine and checked it for messages. Miss Ada's voice was blaring on the speaker of the machine. By the clarity of her speech, Pearl could tell the old woman was in possession of her false teeth. "Pearl, get that money we got socked away in Zorita's old room and come and bail my ass the hell out of here. You know, I think they is tryin' to pin Randy's murder on me. Can you believe that shit? Hurry up girl, I can't be stayin' here another night. You know how much you mean to me; besides, we can't be away from each other for any length of time."

The first night of Miss Ada's incarceration Pearl slept on the sofa. She found it to be very uncomfortable so the next night she took over her daughter's old bedroom. She never slept in the bed she'd shared with Miss Ada after the woman was thrown in jail. Long ago Pearl had tried to break the bond of Miss Ada, but she never could. Now the old woman found herself locked up and looking for Pearl to get her out. She looked around at all of the beautiful things the big woman provided for the both of them. She sadly shook her head. How could she have been so shallow? Now it didn't seem as though having somebody else take care of her had been worth it. She felt she had messed up her own life; and would have ruined her daughter's as well, but Zorita was too strong-willed to let that happen. Secretly, she was proud her girl had been smart enough not to get tangled into Miss Ada and Slick Rick's snare.

Two weeks later Miss Ada was found stabbed to death. Two other prisoners rammed shanks into the woman while she was showering. The day Miss Ada called for Pearl to bring the bail money, Pearl knew she would not. She was experiencing a taste of her freedom, and freedom tasted real sweet. She had been afraid of the woman most of her life. She did not want to experience another one of Miss Ada's beatings. She had tired of being used as a punching bag, and then a love machine after the fights. She had tired of fake penises being rammed inside of her, and pretending to have organisms. She wanted to be on her own and she wanted a real man. It was something she had wanted for decades; but Miss Ada put such a fear in her, she simply gave up the quest.

When Pearl found out about the death of Miss Ada, she fell into depression. Out of desperation to talk to someone she went to visit her daughter at the inn one morning. After listening to Pearl, and even feeling a bit sorry for her at times, Zorita began asking Pearl questions which she needed answers to. Without hesitation, Pearl told her everything she could remember; from her first involvement with Miss Ada to the deaths of Zorita's husbands. When Zorita asked Pearl who was her father, Pearl told her what little she knew about the man. She told how Miss Ada convinced her to get pregnant by the white man. Miss Ada and Pearl never had a clue the man was simply passing himself as Caucasian. She told her the name of the town and the name of the tavern where the older woman found him. She swore she did not know his name because it was a one-night stand. She confessed Miss Ada had killed people and defrauded the insurance companies. Pearl told Zorita that Miss Ada felt that good guys really do finish last and she would do whatever she had to do to get whatever she wanted for the both of them. When Pearl was finished explaining all she could, she ended by defending her lover. She justified, even though Miss Ada had a lot of bad qualities, deep down she had been a good person to she and Zorita in happier days.

It had taken Pearl almost a lifetime to realize she could have been a successful, productive member of society. The only thing she had successfully accomplished was having Zorita, a daughter who had the sense to march to her own cadence. Pearl was fifty-three years old now, an old woman by any standards. But now Miss Ada and Slick Rick were gone and she felt her life was just beginning. With sincerity in her voice, she told Zorita, "Now that Miss Ada's gone, the big, black body of the headless snake has finally stopped floppin' around."

After the dust settled, Zorita sent for her daughter and Widow Paulette to return to the inn. When Ramona returned to the establishment, she put applications in at Foto-Mat and Sears Photo Gallery to earn more money for her stay. When Zorita got word of this, she approached her child. "Ramona, why are you trying to get a job? What does it look like with me charging my own flesh and blood room and board? There's no need for you to work."

But Ramona did not want to infringe upon the innkeeper's generosity, "Zorita, I don't want to be a bother to anyone, especially you. I've got enough money for one more week of room and board. I need to get a job so I can stay here. Besides . . ." she lowered her head, "I don't want to be away from you."

"Then sweet child, stay here and work. I'm sure Betty can use an extra hand. I know I can use you in this bar and lounge area. Your work will pay for your room and board." She continued with her plea, "I don't feel comfortable with you going to work in town. Please take the job I'm offering you. Honey, please."

Ramona took Zorita up on her offer and became Betty's assistant in the kitchen and aided Zorita in the bar and lounge areas. Zorita even paid her a wage and the girl saved enough to purchase a professional Polaroid camera that came with accessories.

On band nights, when the bar was busy, Ramona dressed herself in a white silk blouse, a plain black satin skirt and wore a red silk rose in her hair. She would go to the lounge to take and sell pictures for the customers. The young lady even sold silk roses to the men to present to their ladies. Ramona chatted briefly with some of the women and men whom she photographed. The wife of one of her customers complimented, "Why look like me and Jimmy done went to one of them fancy photography studio. Look at you, Jimmy, standing by that big peacock chair I'm sittin' in, and me holdin' that long-stemmed rose. Look like you's the king and I'm yo' queen. Ramona, why this here is what I call real professional photo-graffin' girl. You is good." The women patrons liked Ramona; they did not fear her as a threat to their relationships. Though the men secretly admired her beauty, they knew not only would they have their wives and girlfriends to contend with, but Zorita as well. Ramona emerged from her cocoon into a beautiful, vibrant young lady and she added great joy to Zorita's life. Some of the innkeeper's customers told her they could see a great resemblance between she and the child, proving they were definitely mother and daughter. This made the big woman beam with pride.

Pearl wanted to share time in her daughter and granddaughter's life. But after Zorita finally got around to introducing the granddaughter to Pearl, the grandmother noticed Ramona was simply polite to her, and extremely devoted to her mother. Rarely did Pearl see her granddaughter, even though she made a point of trying to catch Zorita and Ramona together at the inn. For some reason, the girl seemed to always be busy, either working in the kitchen, upstairs, or off somewhere taking photographs of mountains, people and trains. The girl branched out for the sake of her photography, in spite of Zorita's concern for her safety. After repeated phone calls and visits to the inn for breakfast, Pearl only managed to have general conversations with her daughter. The verbiage went as such, *"Mornin' Zorita,"* *"Morning Pearl. How's things going,"* *"Good, how's it with you and Ramona?"* *"Another cup of coffee, Pearl,"* *"Yes Zorita, thanks."*

On a crisp, fall morning, Pearl asked her daughter, "Are those some more of Ramona's pictures she done took over there?"

"Yes they are, go take a look," Zorita told the woman.

Pearl had longed to have her picture taken with Zorita and Ramona, but she was so afraid Zorita would say no. Regardless, the words spilled from her mouth. "Gee, I wish Ramona would take a picture of the three of us."

She was surprised when Zorita responded, "I'm sure she can. She's got one of those expensive cameras. I'll bet it's got a timer and everything on it."

Feeling awkward about imposing upon her granddaughter, Pearl backed down. "Oh that's alright, Zorita. I know how busy the girl is."

"Nonsense! I think it's a great idea to have a family portrait made. Today is as good as any day."

"I guess you're right, Zorita. You know the old sayin', *don't put off today what you can't do next week.*

"That settles it then. The next chance I get I'll ask Ramona if she'll . . ."

"Ask me what mama?" Ramona put the bottles of ginger ales into the mini-frig behind the bar. "What is it you want to ask me?"

"Why your grandmother want to know if you can take a picture of the three of us."

The girl looked at her mother and could tell it would mean a lot to her. She had heard so many wild stories about her grandmother and figured it best to stay far away from the woman. But now her mama seemed to be asking her for this one favor, without really asking for it. She quietly sighed, then said, "Of course I can take a picture of the three of us. Give me fifteen minutes to set up a nice area for the photograph." Zorita looked at her mother with an air of pride. She nodded to Pearl, as if to say, *See, Ramona don't mind at all.*

The young photographer took photographs of the three of them. Then she took individual portraits, then clicked pictures with Zorita and Pearl together. Next, with her and her mother, then her and her grandmother. When Betty came out of the kitchen to see what the excitement was all about, Ramona took shots of the cook also. It was a wonderful morning. In fact, Pearl felt it was one of the best mornings she had ever experienced.

CHAPTER 42

PACKAGE

Winter of 1978 arrived frosty, frigid, and fresh. The snow flurries, fluttered, whirled, and whipped The Inn at Walnut Valley; and from a distance, the property resembled a beautiful, round snow globe. The first snow storm draped Timberland like a white, fluffy, cashmere blanket and all of the residence were snuggled in for the long season ahead. The trees on the surrounding hills and mountains were white-haired, and the snow coated the bark on their strong, bulky trunks. They stood boldly, protecting the tiny village from the wind shear of winter's fury. The beauty of the fresh, fallen snow was enchantingly blissful. The squirrels were safely nestled and amply prepared for winter's visit. The large snowflakes were so magical that the kids could almost see their snowmen come alive. Even the beautiful snow angels, the children made in the snow, created a spiritual aura. The bushes and trees were covered with the soft snow and all around the town the people hustled fast to get out of the winter's chill. The lone house on the mountain, which had been in plain view during the spring, summer, and fall, could no longer be seen from the valley of Timberland. It too had taken winter's queue and gone into hibernation.

The winter of 1978 brought about renewal for everything and everyone. Especially Zorita and Ramona. It represented a new slate of life, a slate wiped clean; a new beginning for a chance to love. An opportunity to go on with life, the way life intended.

The arrival of winter had also brought about renewal for Pearl. She had been reborn since the serpent was completely dead. Just as winter wrapped its arms around the town of Timberland, she knew God was sheltering her with his love, and her life would only get better. Though Pearl was propelled onto a happier plateau of consciousness, she knew there wasn't a place in Zorita's life for her. Sure, Zorita treated her cordially and never again threw it in her face of how twisted Pearl had raised her; but cordial was all she got. Cordial conversation, cordial acknowledgement, cordial pleasantries; why should Pearl expect anything else? Deep down, she knew she shouldn't. The woman came to the decision to accept the fact her daughter and granddaughter only needed each other. She would no longer feel compelled to insert herself into their lives. She had her chance at being a mother, only to mess it up royally. Pearl decided she would stay long enough to spend Thanksgiving and Christmas in Timberland, with hopes that she could spend the holiday seasons with Zorita and Ramona. She was thoroughly pleased when Zorita invited her over on both holidays.

When New Year 1979 rolled around, she made a bold decision to call her brother, Ted Frazier. She hadn't seen, nor spoken to him for almost two decades. She told him of her breakup, the murder of Miss Ada and how Ramona found Zorita.

"But how are you holding out, Pearl?" Ted asked.

She had a smile in her heart when she answered, "Tough. But you know, Ted, *when the going get tough, the tough put on boxin' gloves.*"

Ted Frazier laughed. "Stop with the jokes, girl. How are you really doing?"

She answered, "Miserable."

"Then you might as well come on home and be miserable with your family," he sincerely offered.

There were a lot of things she had to set into motion and she could not afford to waste any more time. She was sure losing Slick Rick and Miss Ada was God's way of setting her free from hell. It was a hell she had willingly placed herself in over three and a half decades ago. She was determined there was no way she would ruin this gift of freedom. Pearl put the house and all of its contents up for sell. As soon as she sold the house, she purchased a one way ticket to Macon, Georgia. Right before she got on the train she made a delivery.

She hand-delivered the package to The Inn at Walnut Valley on Thursday afternoon, five months after Miss Ada's life had been taken by the inmates. The box read, ZORITA THE IN-KEEPOR. Spelling was never a strong feature of Pearl's. The woman wanted to address it by using the name she'd given her daughter at birth, Zorita Frazier. She decided Zorita the Innkeeper sounded more appropriate. Because when she thought about it, once her daughter was released from the confinement of the basement in Macon, Georgia, Zorita became the innkeeper of her life. It had taken Pearl all her life to realize she too could have been her own innkeeper. When Pearl hand-delivered the box to her daughter, she simply said, "I love you Zorita, you and your Ramona. I'm going back to Macon. I'm going home." She leaned in and kissed Zorita on the cheek, turned and walked out of her daughter's life.

Zorita asked Betty to oversee things while she went to check on something upstairs. Behind the locked door of her room she took a pair of scissors and ran the blade along the edges and down the center of the box. She found a note on top of the cold, hard cash. It read:

March 18, 1979

My Dearest Zorita,

It's a lot of things I need to tell you and a lot I wont to do for you to. But mosly I just wont to tell you that I love you Zorita. I reelly do even tho I didnt never tell you them words before. I did not do nothin wrong. I did not kill neether one of your mens ether. You can blaim Miss Ada and Slick Rick for them things. Just don't be putin me in the same class as thos murdorers. The only reeson I stayed all them yeers was coss Miss Ada said she wood murdor you to if I lef her. Beleeve me that was the only reeson.

I got my self in this mess long time ago. I'm the blaim for my own dumness. My family don tole me to leeve the old woman alon, but at 18 you think you no it all. I never wonted to work cause I figar I wood not be smart enuf to get me one of them good secreetery jobs. I just figar I wood let Miss Ada take care of me. I dont hate her to much. How could I? cause of her—you was born. I always did loved you even if you dont beleeve it. I did every thing Miss Ada tole me to do. *Oh well too late to cry over spilt butter milk and cornbread.* I'm old and Miss Ada is gone. And dont ask me why but I think I kind of miss her. Even that old devlish Slick Rick.

Anyways, you dont have to be a feerin bout me comin round. I wont bother with you and that purty baby of yours. I am goin back home to Macon and maybe find me a little house so I can live in som peece. I will rite you agin when I get a place.

Use this money for how so ever you wont. I'm sorry for what I did to put you in so much pane when you was a kid. I just follow Miss Ada's rules coss we had to servive and I never thoght I could take care of you by my self after she don made me have you.

Love,
Pearl Frazier

There was so much money in the box it took a very long time for her to count it. When she was done she had counted thirty-thousand dollars. Zorita added the money to the cash she already had in her second safe deposit box and went on about her life at the inn.

In May 1979 business at the Inn at Walnut Valley picked up tremendously. A large factory, Eleimex Plastics, relocated from New York to Pennsylvania to take advantage of the state's lower corporate tax rate. Eleimex Plastics' transferred employees had utilized all of the room at the Holiday Inn and The Inn at Walnut Valley. The overflow of employees was registered at Slumber-Time Lodge, in LaVala. With the large industry setting up shop on the outskirts of Timberland, property values soared sky-high. Some of the poor families soon discovered their humble homes were worth a fortune. This is because the New York employees who had relocated to Timberland, Pennsylvania readily searched for homes to purchase.

On August 11, 1979 Ramona informed her mother she was taking an extended vacation to see her father. Over the months of being with her natural mother, Ramona had forgiven her father for withholding the information regarding her birth. This pleased Zorita. She was also relieved her daughter was leaving Timberland because the girl had started talking about finding a job outside of the inn again. So much time had passed since Slick Rick had died. The innkeeper sensed no one really cared about retaliating against the death of the man-like woman. But still she worried for the safety of her daughter. With Ramona returning to Little Rock it would take a load off of her mind.

Zorita kept in touch with her daughter each month by phone. One day in November of 1979, Ramona called Zorita and informed her mother she would be spending not only Thanksgiving and Christmas with her father, but she would also celebrate New Year's Day 1980, with him as well. The young lady asked Zorita to let Betty run the inn so she could come to Little Rock to reacquaint herself with Kashif and meet her new stepmother. The innkeeper declined.

On January 3, 1980 Zorita received a call from her daughter. Anxiously, Zorita asked Ramona when she would be returning to Timberland. When Ramona admitted she did not know, Zorita said, "Well I certainly hope you make it back to Timberland before February 22. I'll be thirty-five and I'm going to have Betty throw me a surprise birthday party."

Ramona thought for a moment, then said, "Mama, how can Betty throw you a surprise birthday party. It's not a surprise if you know about it." Ramona added, "Besides, isn't that being deceptive?"

Zorita heartily laughed, "Ramona, I'm joking with you. Where's your sense of humor, child? The only surprise I'll have is the fact that I made it to age thirty-five. Lord, where do the years go?" Zorita confessed, "I just want you to come back to Timberland in time to help me celebrate."

Ramona, who was almost always serious, said in a gentle voice, "Mama, all you have to do is ask me to be there and I will be there. I don't appreciate when people are dishonest with me. My parents deceived me for almost eighteen years. Please don't mislead me. Not ever. Not even as a joke."

What had Zorita been thinking? She missed her daughter for almost six months and wanted her back in Timberland. She'd forgotten about the deception of Sally Mae pretending to be Ramona's mother, until the woman was dying. It escaped her mind that Kashif went along with the dishonesty by letting her think he was her stepfather. She didn't even know why she said Betty was giving her a surprise birthday party, because it wasn't true. Zorita was giving the party herself, but she thought it would let the girl know how desperate she was for her to return to Timberland. It was a joke, and the joke bombed. She apologized, "I'm sorry, Ramona. I really am. I want to see you again, soon. I do want to throw myself a party for my thirty-fifth birthday; I've never had a birthday party. I was hoping you would soon be back in Timberland so you could make it to my party."

Still disappointed her mother felt the need to trick her, Ramona quietly said, "Don't worry mother, I'll be there."

~ ~ ~

Ramona returned to The Inn at Walnut Valley a week before Zorita's birthday bash. She and Betty worked feverishly getting things in order for the upcoming celebration. Betty's husband did some touch-up painting in the lounge and bar areas.

The day of the birthday party, Betty plastered the number thirty-five all over the walls and on the mirror. She made sure all of the café tables had birthday tablecloths and party hats and favors. On both of the large café windows she wrote HAPPY 35TH BIRTHDAY, ZORITA.

On Friday night, February 22, 1980, most all of Zorita's customers showed up for the innkeeper's birthday celebration. There were so many people at the inn it was literally standing room only. Zorita looked around at the crowd. Black and white patrons were there to wish her a happy thirty-fifth. Max and most of his crew from Queen City Taxi were there celebrating with the innkeeper. Previous bands and their friends came to the party. The rear parking lot of the inn was completely filled with cars, and the street was lined with taxis and privately owned vehicles. Zorita was elated that so many of the town people came to her party to wish her well.

Ramona photographed every detail of the party. The large, three-tier birthday cake with whip-cream frosting, topped with the red, waxed number thirty-five was purchased from M & N Bakery. She photographed the cake from four angles. She also took pictures of the buffet counter, which Betty, with the help of Sissy's Catering Service, put together. She snapped the mound of birthday presents given to her mother by friends and patrons. Ramona also photographed every guest who had given their time to be at the birthday celebration. She would send thank-you notes later with their photographs inside. Betty and her husband made sure Zorita enjoyed the musicians and partook in the dancing and festivity of foods. And yes, there was even walnut ice cream Betty made from

Nick's recipe, which she had figured out long before he quit. The night of the party was exceptional. Everyone had a wonderful time and though the inn normally closed at one o'clock in the morning, it was opened well until three.

Zorita was now thirty-five; she decided it was time for her to make a change in her life. She was ready to leave Timberland, Pennsylvania and hoped her daughter would join her. After breakfast she approached the young lady.

"Ramona, what would you say about us moving away from Timberland?"

"Move from here, why would we want to move from Timberland? You've been here for so long; where would we go?"

"Ramona, I'm sure we can find a place. I just know, I'm ready to leave. Now if you want to stay here, or go back to Little Rock or anywhere else, that will be alright. My main concern is for you to be happy, no matter where you are."

She left her child alone to think about what it was she wanted to do. The following day Ramona told her mother, it didn't matter where they moved to, as long as they were together. She was ready for a change in her life as well.

CHAPTER 43

GOOD FRIEND

Springtime 1980 arrived in Timberland with a big, beautiful rainbow arched from one end of the small town to the other. Crocuses covered and caressed the ground's canvas; as daffodils diligently danced into dawn. Towering, tall tulips tempted the townsfolk to touch their treasured treats; and hardy hyacinths' pleasant perfumes heightened the happy hearts. The beautiful, green grass gracefully bent towards the gentle breeze. And the sun was like a satisfying friend, looking over your shoulder to give you a touch of brightness to glide you on your way. Spring, such a beautiful season. A beautiful season to leave Timberland, Pennsylvania.

Zorita drove her old car to the bank for one last time. She would no longer do business with Timberland Savings and Loans. She was moving. She had gone to see the manager of Timberland Savings and Loan two weeks prior. She told him of her desire to close out her account and empty the money from her two safe deposit boxes into a suitcase. When she mentioned she would be taking a flight and carrying the case of currency, the manager almost passed out. He was determined to convince Zorita how unsafe it was for her to travel with tens of thousands of dollars stuffed in a suitcase. "What if that bag of money get lost?" he explained, "Mrs. Thurman, you will never see that cash again. It would be best to wire-transfer your funds." She knew he was right. She mailed the Bank of Hawaii a check for one-hundred dollars. In return, they sent her the savings account book showing her deposited funds. After a few days of running it through her mind she decided she would take the bank manager's advice.

"Ma'am, are you sure you want to close your checking account. There's over three-thousand dollars in the account," said the new bank employee, who sat smugly behind her desk.

"Yes, I am. I have a new account in Hawaii. I want you to transfer the funds I have in my checking account, plus this money here." She placed the carpetbag on the desk and pulled it opened.

When the woman tipped the bag towards her and looked inside she said, "Whoa, my god; how much money is this?" It was all the money Zorita had tucked away over the years in her two safe deposit boxes. She had closed her account for the boxes out.

"There's seventy-two thousand dollars there. Like I said, I want it all transferred to this Hawaiian account," she looked at the woman's name plate, then added, "Mrs. Hillenson." She presented the book to the woman.

The lady looked at the bag of money and then suspiciously stared at Zorita. Arrogantly, she said, "S'cuse me for one moment." She left the bag of money on her desk and Zorita holding her bank book in midair. Zorita could hear the woman's heels as they click-clacked quickly across the marbled floor towards the manager's desk.

The manager followed Mrs. Hillenson back to her desk. He said to Zorita, "Hello Mrs. Thurman, it's good to see you again." To add humor to the situation, he said, "I see you've decided to empty your piggybanks." He looked into the bag of loot, shook his head, then added, "Pity you didn't put this money into one of our high interest-yielding, money market accounts. Remember, I tried to get you to do that when you opened your checking account a few years ago?"

Zorita stayed seated and shook the manager's extended hand. "Hello Mr. Whitman," she spoke up towards him. "You know what I told you when I signed up for my first safe deposit box. I really . . ."

Mr. Whitman finished her sentence, "I know, *'I really don't trust banks. I only want to stick my money into one of those safe deposit boxes.'* Yes, I remember."

Mrs. Hillenson looked at the two in total astonishment. She asked, "Mr. Whitman, you mean it's okay for me to make the wire transfer? What about all of this cash money? Where did she get it from?" she abrasively pointed to the satchel.

The manager looked at the brunette; he justified Zorita's actions. "As you heard, Mrs. Hillenson, Mrs. Thurman is a lot like many of our citizens of Timberland who do not trust banks." He looked at Zorita and apologized, "No offense Mrs. Thurman." He resumed the conversation with the bank clerk, "I'd much rather she put her money in the safe deposit box then tuck it beneath a mattress. At least in a safe deposit box it won't get stolen. When Mrs. Thurman told me she was moving to Hawaii I told her to contact the Bank of Hawaii to open an account with them so she can transfer her funds into her new bank account." He scratched his head. With a slight scowl he lightly chastised, "It's no concern to you as to how Mrs. Thurman came about her funds. It is your concern to provide the service she has requested concerning her money. So Mrs. Hillenson, if you can't handle the wire transfer, by all means step aside and I will take care of it myself."

Zorita was pleased when the woman snootily excused herself and click-clacked across the glazed floor to stare out of the window. Enviously, the bank clerk mumbled, *"Moving to Hawaii; must be nice!"*

Mr. Whitman took over the task of transferring the funds. He updated her savings account book and placed the transaction slip into her bank book. The manager double-checked by calling the Bank of Hawaii to make sure the funds had been received. Upon completion he stood and extended his hand, "Nice to have known you Mrs. Thurman. Hawaii's gain is definitely Pennsylvania's loss." Zorita shook Mr. Whitman's hand. She put her account book in her purse, grabbed her empty carpetbag and walked out of the bank with her head held high.

The innkeeper returned to the inn, went to her daughter's room and told her to start packing because they were moving. She was giving away The Inn at Walnut Valley and the two of them were leaving Timberland, Pennsylvania to make a fresh start in Hawaii. Zorita stood in shock when Ramona unexpectedly grabbed her and gave her a big hug and a kiss on the cheek. Zorita, not use to experiencing female affection, casually accepted the show of appreciation. She encouraged her daughter to get a move on. "Now you got a lot of packing to do so hurry it up and get started. Me and Betty got some business to take care of within the next day or two. When we're done, I want us to be on that jet plane making our way to our new home."

"But Mama, how am I getting on a plane? I'm really scared to fly," Ramona reminded her mother.

Zorita comforted her daughter. She looked into the girl's young eyes and said, "Ramona, I've never flown myself, but I'll be with you every step of the way. Life is sometimes scary. Somehow, we've got to be brave and fly right through it." She patted her daughter on the shoulder. "If we don't, we might end up living a mundane life. Then we'd never experience wonderful things heading our way, all because we're too afraid to fly. Is that what you want, to let life pass right by you?"

"No ma'am. No that's not what I want." She leaned in to hug her mother and this time Zorita casually hugged her back.

On the drive to City Hall Zorita thanked Betty for all of her help and told her she was signing her old piece of a car and the inn over to her. When they were done at the Motor Vehicle Department and City Hall, Betty asked, "Are you sure you want to sign the deed to your inn over to me?"

"Yes Betty, for the third time, yes I'm sure. I already signed the deed over in your name, remember? Or were you daydreaming when we took care of that? I've paid the taxes for the remainder of the year so you don't have to worry about that. You practically run this place by yourself anyway." She looked at Betty with great admiration; she said, "Betty, you have acted like my right hand throughout good and bad times. When the club was bustling with business, you were there. When I needed errands ran, you ran them. When Nick quit working for me, you came through. When he left this earth, you stepped right in and made sure everything went the way it should." She touched Betty's shoulder to reassure the woman that she knew she had made the right decision. Zorita continued with the praising of Betty's dedication. "When the factory moved nearby and the inn's business became very profitable, you were right there to help me through. You're a good friend, Betty. This is my way of showing you how much I appreciated you taking time out of you and your family's life to assist me in keeping the inn running successfully. I couldn't have done it without you." Then she smiled and said, "Thank you Betty for being a friend, when I didn't even know I needed a friend." The tears were streaming down Betty's face. Zorita took tissues out of her purse and gave them to the woman. "Now if you find it's gonna be too much for you, then put the thing up for sale and use the money for your retirement. It's worth over eighty-thousand dollars. You and Rick can come visit me and Ramona in Hawaii. I'll send you our addresses when we get settled. Well, at least I'll send you my address 'cause Ramona and me will be having our own separate houses. My Ramona, you know, she's a young lady and she's gonna have to know how to think for herself and not depend on somebody else's way of thinking. So my home is open to you if you come for a visit."

"Lord, I ain't never thought I'd own this here inn. What a blessing! And you inviting me and Rick all the way over to Hi-waa-eee to see you, this is just hard for me to believe. Lord, I'm tellin' you, God is good! If I'm dreamin' then I sure don't want to wake up."

Being a business woman no longer appealed to Zorita. She knew she could have received top dollar for the inn. But the Lord had delivered her daughter to her and she was a mother now. Feeling a great debt to God, she felt compelled to give the inn to her dear friend, Betty Morgan.

Zorita and Ramona were packed and ready to take a cab to Oaktown to board the Greyhound Bus. They had to take the bus to Pittsburgh to catch their flight headed towards Hawaii. Betty and her husband were at the inn to see the two ladies off. Rick seemed pretty calm. She was still in awe about the newly-acquired inn and her nerves were jumbled. The woman said, "What can I ever do to repay you for being so generous? You name it, Zorita."

Zorita said, "As a matter of fact there is something I need for you to promise."

"What is it Zorita, tell me, what is it? You don't know how happy I have been since you gave me and Rick this opportunity, so you name it. Right Rick?"

"Absolutely! Of course," he answered."

Zorita looked at both Betty and Rick and then glanced back to Betty. The ex-innkeeper had a serious air about her, as Betty held her breath in anticipation. In a gentle voice, Zorita said, "There are things I need for you to promise while you are the owner of The Inn at Walnut Valley and all three are equally important. The first thing is don't ever change the inn's name, The Inn at Walnut Valley. The second thing is don't cut down any of those walnut trees planted around the inn. Jack of Diamond planted those trees and they meant the world to him, that's why he named this place, The Inn at Walnut Valley."

Betty clutched tighter onto her husband's arm. In a fit of jitters, she said, "Zorita I promise, I will never change the name of the inn and I won't ever bother them walnut trees. What is the third thing, Zorita? What is left that you want me to promise you?"

Zorita had a slight smile on her face. She said, "Betty, Fred saved my daughter's life. You've got to promise me that as long as he wants to live here you will let him stay and eat free of charge. Promise me that you'll give him free room and board as long as he's here, and don't ever back off of that promise. A deal's a deal." The three of them glanced over at the gazebo. There sat Fred, talking to the widow Paulette. Zorita remembered two weeks after the elevator had been repaired; it was the first time she had ever seen Fred come down from the third floor for a meal. Though he didn't speak to anyone when he initially came to dine, the tenants were happy to see him amongst them. Zorita, added, "Look at him. My goodness, he's come a long way. I'm so proud of him." Betty nodded in agreement.

Betty released Rick's arm and said, "I promise, I promise to everything. I will always let Fred have free room and board, even treat him like family." She reached to hug Zorita, but Zorita stood steadfast and extended her hand for a handshake to finalize the deal. "Thank you Zorita" she said as she vigorously shook the woman's hand. "Thank you from the bottom of my heart."

Ramona was in her room getting all of her cameras together and checking to make sure she had everything. Even though she didn't want to leave beautiful Timberland, Pennsylvania, she knew it was time to go. Soon they would be living in Hawaii. Ramona knew, if she worked hard on the island state, maybe she could manage to open her own photo gallery. But it would have to be done on her terms, with very little assistance from Zorita. Ramona had arrived at The Inn at Walnut Valley in the fall of 1978 in search of her mother. Now it was spring of 1980 and she and her mother were on their way to Hawaii, a place she had only known in her spirit.

Max took one of the cabbies off of the job and had the man dispatch while he drove over to The Inn at Walnut Valley. When Max pulled up, he saw Ramona moving about with the camera to her face taking photographs. It was her way of preserving the memory of the inn for her mother. He noticed Zorita at the gazebo with Betty and Rick saying the last of her goodbyes to Widow Paulette and Fred. He waited patiently for Zorita to finish with her farewells.

Betty and Rick walked Zorita towards the front of the building. The new inn owner asked Zorita if she wanted to go back inside to take one last look. Zorita declined; she knew she would miss The Inn at Walnut Valley. The woman stood looking at the big, boxy, brick inn and smiled. And for a moment, just a flicker of a moment, she could have sworn the porch and the windows of the building smiled back at her, as if to say, *Don't worry Zorita, I'll miss you too*. She admired the grand building and remembered the first time she had ever entered the distinguished inn with her beloved, Albert Manning. From the town's chatter, Zorita found out it had been the consequences of living by Mouth's standards that had done Albert in. Regardless, she loved him even after he left her. She knew she always would. He had met her on their very first date inside The Inn at Walnut Valley. That is where she had come to know the owner, Jack of Diamond. It was through Jack of Diamond's urgent need for money that she had the opportunity to purchase the inn. The purchase of the inn was a great diversion for the pain in her heart. It had taken her mind off of the bludgeon of her first husband, Randy Banks, who was really a criminal named Samuel Lynch, the murder of her second husband, Percy Thurman, and the abandonment of Albert Manning. The three men ran through her thoughts as she looked at the building. Zorita's customers and friends flowed through her mind. She had showcased a lot of talent, both black and white, at her place. She remembered the bi-centennial celebration when Junior Walker and the All-Stars bought the house down. She laughed to herself how Two Thumbs always thought he had everyone fooled into thinking he was a world traveler and even a great investor. Yet the man's travels extended no farther than Oaktown, Pennsylvania; and his portfolio overflowed with I.O.U. notes and unpaid bills. Happily, she reminisced of the Classes of '76 when the Ohio Players and The Righteous Brothers rocked the graduates' celebration. The graduates of 1977, 1978 and 1979 used the inn for their parties as well. She thought of the fun she had shared with Nick the Chef. Then her heart became heavy as she remembered the moment he angrily walked out of her inn with all his belongings in the two shopping bags. It had been in her heart to beg him to stay, even remain rent free as he had been doing. She just couldn't swallow her pride and admit she had been wrong to break her promise. Zorita had never forgiven herself for Nick's death. She remembered the insecurities of Popeye and the beauty of Olivia. It was magical to see the once, self-conscious guy become a totally proud and confident man. He found so much pride and happiness in his life because of the love Olivia had given him. Then there was the evening of Nick and Olivia's memorial celebration, a tribute to their lives which had been tragically snuffed away. That was the night she discovered Ramona was her daughter. She thought of the happy times she spent making amends with her mother, Pearl; and the effort Ramona took in photographing the three of them as a family. Pearl, Zorita and Ramona; individually different in every way; yet they are family. And though they are not perfect, few families are! they will forever be connected by the blood in their veins. She thought of Widow Paulette, the overly-friendly tenant, who had taken on the task of being the inn's matronly mother and lovable busy-body. The woman was always around whenever needed, and made sure Fred had his meals each day before he finally ventured from his room. And then there was Fred, who most had her heart. Even though he had once been the inn's recluse, she loved him dearly. Though people had rarely seen the man, he made his presence known the night he saved her daughter from Slick Rick. She remembered Betty, a real talented woman. She could sew, cook and move with lightening speed when it came to taking care of the inn. Betty also had no problem getting her husband, Rick, to lend a hand whenever work had to be done around the tavern. She remembered William, the young man who helped her around the inn before he joined the army. She hadn't heard from William since he left the small town for boot camp almost a year and a half ago. She could only pray God kept him safe as he served his country. She had made a lot of friends at the inn and she knew she would miss them all. In her heart, she knew she would forever cherish the memories. Because, with the exception of the murders of Nick and Olivia, her memories of The Inn at Walnut Valley placed a beautiful treasure in her soul. In a way, the inn brought out the joy that was meant to be in her life. The woman had the sense to realize, at each and every fun-filled moment at the inn, she was having the best time of her life. She made a difference in the neighborhood. She had given the town of Timberland, Pennsylvania a decent inn, The Inn at Walnut Valley. It was a place where the people, no matter what their color, could let their hair down and have a good time. She had given the town the best she had to offer. She had given them Zorita.